Confessions of a Sage Woman

by Milele

Confessions of a Sage Woman

For more information, contact Milele Enterprises

Executive Editor/Interior design by
Veronica L. Banks, M.A. Communications,
Uhuru Lifestyles
Cover design by Stephen Bruce
Front Cover photo by MwazaCarol Art
Back Cover photo credit "theblxkblonde"

ISBN-10:
0-9978869-0-0
ISBN-13:
978-0-9978869-0-0
FIRST EDITION

Foreword

African Cosmogony
By Kujaliwa Kennedy

In Afrikan cosmological traditions all physical reality is seen as a manifestation of spirit. Each manifested spirit arrives in this realm with work to do, things to express the needs of the divine. From this view point the people and objects that we see are an expression of an invisible force desiring to be. Each of these spirits has its gifts and its needs.

In most Afrikan traditions to ignore the spirit that caused a physical thing to be is to ignore its true essence. Ignoring the spirit that cause a thing to be ignores it true existence and can deny a community its gifts.

Confessions of A Sage Women acknowledges the inner spirit that causes a specific manifestation as well as gives attention to the interaction of these spirits (people) as they each attempt and desire to be all they came to manifest. Confessions acknowledges this interplay and how they each affect one another toward change and evolution. These spirits are in fact human beings who from the Afrikan cosmology are gifted, invisible forces covered and housed in flesh and bones.

Confessions explores the needs of these spirits as they seek higher expression and deeper meanings. As they attempt to rediscover inner divinity and deeper connections with one another. Confessions dares to challenge the commonly accepted views of life, sex and sexuality and pushes the reader to consider a paradigm of thinking and living. It pushes readers to no longer see life as a finality but an eternal divinity and through story suggests that even our sexuality and sex has a spiritual bases and function. Yes, Confessions is sexy, erotic and challenging.

Milele has dared to be different. To write about what some would think is the unthinkable and share stories that could knock your socks off. Enjoy the ride. Open your mind. Allow yourself to perceive and be ready to learn and think differently.

Prologue

Unveiling the Sage Within....

To understand the title, "Confessions of a Sage Woman" let's first talk about the role of 'sages' in history. According to Kemetic theories, the sage person is a "thinker" – someone who is very wise. They embrace *the fulfillment of what exists. A "sage" breathes, thinks, feels, lives and speaks truth"* and that is what I have attempted to do in this book.

This series is called "Confessions..." because when we "confess" we speak our full truths while acknowledging our right to live, think and act freely. Through our "Confessions" we also admit our understanding of the responsibility of our actions, words and energy. The ultimate goal of the "Confessions..." series is *to raise the level of humanity* in people through sharing, entertaining, teaching, enlightening and arousing the readers.

"Confessions of A Sage Woman,"(COASW), the 2nd book in the series, is a journey of the freedom and evolution of spirit. It expounds upon "Confessions… of a Faithful Woman" as it goes deeper into challenging commonly accepted views and practices surrounding: sensuality, sex, relationships, self-validation, wholeness, wellness, gender, intimacy, spirituality, love and being human by educating readers about timeless worldly practices, traditions, philosophies in a deeply intimate and erotic fashion.

This book is a "rite of passage" of sorts…working upon the understanding that humans are divine beings born with an innate connection to The Universe; yet as we grow and begin to focus more on the physical/visible world we disconnect from the spiritual/invisible world. This physically focused existence is necessary for us to be able to learn to function and operate in the physical world as we grow from infancy to adulthood.

However, understanding the invisible is just as crucial for us to be full human beings. This is why most people develop bush schools, rite of passages, initiations, and any other spiritual pursuits designed to reconnect people to the invisible world (which is simply The Great Intelligence that exists in all things). Through these systems/initiations we learn how to tap into the spiritual **through** the physical (sex, dance, trance, herbs, "spirit" song, etc.). As we become more in tune with The Divine we better connect to all things with an intimate knowledge and understanding of ourselves. Without the connection to The Invisible world, life is less than half of what it is intended to be.

"Confessions of A Sage Woman is written to help us to reconnect to those ancient understandings and practices while arousing our mind, body and spirit. "COASW" can also aid in getting us past pre-conceived or imposed limitations about sex, love, gender, relationships, life, Afrikan traditions, culture and what it means to be a man or woman in this world. Many characters created in this book experience their awakening into a new phase in their lives. If you find yourself relating to your awakening into a similar phase – Embrace it fully.

There are also "Sage Wisdom: " in "COASW" which is food for the soul. The Sage Wisdoms in this book are a collection of information Milele has received through research, studies, initiations and personal experiences with other sages. These "Sage Wisdoms " will enlighten the reader about ways to foster an understanding about "wholeness" from a healthy and intuitive perspective. There are also pages for journaling throughout the book so that you may jot down your thoughts and feelings.

Since this book is meant to be a full experience, it is recommended that you prepare your space for reading. It can be as simple as taking a moment to meditate or as elaborate as adding candles, incense, food, drinks, toys and friends to the experience. Challenge yourself to step out of the box and experience a heightening of your "senses" as you read. Have discussions and group readings, read it with your mate(s), read it by yourself, read it more than once, or change the story to fit you.

Always keep in mind that our thoughts, our energy and our words are powerful and they leave traces of us wherever they are directed. Enjoy the freedom of spirit that we all have and expand your thinking. This is a fictional series, despite the fact that it has actual lessons, rituals, rites and practices. As with all things you must use discretion about the use of the cleansings, essential oils, baths, etc. so that you do not cause harm to yourself or others.

"This is but one stop on the journey of my spirit. I will enjoy it fully; learning as I live, incorporating Sage Wisdoms and being in alignment with my Universal purpose."
~Milele

Contents

Us and Him

A beacon of light spreads across the night. The "Women of the Red Lotus" gather in front of the palladium. Nasiya speaks first: "I dreamt of a high man...one who is honest, honorable and true. This man is taken from his bed, bound, gagged and put on a horse. Now, he is a great distance from his home; darkness feeds on his spirit. He is alone, hurt and could die. If he dies... all of his knowledge is lost."

Mfiyah raises her melodic voice to say: "If he dies...we will be at a loss as a people. His powers are strong and vital. This is why he was chosen. He must be saved. We can't allow them to break or kill him. Is there two amongst us who will go to save him? The journey will be treacherous and taxing. There is no room for mistakes, hesitations or delays."

Sekele is the first to raise her blade. Since the last time, she has longed for another rite of passage. Her mate Kershay also does not hesitate; she simultaneously raises her blade into the air. Before departing they sit with diviners to receive insight, prophesy and knowledge. Before they depart they are given a magic crystal to guide and light the way, magical dust to conceal themselves and healing waters that can be used for him when they arrive. They depart after mounting Shash, the fierce eighty foot snake that everyone in the order fears and dreads, except for them.

Shash is their trusted friend and protector. The continuous hiss of the snake is a faithful companion as they travel high above the lands. On the way, Shash gives them knowledge of the hidden under-workings of the world. It is decided that Shash can only travel so far before being detected. In the distance, they spot a compound where they may dismount Shash and travel by foot. The serpent burrows deep underground to travel with them, yet beneath the surface.

Kershay and Sekele travel swiftly. They face many hazards as they make their way across swamps, hills and even a fiery lake. They are nearly at their destination when they feel the power of the sun as it rises in the east. Their bodies tingle with both warmth and light from the sun's rays. Looking ahead the two warriors feel both confusion and amazement. They are faced with a magnificent labyrinth carved into a mountain range. They pull out the crystal and hold it up to the sky moving around until the prism catches sunlight. The crystal begins to glow. The two lovers share a private smile with each other. Because they now know the direction he is being held.

The crystal glows brighter and brighter as they approach their destination. Travelling silently through the labyrinth, they slay many agents of darkness. They pour magical dust over themselves to hide their physical presence from their enemies. Then they place explosives at every exit, set to go off minutes apart to make sure there is no pursuit. At the end of the labyrinth, they arrive at a 10-foot dark mahogany door. Everything they see is exactly as they were told by the diviners back at home. They whisper the ancient incantations designed to break through any physical and cosmic barriers. Slowly the massive door opens after several locks turn.

He sits in the far corner poised and ready to fight. His eyes seem unafraid and his body is coiled to strike. You can tell he has experienced horrors that could fill up stories told late into the night.

They tried to break him. They tried to sway him. They tried to turn him evil. They tried to steal his essence. None of their efforts were successful. Faced with his indomitable spirit they refused to release him. Instead, they repeatedly beat him, raped him, tortured him and starved him. His physical body was deteriorating but his spirit was still strong. The failure to break him drove them further into the sickness/madness that consumes their lands. The women enter and approach him slowly. Sekele quietly addresses him. "Brother, we are the "Women of The Red Lotus." Our mothers have sent us to free you. You are safe now but we must leave here quickly."

Sekele reaches for him and hands him the container they brought filled with the healing waters. He drinks the water thirstily. Accidentally, their hands touch. She feels an electric current that is new to her; it is thrilling and frightening at the same time. She pulls her fingers back from him. Then before they move, BOOM!!! The first explosion goes off. They grab him and run out of the door. One by one, each explosion ignites causing panic and chaos to his captors and everyone around them.

While fleeing they stumble across the Elos, Beings of Magical Winged Lights, who were also imprisoned by the same evil ones. With one last explosion they free them as well. The Elos descend upon the darkness with unrestrained wrath and might. Kershay uses the magic crystal to guide them back down the labyrinth as they carry him along. When they move out of the darkness, Shash springs forth from the depth and the three mount quickly.

Fire and molten rock lights the sky and all around them as they successfully flee the darkness. The journey is quickened by magic incantations that they whisper to the serpent. They hear the horn of victory as they approach the outer gates to their home. The healers gather around to await their arrival. Shash falls quietly on her side; she is exhausted. The warriors feel travel-weary but their victory invigorates their spirit. There is very little life left in his body so the warriors gently place him in the arms of the healers who survey the womens' wounds they part ways. The healers take him to the prepared special healing hut.

Sekele and Kershay return to their normal way of life. They go back to their daily routine of loving each other, warriorship training and growing foods on the lands. They spend their nights in each other's arms and their days waiting for their nights. As is their custom, Sekele visits him daily to check on his healing. Based upon village traditions, it is her responsibility to make sure he makes it back to his home safely because she was the first to volunteer to retrieve him from the soulless lands. She walks to his window and sees for the first time he is awake and moving about.

She greets him and waits for his gesture to enter. "My brother, I am pleased to see you up and about. How is your spirit and body?" She introduces herself to him. "I am Sekele, one of the ones who came for you…" He cuts her off with a big hug, "I know who you are, I dreamt of you and your people before I was taken. Holding her tightly in his arms, he says, "Now, I have a name to go with your alluring image… Sekele." He speaks her name reverently. They stand in silence for a moment gazing into each other eyes. Sekele smiles graciously and steps back from him. Then she grabs his hands. "Your presence greatly honors my people. I will return you to your home when you are ready. Your people know you are with us and send their blessings and love. They are preparing for your return."

With deference he bows his head and expresses thanks. For a moment he is quiet, and then he asks a question. "I have not seen any men within and around. Why is that?" Sekele burst out laughing. He is captivated by her spontaneous laughter, it sounds like bells on the wind. He is immediately aroused. "Have you not looked at a mirror?" she asks in reference to his presence. He chuckles aloud composing his body's reaction to her but waits for a response.

Finally Sekele responds. "No men live here. Some visit their wives, mothers or their daughters but none live amongst us. Unless they are being cared for as you are, no men are here." He focuses inward and instantly his ancestors flood him with images, smells, sounds and knowledge of how things work, who she is and why she is chosen for him. One of the reasons the soulless ones tried to corrupt him is because he is a "Seer" "Gifted One" who sees things as they really are....have been... will be in the future. Some call him an "Oracle." His eyes dilate and his timbre becomes deeper when he speaks again." Sekele, when you return home with me I have a gift for you. I prepared it before I was taken. I knew you would be coming for me. Meeting you finally confirms that the gift is for you."

Sekele smiles showing her beautiful white teeth and takes her leave. That night as she lies wrapped around Kershay panting after their intense love making, Sekele is awakened by a glow that is both warm and cool. Not wanting to disturb Kershay she slides from under her and walks towards the light. It leads her to the sacred River of Knowledge which flows steadily but silently. On the riverbed she approaches him while he takes a drink from the sacred water.

She is immediately seized by anger. Sekele darts towards him and knocks the cup from his hands. She is offended and fearful by his sacrilege of her people's traditions and customs... *"Men are **not** allowed to drink this water. It could kill you. It is a gift given to us thousands of years ago from the Grand-Mother of all things. Her one rule is that no man should drink from these waters directly. Why are you even out here?" She demands. "I'm not*!" he mysteriously responds. Then he fades into air.

She gasps as Kershay shakes her awake. Trembling and wet; for different reasons this time, Kershay looks deeply into her lover's eyes. "What is it, love? What did you see?" Sekele relates her vision and rushes to the healers to physically determine his state. He is not surprised by her arrival. "I see you can't sleep either. Sit with me. Shall we play the game, the bean game Awari?" Momentarily, Sekele is confused but she sits down and they begin to play. Sekele listens as he shares his story while they play the game. She shares her story. They laugh and even cry together before she returns home many hours later. The elders are unconcerned. Kershay is only mildly irritated.

Something between them shifts. During the next week she spends most her spare moments with him. Sekele greatly desires to share him with her bond mate Kershay but the diviners tell her that "he is not for Kershay; only for you Sekele." You alone must learn from this journey and grow with him." She discovers day-by-day that he is more than a friend. Sekele is almost saddened by his swift recovery. Before she realizes... it is their last night together. Sekele passionately kisses Kershay good night and walks the path slowly across the village to spend time with him for the last time.

He senses her sadness but says nothing. They say very little while playing their favorite game Awari. They have spent much time together during his recovery. He decides it is sufficient. He knows of the ways of the "Women of the Red Lotus" and will not risk offending their customs because of his desires.

After playing in silence and enjoying time together she finally speaks. "I want you to be the one to heal me inside. I wish to have a daughter one day. I lost the gift of life during a period when others forced me to experience indifference, harshness and pain. I want you to heal me; to plant your seed inside me. I have spoken of this to my bond mate Kershay and also to the elders. They all agree that it will be a beneficial thing."

Sekele has more to say but is overwhelmed so she decides to stop and wait for his response. He continues to play the game without voicing any words. Patience is a virtue she lacks but with him she is learning its value. As they continue to play; she too is silent. He contemplates her words for a long time. Finally he speaks. "Are you sure this is what you want? Sekele, I will have to blend with you several times for this to happen. And if my lok impregnates you -- the child will most likely be a male child. He will be unable to live here with you and your people."

She looks into his eyes seeking more. He shields his deeper thoughts. "You will have to live amongst my people during your pregnancy and for many months after the birth. He will be raised by my people and know nothing of your ways." He thinks she will be surprised by his words. She responds immediately, "I have considered all these things and my decision is still the same."

Instead of leaving immediately, it is decided for his stay to be extended. Within days, a sacred space is created for the joining. The elders and Kershay begin the ritual in the ways of old. They raise their melodic voices in song, whisper cleansing incantations and sweep with strong bark branches to remove spiritual and physical impurities. Next they pour libation to the 'Grand Mother of All Things,' lay jasmine scented thick rugs across the ground and hang lighted talisman in the space for positive vibrations. Both he and Sekele bathed and dressed in ritual cloths. When Sekele enters the space, he is waiting. She feels enshrined.

He is sitting with his spiritual items and looks up at Sekele. He has used his own divination tools and is certain of their wisdom. Neither of them speaks. He begins to pray quietly in an ancient, but familiar language. With a penetrating look, he asks her quietly, "May I?"

At first she does not understand. Then she realizes he is asking permission to touch her intimately. Her hesitation is brief. She is not afraid; but apprehensive. She nods, yes. Slowly, he reaches for her. An electric current runs from his hands. It is the same as when they first touched. Sekele begins to tremble at the core and essence of her being. The trembling turns into a whirlwind of desire. She feels hundreds of hands touching every inch of her exposed skin. She is on fire; her mind; her senses; her soul suddenly feels too big for her body. The fire consumes her. It awakens a need deep guttural moan that escapes her lips.

Within minutes Sekele's trembling becomes erratic and in one deep thrust his massive tekken enters her deeply sheathed by pools of her dripping warmth. Sekele can no longer hold onto to her thoughts as their movements reach pinnacles of light and sound connecting endlessly. After days of joining together her endurance and heightened arousal is spent. The connection is so deep it is painful.

Shifting the energies, he uses one fingertip to touch the center of her head; light explodes behind her eyes. He places one of his massive hands on her stomach and the other on her heart while aligning their limbs skin-to-skin. He takes his time intoning ancient words in her ears, suckling her breasts, kissing her lips, nibbling on her neck, gently biting behind her thighs, placing open mouth kisses on her stomach and hungrily licking her nectar to 'seal the healing.'

At first she is sobbing, then her sobbing turns into tears of joy that cascade down her face. He shifts her body on top of him, matching heartbeat to heartbeat until he feels peace exude from her. He holds her while she sleeps. They perform this rite many times before she is impregnated.

The time to return to his home arrives. The "Women of the Red Lotus" send word across the land to his people about his safe return and the "new life" that accompanies them. The trip is harder for Sekele because she is unfamiliar with sickness. Of course, she desires no sympathy or special attention as they travel over the bumpy paths. After days of travel they arrive to colorful banners waving all across the land. She is greeted by his mother first, and then each of his people personally greet and thank her for saving him. Healers approach to touch her stomach to ask the Creator for blessings for the child. That night at the feast he stands before the fire with something wrapped in cloth. It is her gift.

He approaches her and hands her the woven cloth. Inside the package is a beautiful golden anklet with three charms: a mountain (where they met), a snake (that carried them to safety) and an ankh (symbol of life, masculine and feminine principles joining). She lowers her eyes and looks at the gift, then looks at him in astonishment. "I am confused. You told me about your people's traditions. I thought a woman is only given an anklet prior to her wedding ceremony." Sekele looks at him intently without recognizing the festivities surrounding them. The women of his people gather around her and begin to prepare her for the Hymeneal Rites. Before she blinks, the women wrap Sekele in blue cotton and her clothes are removed. She is guided back to the women's house where she is bathed, rubbed with fragrant oils and prayed over. Sekele does not resist. She understands that under the customs of his people, all the children are born as a result of the joining of two houses – hymeneal rites.

She is not concerned about the rites. Her only concern is Kershay, who she loves deeply. They share a bond that is irreplaceable. Yes, his efforts brought complete healing and the planting of his seed but Sekele is/will always be life mate to Kershay. There is no doubt in her mind about that truth.

One of the elders stops praying to speak to her. "Child, it is our belief that marriage is a sacred commitment between two individuals/families or more who vow to respect, care and work together towards the benefit of each other while perpetuating the good of the society.

You carry his child. As so, you agree to connect your two families, honoring our way, joining together by these hymeneal rites. You two will forever be connected. Our people will always protect the spark of life that you now nurture and will leave to thrive and grow here with us. You and your child will be honored and loved in our sacred spaces even if you return to your people." The elder's words bring clarity and helped to ease her troubled mind. Sekele is finally prepared and led back to the circle of fire where a beautiful ceremony is held. In the ancient way the two are united.

Months pass and it is time for the birthing ritual. Kershay and healers of the Women of the Red Lotus travel the far distance to be with Sekele during the birth. All the women gather. They ask the guardians who stand in the birthing chamber for guidance, protection, insight and blessings. After several hours Sekele gives birth to a strong and willful baby boy. Kershay stays with her for several more weeks as she nurses the little one and recovers. As is the tradition -- only an elder woman of his family is allowed to see the little warrior until his coming out ceremony.

Kershay is also allowed because she is Sekele's chosen life mate. Both people share the tradition that Kershay is considered the child's second mother. By the time Kershay plans to leave, Sekele also begins to prepare to return home. She stops nursing and allows her milk to dry. Part of the process involves the baby being nursed by the woman who will eventually raise him.

During the transition, Sekele, Kershay and the baby's baba (father) become very close. The three of them spend their days and nights side by side. After the child's coming out ceremony Sekele pours Libation to the Creator for giving her life – granting her healing and the wealth she was bestowed by meeting him. Next, she prostrates herself in front of him in thanks for his sacred act of helping her to heal; restoring vitality and life to her womb.

She ceremonially presents rows and rows of colorful textiles, succulent fruit and dried meat to the village leaders, women and healers for the women's care and acceptance of her and newborn child. They begin the journey back home to the "Women of the Red Lotus," leaving her son in the care of his father and his people – content to provide "life for the ability to give life." She has "sacrificed" her first born not realizing that he has also implanted the baby girl she desired.

Sage Wisdom: **Meditating with Crystals**

Meditating with Crystals

Crystals can be used for cleansing, healing or to ground yourself. Many people use crystals when they are meditating to help them focus. Pick a mineral or rock based upon what feels right. The color of the crystal makes a difference; it will carry the energy you seek. See the *Sage Wisdom: Colors in Healing and Stones.* If you want to clear the energy of a crystal, wash the rock with water and sea salt and pray/focus to remove all negative/unwanted energy.

The Pyramid Meditation

Sit with both of your feet flat on the floor or in a lotus position. Take your crystal and place it in either hand or you can rest it in your lap.
Close your eyes and visualize what you desire. Take three short breath and hold each breath to the count of three. Breathe in through your nose. Breathe out your mouth. Repeat this breathing exercise two more times. You might experience a slight lightheaded-ness so don't overdo it.

Count backwards from 10 to 1 while you set up a natural pattern of breathing. Continue to visualize what you desire. With eyes still shut, choose a color that best suits your present emotional state.
 Sit in a Lotus position and flow with your positive energy. Relax your body as fully as you can. Mentally direct more colored energy to any area of discomfort, pain or tightness in your body. Try and allow all your thoughts to flow freely. The external noises around you will cease to be a part of your awareness as you meditate deeper and deeper. Enjoy your peaceful state of awareness. This may take several sittings before you are able to meditate to the level you seek.

Hold the picture as you meditate. After about 15 minutes, bring yourself back to full consciousness. You will be surprised how accurate your bio-timer will become with practice. Open your eyes.

You should feel refreshed and peaceful so you can begin your day. Stretch your body and give thanks to the Creator for the meditation. Wash off your crystal, dry it and put it away after you are finished.

Five Days

Work Schedule

Monday
I made vegetarian pizza and served it with sweet red wine for him when he arrived home from work. I ran a hot bubble bath and bathed him slowly using my hands roughly to touch his dark muscular body. I spend extra efforts concentrating on his glistening thick elongated dick. After bathing him I dried him off, expertly led him into the bedroom, and then slowly sucked him until he begged me to put it in. His dick is so delicious. I enjoy it every time! He continued to beg but I made him suffer. At the point when he was about to lose it... I entered heaven; he watched my body movements as I repeatedly hit his anal walls.

I then squeezed his beautiful ass and licked his neck while I continually entered and exited heaven. He responded by moaning loudly as I watched him succumb to me.

Tuesday
He arrived home late from his job. I coaxed him to lie on the floor on his stomach and massaged his feet. I pressed my index fingers and thumbs between his toes. I firmly massaged the heels and sides of his feet; massaged his lower and upper calves, his thighs, his back, his arms, his neck, his head, and his eyes. All tension gone from his body, I then entered his ass from an angle that required him to feel the fullness of my member. I did this... oh so slowly. After pumping his ass time after time, I finally spewed life inside him. I then kissed and licked his dick until he came, tasting a bit of my own semen.

Wednesday
I picked him up from his job, took him home, and pushed him into the house. I ripped off his shirt and pushed him up against the wall, gripping his wrists in one hand so that he couldn't move. I immediately put my other hand over his mouth and muffled the scream that simultaneously erupted when I penetrated him roughly from behind. I continually pushed my dick into him hard and fast until we came together.

Thursday
He entered the house without my knowledge while I was still asleep. He licked my nipples, thus making me hard and began to ride me while choking me at the same time. His grip was so damn tight I was about to pass out. With a guttural sound from all the exertion, he asked, "whose is it mine or yours?" I could barely breathe but I still bit out the word "Mine!" He slapped me. This made my lok larger and harder. He turned around and rode me until he came. Next he moved his ass back and rode my face until my jaws were sore. Leaving nothing untouched, he then forcibly jacked me off saying, "I don't suck dick".

Friday

We woke up making passionate love that was so intense that neither of us went to our jobs. We started in our favorite 69 position touching and tasting each erogenous zone that had us dripping wet with sweat and continuing until we both came.

Then I kissed him in a hungry passionate way that always makes him growl; both of us fought for dominance between teeth and tongues. My dick grew thicker and longer... as we fondled each other's family jewels and sacred phallus. We embraced tightly while he dug his nails into my back. I stuck my two fingers into his rectum sliding them methodically in and out.

I bit into his nipple real hard – then licked the pain away. His dick exploded as he screamed my name. All I could think of was....MINE! So I pushed him on his back and continued to make love to him until he experienced multiple orgasms. After this he laid me on my back,   put his mouth on my tip and alternated between licking, sucking, nibbling, deep-throating and blowing on my dick. This continued for the next two hours until he commanded me to "cum." I almost fainted when I did.

Black Man

You are the sun rising in my morning bringing light to the world. You are the seedling sprouting forth from the depths of the earth determined to live and grow.
You are the lava bursting forth bringing your fiery force to all things that you touch. You are the feral force of the warriors that protect our people. You are the potent herbs used to heal the deadliest ailments.

You are the relentless push that causes the mountain to rise. You are the screaming whisper that causes justice to be heard. You are the penetrating arrow that pierces the deepest mahogany. You are the masculine physical manifestation of The Creator that easily transcends all realms.

You are the bass in my baritone that vibrates the foundation of the human spirit. You are the voice of dignity that brings things to light from dark. You are splendor; every element of your existence is arranged in the divine essence of masculinity. Your energy causes the stars to align themselves to tell your story in the cosmos. You are the algorithm.

Your vast manifestations, attributes, perspectives and essence converge into infinite possibilities for divine victory. You add flavor to all you touch. You multiply life and new ideas. You subtract all doubts, fears and worries. You divide virility into molecules of womankind. Whether you are stating facts, statistically speaking or theorizing about probabilities you open the mind and spirit to the universal truths. You are beautiful, black man.

Fall into me....

Slowly pulling out.....causing red, orange, yellow, green, brown vibrations to permeate and my subtle preparations for a long night. Amassing my nuts one by one by one allowing my juices and berries to accumulate so that I may accommodate him even more~and I can never get enough. My defenses fall one at a time to reveal a vulnerable me that houses many things roaring up inside me awaiting his bitter blows. When he hits me with his best shot I'll stand strong although I may want to buckle and break. Leaving his reflective attributes all over me from top to bottom I am covered in his bone quivering expressions of love.

His presence causes a death like silence that allows me to hear those things stirring inside of me looking for fuel, nourishment, comfort, warmth... hell anything at this point. Just when I think I cannot take any more I feel him rising up inside me bringing life back to every inch of my being. He causes me to burst open and share my beauty with all those around me. And while he stimulates me he saturates me from head to toe encouraging me to dig deeper looking for new secrets. I am content with my newness, but he is not done yet he continues to get me hotter and hotter and hotter until I am wilting pleading for him to release me from his intense stare...a blow causes me to sway and dance and shake. I turn upwards as he pours his blessing upon me to nourish my soul.

Knowing that in but a blink of the eye I will be amassing my nuts again.

Sage Wisdom: Spiritual Intimacy

"Intimacy in general terms is a song of spirit inviting two people to come together and share their spirit together...."

"....each of us is seen as a spirit who has taken the form of a human in order to carry out a purpose. Spirit is the energy that helps us connect and helps us see beyond our racially limited parameters, and also helps us in ritual and in connecting with the ancestors....

"THE SPIRIT OF INTIMACY: Ancient African Teachings in the Ways of Relationship" Sobonfu Some

Divine Spirit and Sex

What is **divine spirit**? Does this have anything to do with sex? This is the aspect of self that many people describe as "vibe," "aura," "energy," or "essence." Truly, this must be the capacity to operate at my higher self, my consciousness and connection to the Creator, my Ancestors, Mother Earth, etc. How does this connect to sex? For me it has everything to do with sex. It is the divine spirit that seeks fulfillment; to always achieve oneness... to be whole and complete. "There is a great deal of talk about sex, sexuality, sensuality, climaxing and joining – more today than in past generations. Many people speak in hushed voices about that so-called "cosmic cummin" that only one in a million individuals may attain when sharing intimacy.

Why is that? Have you ever wondered why so many seek "fireworks" in sexual connections but rarely talk to each other and share true intimacy, divine spirit, cosmic love or erotic-spirituality?

Oftentimes, we forget what happens when we "make love" or "connect spiritually. " Many of us still focus entirely on the physical desires to chase a temporary **physical** pleasure or "orgasm." What might happen if we sought to experience a **spiritual joining** or **oneness** that connects us to spirit and to the Creator?

These are a few questions you might want to ponder as you read through the pages of Confessions of a Sage Woman. Who Am I? Am I ALL that I choose to be in this lifetime? If I seek to understand **intimacy, what should I do; what should I study and understand so that my relationships can manifest true connections**. Is my physicality simply a portion of my consciousness or is it all of it? What is my level of openness... Will I allow myself to become engaged in experiencing, sensing, appreciating, understanding, accepting and loving myself? How can I openly share my "unloved" self with others? True intimacy is being open and receptive to connecting spiritually with another person in a loving manner – this starts with being connected and loving to my spiritual self?

In life we must remember our "spiritual" journey as well as our physical journey. We are born as divine beings ready to experience life fully. To experience life fully one should incorporate the visible (physical) and invisible (spiritual/energy) aspects of life. We are experts of having physical experiences, yet we often ignore the spiritual aspects of those experiences. Our spirit animates our bodies and without it we would not exists.

With that in mind we can spend some time on pursuits that ensure our spirits are healthy and that we are experiencing life to the fullest. Each of us should be interested in spiritual wellness. Right? To improve your spiritual 'wholeness' there are many avenues. Here are a few suggestions: Spend time each day allocating time to do praying, meditating, fasting; or assisting with shrine work, divining, mediumship or other paths to spiritual journeys.

There are many different systems or approaches to spiritual intimacy. You just need to find which is best for you. In the meantime this visualization can be done to enhance your spiritual experiences.

Visualize a Heightening Experience....

Visualize what energies you desire to raise through the sexual act. Our bodies are our temples because they house our divine spirit (soul). Before we let someone into our temple or go into someone else's temple we should make sure we have the proper energy and mindset.

Bathe your partner before the sexual act; or make sure both of you bathe and pray together....asking the Creator for the "joining" to be blessed. Pray over your partner(s) before sex. The joining; symbolic of sex as a spiritual act. Whenever we "consume" or take something into our bodies we should pray over it.

Set up a shrine that represents the beauty, joy, connection, arousal, peace, vitality, enlightenment and heightening energy that you want to use after the sexual act. These are simply suggestions of course... but it can't hurt to have a higher intent than simply....culmination.

When we add prayer to our sexual experience we welcome our spirit to fully participate in the act and make it sacred. Don't believe me? Try it.... Then let me know how it was...

A prayer simply focuses our minds on something we desire and putting consecrated thoughts towards accomplishing it.

Prayer or Meditation

"My life is my prayer. I live in a manner that is holistic, reciprocating, connective, collective, beneficial and positive. I speak words of beauty to loved ones so they may feel uplifted and inspired. I show my appreciation for the wonder of nature by growing things, recycling, reusing, and leaving little to no carbon footprint on this earth.

I support people, organizations, businesses and ideas that work to improve the state of the world. I celebrate life by honoring all living things. I recognize my divinity and the divinity of others and use that to guide my decisions, relationships and behaviors. I reinforce my optimism and an understanding of how the universe works and my role in it. My life is my prayer Ashe!" Milele

My Desires for Spiritual Intimacy...

Marassa

The cool soft mud from the river bank was a nice contrast to her warm leathery skin. Although the mud completely covered her anklet it still had a magnificent shine that mesmerized him. The sun rose over the peaks of the mountain to burst through the tops of the trees. This is what she thought of as she slowly rubbed her right thigh with her left hand, then her left thigh with her right hand. She crossed her arms over her chest and fully caressed her breasts. She bent over and rubbed more mud on the outside of her legs starting at the anklet and gliding upwards until she covered her hips.

At some point she slid her hands around her hips, over her cheeks and then back up her crack. Now from neck to claws mud covered everything; nothing was shown except her anklet. Caught up looking at the *anklet and pendant he barely notices how she lays in the sun allowing the mud to warm and harden all over her.*

The sun beams danced around her body to blast off her anklet then back into the sky as if they were having a conversation. As the mud dries it cracked and split when she slithered her body into the river like a serpent.

Her body was visible beneath the waves of the tide. She swam the rapids like a fish -- occasionally springing up for air with her anklet always beaming. She disappeared beneath the waters and suddenly appeared behind him, licking his neck and hissing.
Enjoying?
Umm, yes, uh, no I mean. . .
Why do you ALL wear the anklets? Where did they come from? He fumbled over his words. "Many moons ago...we got a visit from a conjurer whose village we visited habitually. There were many wicked among them and we feasted upon them. She licked her lips as she recalled. One evening one from the village journeyed to our mountains to request a favor amongst us. She brought us many gifts and charms. Among the gifts were these pendant anklets."

What do they do? They are magical. They permit us to become human while on earth.
I don't understand. Aren't you all shape shifters?
"Yes, we do shift into entities: mist, water, wind, fire, serpent, feline, canine, many different archetypes and forms; excluding human. Becoming human is a more intricate transformation that cannot be done without assistance from humans. That has kept humanity safe. The spirits whisper the herbs and prayers for us to her. We accept, inform her of the duties of the villagers and then there is peace."

Can I See?
Within moments, before him appeared a fully grown bare bodied woman. Her breasts were still round and supple, the muscles in her legs still shown but her skin was brown; not grey, it was soft not leathery and her fangs and claws were no more.
How long can you stay in this form?

"It is un-timed, as long as needed. We age, live, eat and exist as you do."
Are you human completely or do you just appear to be human?
He reached his hand out and put it to her breasts. Then he slid his hand down her body which caused her to squirm. She had never been touched by a man in this form. His touch felt unusual, but she did not desire him to stop. She leaned her face towards his hand. She wanted to feel his touch all over. He instinctively took her hand and walked her back to the nest that he made for himself. The fur that covered the nest tickled her as she laid down on it. With both his hands he readjusted her "human body" by putting a pillow under her head. It would be different for them both.

He softly kissed her. His saliva encased her nipples as he slowly suckled her breasts. He followed her moans until he reached her inner desire to

*receive pleasure. He did not anticipate that this would be her first time,
but it was. At the first thrust, she bit down hard into his shoulder.*

"Sorry, I did not know."

*She did not respond. She was quiet. She waited for his next move. He
opened her legs a little more and rubbed his hand over her clitoris.
Moisture flowed easily from her center. He tried to slide a finger inside her
but the pain caused her to wince...so he retracted it. She did not respond.
She was patiently waiting.*

*She had possession of the anklet for more than ten centuries... so, time was
of little consequence. She desired his penetration and patiently waited for
his success.*

*For nearly an hour he tried to be gentle. He wanted it to be painless so he
gently pushed into the core of her being... but it was without real success.
Finally, he made the decision to simply do it but make it quick. He
instructed her to relax as much as possible and hold him tight. He looked
deep into her eyes until she was calm, then with a mighty thrust, he pushed
inside her with all his might. She moaned so loudly it echoed for miles -
bouncing from mountain to mountain - in and out of caves and traveled
across the wind. He waited until she was calm again. Then he slowly
moved inside her. He barely moved. He took into account that this was
her first time having intercourse in human form. After only a few strokes he
exploded inside her. He began to retract himself but she purred and pulled
him closer.*

"You will rise again. It is better for you to grow than burst inside."
*Her stomach began to sink as he rose again. He began to pump slowly.
This time it felt much different. The sinking intensified the faster he moved
and she began to experience a pleasant sensation within her body. She felt
her "other" approach. The intensity of the two of them joined together
intimately had startled her awake. She and her mate both jumped when
she awakened from the vivid dream.*

"Raba? Are you okay? You were moaning and tossing around in your
sleep?" Naraba was disoriented and couldn't remember her dream. Instead
she spoke to her "other" inside her head. "I am fine. It was just a crazy
dream. You know how things are around my birthday." She shrugged it
off and walked into the kitchen. Naraba peered outside to look at the entire
city. She absentmindedly rubbed her fingers across the pendant which
hung from a gold chain around her neck.

Naraba sighed loudly and wondered why she had recently been so unsatisfied with her life. She sensed her sister Nifisa who prepared for the day in their bedroom. The apartment they shared was a three bedroom loft on the 27th floor. Their bedroom was the largest room; two smaller ones were shrine rooms. One room held a collective shrine for the shujaa (victors) of their people; the other shrine was devoted to Naraba and Nifisa's energies.

When Naraba and Nifisa met, some twenty plus years back, they did not know that their relationship would define the sum of their duality. Today, everybody knows it. They dress alike, sound alike, smell alike, think alike and have mannerisms that are mirror-image. If you didn't know it; you would think them to be fraternal twins. They are inseparable. Because of their unique oneness and connection were called "Marassa" meaning Divine Twins.

Marassa discovered during their rite of passage training that they had been close in another life path; or "life manifestation." It was interesting to hear in a divination sit that the two women came back to finish work started in previous past lives. They were also told if they became more in alignment with their destiny they would recover more memories of their past lives. After completing their womanhood rites, they both received items to start a new home. The items they were given were intrinsic to "new beginnings" in a new home. They were both gifted: books, tools, cowrie shells, incense, honey, a kinara, a broom and a bag of rice. They were both pleasantly surprised when they received a lump sum of money to buy a new home. They were honored to also receive a House Blessing Ritual for their new home – one that had been passed down through generations of their female ancestors. They decided to wait until later to build a home; so they got an apartment together.

This day was their anniversary. A decade ago they had completed their rite of passage transition into womanhood. Tonight they were going out to celebrate their victory. Naraba's head was filled with so many different images it seemed almost confusing. Nifisa's aura vibrated enthusiasm and excitement. She couldn't wait to go out and celebrate. Naraba was more excited about re-enacting the ritual. They had planned to do that tomorrow. They had re-enacted the ritual many times over the years but this time it would be different.

This time Naraba would re-enact the ritual as a "full-fledged" adult. In addition to their anniversary Naraba had recently celebrated her 28 birth cycle – meaning she was finally considered a full adult woman - based upon Afrikan values.

According to their traditions it takes the stars 28 years to align to your birth cycle. Every seven years marked a different transition of one's life. Nifisa shouted out "One full cycle of the stars Raba." Naraba sighed again. "You would think I would feel something more than simple trepidation. Spiritually, I should feel something powerful, something greater. I really don't want to go out and be with others. I would rather stay home and astral project."

"But Raba this time for you is sooo... special. When I made my transition you were right by my side. It was you who ensured that I celebrated my transition fully. You must allow me to do the same for you. Plus I have a good feeling about tonight."

Naraba conceded reluctantly....."Fine, but you must drive." They drove in a comfortable silence to the gathering place. Naraba looked out the car window and watched the street lights buzz past her. Suddenly she turned to her twin and said, "I have a weird feeling about tonight." Nifisa squealed and interrupted her "I KNOW! ME TOO! ISN'T IT WONDERFUL?! I had no idea I would be feeling our transition so strongly. My entire body is tingling...."

She continued talking while Naraba turned back around to face the window. Naraba did not share the same perspective about what would happen during the evening. Her sister's voice sounded like a flock of birds singing. Naraba closed her eyes and drifted away to an inner tranquil place.

She began to remember bits and pieces of her dream. She even recognized that the creature was wearing her pendant. Well, for the sake of an argument, both she and her sister were wearing the pendants. They received their pendant as a part of their "coming out" ceremony when they were recognized in their womanhood rites. They were told that one day their stories from previous lives would be revealed to them.
As a part of their transformation, they had decided to add charms to their pendant. They purchased a Bennu charm to represent "renewal, blessings, protection and attraction."

She knew that the new charm represented more than a physical cleansing and blessing of their space. For her, the ritual would bring her those things too. Images of each item and their connotations danced around in her head and flitted across her eyelids. Tomorrow they would re-enact the ritual. The symbolism of the items always brought good vibes and a smile to Naraba. She thought about their meanings as she pictured each item in her head:

Kinara -(Candle holder) connects one to his/her own cultural traditions and heritage; representing the roots of a tree

Broom - promotes cleanliness inside one's physical space as well as within one's psychic self; sweeping away of unwanted things

Books -activates ancient knowledge to connect one to his/her role in the universe; being a consummate student of life

Tools - promotes the ability to manifest into reality all that is visualized/desired; building for the future

Cowrie Shells -promotes fertility, spiritual insight and spiritual blessings; it is also a symbol of wealth and prosperity

Incense -promotes one's ability to rise to their highest potential; higher thinking and divine thoughts

Honey- promotes sweetness, attraction and joy; the good things of life

Bag of Rice - represents transitions, promotes cultivation and harvest; being able to feed oneself and family

Lump Sum of Money- attracts wealth, financial stability and business success

The ritual was very simple. The two placed beautiful African cloth on a table in a designated room; the front room or dining room is best because of its centralized location. All the nine items listed include a symbolic portion of the sum of money (i.e., gold coin, silver dollar, two dollar bill) should be placed on the cloth too. All items should be placed in a circle. Next, a white candle is anointed with Frankincense and Myrrh oil. The white candle is placed at the top of the table (right above the circle of items). A glass of water is also placed out on the cloth (on the right side, in the front). Natural items are always used, such as "glass" or "brass" or "silver", and do not use plastic. Then light the candle and say this simple prayer:

House Blessing Prayer

"Great Creator, It is I, _____, daughter/son of
_____ and _____
We are grateful for the love, sustenance, care and protection that you provided our family and our home this past season. We thank you. We thank our Ancestors and all other friends and guides who have been there for us. We come again and ask for your blessings.

We place these items out today in honor of all that has been provided to us and we ask you to grant us: a deeper connection to our culture/heritage; a more divine and clean energy; opportunities to learn our ancient knowledge; the power to do/actualize our dreams; more insight and spiritual connection; advancement to rise to our higher selves; the sweetness of life and between our relations; the opportunity to reach a new plateau – transition in our lives and financial stability.

Please grant us these blessings, as you have so many times before. May we be worthy and always grateful for all we seek. We ask that you provide blessings, protection, renewal and attraction as we enter this new phase of our lives. Ashe. (so be it; Please, make it so)

Tomorrow, she thought. After the excitement of tonight, Naraba would rise before sunrise and prepare for the ritual. The ritual always gave her peace. She reflected with an inward smile that this time would be different. Inwardly, she intoned: "Because, I am different".

As she drifted deeper into sleep a bright light passes by the window and Naraba began to dream:

Have I ever told you that you make me uncomfortable at times? She inquired.
No you have not. How do I make you uncomfortable? He responde.
I know we have been interacting for years but the things you like about me, the areas where we connect make me uncomfortable.
Are you uncomfortable with those aspects of yourself?

I pause and trace my fingers around the edge of my glass causing it to resonate at a low tone. I lift the glass, take a sip and trace my fingers around the rim again. I smile as the vibrations cause him to shift in his seat. He can feel the energy rising in the room *clearing throat*.
Are you uncomfortable with those aspects of yourself?
   mmm... I guess I am.

You guess? Come now.... surely you know how you feel. And since you began this intimate exchange don't be shy now. You know how much that arouses me.

See that is what I am talking about. Why do you do that? Why is everything arousing to you? Is that how you think of me?

Yes.

I stop tracing the rim of my glass. I push away from the table, stand and begin to walk away. He reaches for my hand to stop me.

Where are you going? You can't run from me. You can't run from this feeling or us. Are you viewing that as something separate from you or outside of you; something that should be controlled? Please realize that it a part of you and me; it has its place. Are you afraid of it? I plop back in my chair and move my kinky coils behind my ear. My fingers trace the stem of the glass again as I search myself for the answer.

Am I afraid of it? I guess...

You guess?

Yes... No. No I am not afraid of "it". But I do see a need to control it. Why do you say it has its place?

You know what this attraction comes through and to us. YOU tell me what is it?

The ringing of the glass, as my fingers slide around the rim, arouses him. I know it does. The vibratory energy in the room becomes more intense and electrifying. I can taste the colors and hear the moisture. The energy within him and I becomes heightened and pulsates. I can feel it bounce from him to me. I continue to rub the rim at a little faster pace. It deepens the sound. I use the pitch to distract him. He clenches his hand tightly then relaxes it again. For a moment I think I should stop. But as much as I don't like to admit it -- I enjoy the arousal.

Are you going to keep doing that?
Smirking Doing what?

I slightly open my legs and my wrap opens; it no longer gathers at my knees. For a moment I desire to reach out for him but contain myself and push the glass away.

It is not something I am doing. I don't make myself aroused. Your mere presence calls forth that energy and when that happens it is arousal. But you already know this. So tell me why you are not comfortable with me.

Because damn it. I can't be myself with you. I don't want to be with you. I don't want to keep calling up those feelings from the past. That was centuries ago and I'm in a completely different place but you always speak of that time. That's not who I am anymore. That isn't who you are. We are both very different now.
I know. I am now of this physical time; in addition to all that was before. I am much bigger now; I am the composite of many, many lifetimes. I know who I am. And I know who you are. That time is as much a part of who we are as this time. Rabai, look at me!

Don't call me that! That is not my name in this life!!
Fine. Beautiful spirit, look at me. Tell me who I am to you.
You are my friend.
And?

My squirming in my seat is all the indication he needs that I am feeling the energy pulsing through he and I. My heavy breathing is the icing on the cake.

And…I don't want this with you. (The words echo in my head). I want the here and now. I want who I am now. Not who I was then. That primal being that I WAS is no longer who I AM.

> *It is no longer who you are?*
> **No.**
> *You don't want this with me?*
> **No**
> *If I were to never speak of the past again, would that make you happy?*
> **Yes.**

Then so be it. I will not speak of the past. I will act as if we did not exist together before now. I will pretend that all the moments we shared from the past are also false. I will erase each thought of your juices on my tongue. I will disregard the times we spent making love for days in the jungles. I will not allow the images from the past to visit me in my dreams whenever you want to be pleased. I will…

I stand up abruptly accidentally knocking the glass over. The red wine glides across the table as if it is alive. Almost in a trance I watch as it pools right at the edge. It glides to the edge and cascades off the table into his lap. He cups his hand to gather it. I watch him in fascination.

I remember watching him drink from the waterfalls when I first came across him. I know how strong and muscular he is and how intense our mêlée is. I get on my knees and cuff my hands under his to catch the last drops. He pours the wine from his hand on to my neck and licks it off. The heat from his breath moistens my center and vibrates through my soul. I can feel me slipping through time.

He lifts me off my knees and tosses me over his shoulder. It has been so long since I let my mask down and let my true essence out. I pull at his clothes and bite his back as he carries me to the bed. My body falls to the bed. He releases me and begins taking off his clothes. The primal force inside me is awakened. It is not going to retreat until this is finished. Hissing and growling fills the air. I hear it but I don't know where it is coming from. The energies position themselves to pounce.

The doorbell rings and momentarily I remember who I am. But his nibbling at my ankles spring me back into the past. Now the ringing goes to banging on the door. I spring back into the presence. He and I leap from the bed and head for the door. I remember that my lover is on the way over. I know she is wondering why I am not answering the phone or the door.

> *Are you okay?*
> *Upon entering she feels the energy in the air.*
> *He's here? Is he here!*

She trots through the house looking for him. My lover's tone changes from inquisition to accusation as she bolts through the house looking for the man who has her mate, me, so entangled in him. I try to run after her but my legs are still quivering from traveling between this time and the other time. I also feel a growing anxiety. As I take a moment to focus I hear the two of them arguing back and forth.

YOU CAN'T HAVE HER! SHE IS MINE NOW! SHE WILL ALWAYS BE MINE!

There is silence and rustling so I fear the worse. I rush to my room to find him on top of her thrusting and pumping. He pulls out and licks down her breasts to her navel. He then inserts his fingers and pumps in and out of her. She opens her mouth as she looks over at me mindlessly; but no sound comes out. He lowers his head more to flick her mound and holds her close as she shakes and convulses. He looks up at me smirking as he brings her to orgasm repeatedly. I stand and watch as juices flow down her legs. My insides throb for him. I prop myself up against the door feeling the primal energy rising inside of me again.

YOU BELONG TO ME! *The words burst from my lips as I bound towards them and pushed him off of her to bite his neck. He pins me up against the wall and I wrap my legs around his waist. My lover watches as he and I move in synchronization together. His energy still engulfs her.*

NOW tell me you don't want me like this. He places his tekken against my thigh and guides it back and forth across my nubbin. My moisture drips down my legs as he holds me effortless in place against the wall. I can feel the strength vibrate across his hands as he holds me securely; I feel protected.

I'm not going to put it in until you tell me you want me. I readjust my hips trying to maneuver him inside me but each time he moves back slightly. It was just enough to brush against my wetness but not enough to enter my depths. He teases me with his girth.... pushing me closer each time. Under my breath I begin to pant. "I want you..." He lowers his ear and listens as I pant his name. As he begins to enter my wetness ...

Naraba is startled awake by the horn of a car.

She sat up panting and looked around for signs that it was real. She focused her eyes to see the clock. She had only been asleep in the car for five minutes. "That was the longest five minutes ever," she thinks to herself.

"I just had the weirdest vision ever just now," said Raba. Tell me about it, my mate said as she rubbed my shoulders. Raba did not want to share the vision immediately. The two of them sat in silence as she contemplated everything. Wordlessly, she continued looking out the window.

Sage Wisdom: **Aphrodisiacs**

"Aphrodisiacs" is defined as any...food, drink or drug that stimulates sexual desire.

Throughout time there have been many foods and drinks enjoyed by people to promote a "happy, joyful, excitable, pleasurable or stimulating" feeling. We call those foods aphrodisiacs. Whether one believes in them or not....we still attribute certain foods/drink with the ability to make sex more pleasurable.

Just for clarity sake, for a food or drink to be considered an aphrodisiac, the food/drink item should be:

- administered orally

- Reliably increase libido or sexual desire (no placebo effect, no diminishment of libido)

- Take effect in a relatively immediate time frame (minutes or hours, not days or weeks)

Check out these common Aphrodisiacs:

Arugula
The high level of minerals and antioxidants, like calcium, folic acid and magnesium, found in dark leafy greens of arugula block environmental contaminates; also boost sex drive

Artichokes
Artichokes are packed with vitamins and antioxidants which are critical to proper body function and blood flow.

Avocado
Avocado is a pear shaped fruit with high levels of vitamin E which promote vigor and energy levels.

Chili Peppers

Chili Peppers are one of the "hot foods" which raise heartbeats, increase sweat glands; similar to being aroused. The little peppers are filled with Capsaicin, a chemical in the body that stimulates nerve endings which act as endorphins to increase your sex drive.

Chocolate

Chocolate, particularly dark chocolate, is an aphrodisiac because it causes a spike in dopamine which induces feelings of pleasure and also has a chemical that stimulates a sense of excitement and wellbeing.

Figs

Figs are a symbol of fertility, sexuality and modesty because of the ripe fruit and abundance of seeds contained within them. The figs are full of potassium and antioxidants which energizes the body.

Honey

Honey is filled with boron, a mineral proven to regulate testosterone and estrogen. A symbol of procreation, honey is made through pollination and it provides a natural energy boost.

Asparagus

The vitamin E in Asparagus activates hormones like testosterone, estrogen, and progesterone, which circulate in your bloodstream and stimulate sexual responses – including clitoral swelling and vaginal lubrication.

Pomegranate

Many people love the bright little seeds enclosed in a thick rose husk of Pomegranates. The fruits are also filled with antioxidants which help blood flow and increases genital sensitivity.

Pine Nut

Pine nuts are aphrodisiacs because they are high in energizing zinc, linked to a healthy sex drive.

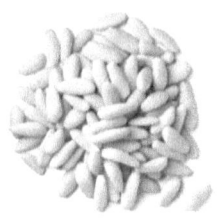

Pumpkin Seeds

Pumpkin seeds are high in magnesium-- which helps raise testosterone levels by making sure more enters the blood stream.

Olives

Olives are packed with antioxidants and a good source of monounsaturated and polyunsaturated fats, that are vital for a healthy heart, blood flow and hormone production.

Oysters

Oysters contain amino acids that trigger the production of sex hormones and are also high in zinc, which produces sex hormones. They act as a double shot to the sex hormones.

Watermelon

Some refer to watermelon as the 'lycopene king' because of its Viagra-like effect on the body, as it relaxes blood vessels and improves circulation leading to better erections.

Bananas

The phallic shaped banana is a powerful aphrodisiac because it is packed with nutrients essential to sexual hormone production, including potassium and B vitamins.

So whether you use these together or individually consuming these can lead to a more intense, longer, deeper and more fulfilling experience, and they are good to your body. Eat up!!!!!!

If...Then

If the words you whispered in my ears were only fabrications to make
my heart sing like the soaring sparrow
Then my love is as a love on stage, based on fake characters, set scenes,
rehearsed Ad Nauseam and fading with the lighting

If the arms that once held me tight are now embracing a new friend,
lover, mate....victim
Then I hold her in my dreams mending a broken heart, wiping away
tears and restoring respect

If you said you loved me because the trip you took into my caramel
made you a lifetime member
Then I know everything about you, yet I understand nothing

If the stories I shared with you were too deep and my tears too intense
Then the essence of humanity must have left with your last climax

If you do love me, but are afraid to open up your heart and let me walk
in
Then I can do nothing but watch as you stay trapped in your emotions
until you are ready to be free

If the words you whispered in my ears were only fabrications
to make my heart sing like the soaring sparrow
Then like that sparrow I will fly higher and higher
Dancing in the sky
Piercing the clouds
Gliding on the wind

Then, I will continue to strive, grow and learn
Then, I will become better every day
Then... I thank you

UHURU
(Freedom)

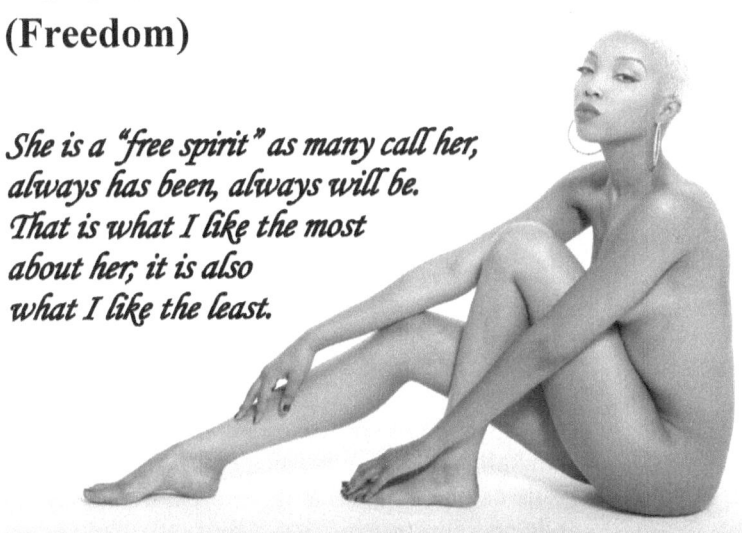

She is a "free spirit" as many call her, always has been, always will be. That is what I like the most about her; it is also what I like the least.

When we met at Progressive Emporium & Education Center she approached me and offered to take me to lunch. The following day we met under a weeping willow in the park (her favorite tree) where she had prepared a wonderful spread of fruit salad, homemade rolls, wine, hummus, salad and several other mouth-watering dishes. As we sat there eating and drinking she shared so much of herself with me without hesitation. It shocked me because so few people are that honest and open.

She told me how she had gotten over a bad break up with someone but it took many years. They had been together for years and then she never heard from them again. She told me how much that hurt. Her words were so powerful. She thought she would never be open to love again. But after spending time with her for only two months she tells me she would like to share her "all" with me. She even wants to give me a spare key to her house. In the beginning we spent nearly every night together and made love every place we went. When I touch her she holds nothing back. She enjoys every stroke as I fully let my intent completely fill her in ways I did not even know was possible. Her moans are so deep and pure that they make my spirit tremble each and every time. "Na kupenda watu wote weusi" was her motto (Swahili for I love all black people) and it is how she lived her life. But there is a catch…. actually there are a few.

Firstly: I am a married man. When I met "Uhuru" as I like to call her, it was at a time that my wife and I had temporarily separated. Although at that time it seemed as if our marriage was over. I wanted something I didn't think my wife wanted to give and I thought my wife wanted to give me something I didn't I want. I am vague for a reason. That reason is once we finally got back together and began to get to truly know the man and woman we had become, none of that mattered. Those faint whispers of dissatisfaction faded quicker than the winter snow on a warm Spring day. The love and commitment between me and my wife has been refreshed and renewed. But…. now I know what Uhuru feels like and I always want more.

Which leads me to the second issue: wanting more. My love of each woman grows daily. My wife and I have a bond that courses so deeply through our mortal fiber; Uhuru and I have a bond that liberates my soul and increases her passion. I want more of what I have with Uhuru with my wife and vice versa. I am neither selfish nor greedy but I want to share them with each other while having them all to myself. Uhuru belongs to everyone, she shares of herself generously. She gives more than I could ever hope to understand or desire to understand. Uhuru speaks of me as if she and I are the only two that exist, yet she speaks of other lovers in her life with the same depth and passion. The thing that I like the least about our "understanding" is that I cannot spend as much time with her as I would like.

The thought of sharing Uhuru is not something I like to think about at all. But one night I decided to use my key to her place, thinking she would not be home. When I walked in I was greeted with the same whispers of pleasure I had so often heard fall from her beautiful lips. Curiosity should be forbidden. I had to know, see, smell, hear and understand with my own eyes. So, I followed the sounds of moans and dripping pleasure straight to the bedroom.

The arousal I felt, when I got nearer, was hot, intense and uncomfortable. As I stood near her bedroom door, I saw her on top of another man dancing rhythms that exploded inside of her; just as she does with me. Light surrounded her body and tingling bells were faintly heard. He had the same look of disbelief I had the first time that I experienced Uhuru.

She turned and looked at me. I will never forget her darkened eyes holding mine while she slightly moved her hand to motion for me to join them. I did not move an inch; well my feet did not move an inch. I could not share her, not like that, not knowing she enjoyed him in the same way she enjoyed me. He and I connected eyes and I saw in his soul that he did not want to share either. That brief connection between he and I -- made me think of my wife.

I thought deeply about my wife. What if it was her lying there, receiving another man, the way Uhuru had received me. I had thought of stopping my relationship with Uhuru many times but couldn't walk away from the feelings she provides. It is so inspiring, enlightening and empowering. She makes me want to be a better man. Uhuru has opened me up to so many things that I never knew existed. Well, I knew they existed but I never thought I could have them.

I continued to watch as her light surrounded him, extended over the entire bed and upward. Her spirit reached out to me. My manhood throbbed, grew bigger and reached out to her; but my mind was in denial. I did not want to share her like that. The irony of finding Uhuru when I wasn't looking for a relationship and falling for her, as I fell in love again with my wife, what does all this mean? And why did I stand there watching him sliding in and out of her soul. I gathered myself enough to slowly back out of the room and I heard her say, "don't leave ..." as I walked down the hall.

I picked up my phone and called my wife aroused and wanting. She was busy, but she assured me that tonight she will have all I need. I sat down and drifted off to sleep thinking of my wife having Uhuru. I was a different man because of her. I wondered who my wife would become once she had experienced Uhuru for herself. I did not hear him leave or Uhuru walk in the room but I knew she was there. There is lightness that always accompanies her and although at times I am frightened of what having Uhuru really means I cannot be without her.

Uhuru touched me, I opened my eyes to see her smiling as she always does and I reached out to touch her. She was fresh out of the tub but I could still feel his energy on her. All I wanted was to replace his energy with mine.

My phone buzzed in my pocket and she reached in my pants and handed it to me. "Answer it love. It is your wife, she needs you". When I answered the phone, I found out that my wife had twisted her ankle and was at the Emergency room. Uhuru was still smiling as she walked me to the door. "Take care of your wife. Let her know you love and appreciate her while you nurse her back to good health."

This brings us to the third issue: honesty. You see Uhuru thought that my wife knew about my relationship with her. Uhuru wants to meet my wife; she believes that my wife wants to meet her as well. I have assured Uhuru that my wife wasn't ready yet and needs some time to adjust to the idea of me being with another woman. But I have not been honest with Uhuru or my wife. Neema and I had always been honest with each other but I have not told my wife about my Uhuru – not yet.

Although Neema believes in "infinite" love and "open" relationships it has not seemed like the right time to tell her about Uhuru. I don't know how to explain her to my wife, who I have loved for over a decade, that I am also deeply in love with another woman – and it happened so quickly while we were separated. This may be too much for her to comprehend or accept. I convinced myself I was protecting them both by not being honest, but I knew that I am also lying to myself. I am selfishly protecting myself from losing either or both of them.

For the next week I tended to my wife's every need, at times I even forgot about Uhuru, but then she would reappear in the recesses of my mind to entice me. "I appreciate you and everything you have been doing for me this last week Chuma. I see you constantly growing and changing. I can't help but wonder what has changed you so much or if I just never allowed myself to see you like this."

My thoughts are frantic and chaotic! She had opened the door. I could tell her now while she is both appreciative and vulnerable. I know it may sound bad but I don't want to lose her. Maybe if I do it now she will consider how well we have been doing and how much I love her. Maybe she will understand that I will never let my Uhuru come first... Maybe.

I took her hand into mine and voiced my thoughts. "I remember when I first came over to see the pictures after the Brazilian government agreed to declare the rest of the rain forest endangered lands. I did not know what to expect. We had been fighting so intensely prior to that but you acted as if everything was fine between us. When you first kissed me, I was so stunned, I could not even move. I thought I had de-sensitized myself against you. Well, I had tried to do so but when you touched me....it felt like Freedom.

He paused trying to clarify his confession. Neema raised an eyebrow and moved closer to him, then brushed his face to comfort him. He scooted back a little, so he could stay focused and continue. "When we were apart..." he sighed and she interrupted him, "we were separated and whatever happened then doesn't matter now." He interrupted her this time, "What if it is still happening?" he asked. A silence fell over the room.

Neema slowly took her hands from Chuma and then limped to the kitchen. He sat still for a moment, digesting the moment and the moments lost, then headed to the kitchen. He placed himself against the counter and watched her busy herself cleaning. "What are you thinking?" he asked her. "I don't know what to say to you. I don't know you anymore," his wife said abruptly.

Her words cut him deeply but he did not try to defend himself. After a moment, she asked, "Do you love her?" "Yes," he answered. "Does she know that you are married?" "Yes," he said again. "She is okay with you cheating." He sighed. "No. She's not that kind of woman."

Neema taunted him, "Well... what kind of woman is she, Chuma? What's her name?" "I call her Uhuru." Neema scoffed loudly. "So I felt like her... all this time since we've been together. You said that about me... and you say I feel like freedom? She limped away again. This time, the silence was deafening. When he heard the front door open and close Chuma knew how badly he had messed up. He was clear Neema would not answer his calls.

Uhuru called moments later. "Hello my love, I felt as if something was wrong. Are you okay?" "No." answered Chuma. "Do you want to come over here?" "Yes" he said yet again. While driving to Uhuru's house, he called Neema several more times. Each time the phone call immediately went to voicemail. When he got to Uhuru's he sat in the car for nearly 40 minutes trying to stop the tears that ran down his face. Uhuru showed up outside his car door and motioned for him to come inside. Chuma walked slowly to the door as he thought of the snowball that he had set into motion. As always Uhuru welcomed him with love.

After sipping peppermint tea, laced in honey, Chuma had calmed down enough to talk. "When my wife and I were separated, I never imagined I could love again, let alone so soon and so deeply." Uhuru smiled as he continued. "With you it all happened so fast. That day in Progressive changed my life for the better and also for the worse."

"Hmmm..." she murmured but let him continue. "I had never lied to my wife before; we have been honest with each other about all things of importance - no matter what the outcome may have been.

But once she and I got back together I could not bring myself to tell her about you. I know that I have told you that she just needed time but the truth is; she didn't even know you existed." Uhuru's demeanor changed as she continued to listen. "I told her tonight and she flipped out and left me. I don't know what to do. She means everything to me. I want to apologize to you as well Uhuru. I selfishly lied to you and my wife, thinking if I took my time I could have both of you the way I wanted. Now I may lose you both." He paused for several minutes to allow time for Uhuru to respond. She did not. They sat in silence for what seemed like an eternity.

When she did speak....Chuma wished he did not have ears. "From the beginning, Chuma, all I have asked of you was for you to share your true self with me and also your honesty. You have denied me both. You have also put me in a situation that I vowed never to be in. I am a woman, I would never do anything to purposely harm another woman, and now you have caused me to violate my own values. I shared with you my issues from past relationships. You heard from my lips how they were dishonest about things and how badly that hurt me. I forgive you because I also promised myself that I would not hold on to pain. But, I'm going to have to ask you to leave. Please leave my key in the basket at the door." She immediately got up and went to her room.

Chuma lingered for a minute contemplating his next move. He ruefully reflected on the gravity of the situation. His whole life was falling apart. When he returned home Neema was there packing her things. He could not bring himself to try and stop her. Before departing Neema asked him, "Do you have anything else you need to tell me?" Chuma shook his head "no" and Neema walked out the door. Chuma's worse nightmare had come true. He had hurt both the women in his life that he deeply loved. Now, he would be without both of them. Chuma felt the honorable thing, that he could still do, was to bring them together, if they so desired. It might help bring peace to both of them. He called each of them and asked them to meet for this purpose; they both agreed.

They wanted to meet somewhere neutral, but hoped for a place that would also allow for open and free conversation. They decided to have lunch in the park. Chuma arrived first. He placed on the ground a huge, colorful African quilt. On top of the quilt, he placed the two gifts that he had brought to give them to make amends. Uhuru arrived next. She gave Chuma a light hug and sat down smoothly on the quilt, eyeing the box with her name on it.

Chuma looked behind them; he could see Neema parking and walking briskly towards them. He stood up to greet his wife and Uhuru began to stand as well. As Neema reached the quilt, Uhuru turned with open arms to greet her. Chuma watched curiously and then in astonishment as Uhuru's face transformed from pleasant to peeved. Uhuru hurriedly grabbed her purse off the African quilt, forcibly pushing past him and going straight to Neema.

"YOU!! You are his wife?" Uhuru asked in an aggravated tone that he had never heard her use. He didn't understand why Uhuru was so angry. Chuma felt like time stood still. Neema and Uhuru argued back and forth and after a while he realized they knew each other. Their argument had nothing to do with him. Chuma felt relief and irritation. Relief because they weren't mad at him; irritation because he didn't matter. Finally, he decided to separate the two of them. Neema stood off to the side, still shaking her head.

Neema finally looked at her husband and said "This is Yasha." "Yasha?" he repeated in disbelief. "The sister you were initiated with that you weren't allowed to see again as part of the rite?" "Yes. No. There was more to it than that." Neema said flatly. Uhuru (aka Yasha) interrupted the exchange and spoke to Chuma. "This is the person I initially told you about, who played with my heart. I guess the universe decided to complete this circle." Yasha (aka Uhuru) became even more pissed. She grabbed her shoes and walked off heading to her car.

Chuma took several long strides and caught up with her. "Uhuru, don't do it like this. You have taught me so much about loving naturally, unselfishly and forgiving myself and others. Can we please talk about this?" Uhuru looked at his beautiful face and paused. She took a few moments to think about it before replying, "We can have dinner together at my house tonight at 7."

When Uhuru arrived home, she immediately used her pent up energy to clean the house. Later, she took a long aromatherapy bath and sat in front of her shrine. Tears rolled down her cheeks while she reflected about the events of the day. She was upset with herself for responding the way she did at the park. It made her recognize that her perception as being "free" was even farther away from the truth. She was not truly capable of loving fully – and "freely" as she had once been long ago. Uhuru realized she had not healed from past hurts but that this was an opportunity for healing, growth and transformation.

Uhuru lit her oil burner and dripped peppermint and a little bit of olive oil in it to cleanse the energy in the house. After the scent filled the rooms, Uhuru lit a bundle of sage and allowed the smoke to envelope her to cleanse her aura from head to toe. The entire time she performed this cleansing rite, she recited affirmations and prayers asking for cleansing, wellness and healing. When she was finished Uhuru grabbed her womanhood beads, placed them around her, then moved to the kitchen to prepare dinner.

Back at the park, Chuma and Neema had separated unceremoniously. Chuma drove home to rest. Neema went to the lake to pour libation. At the lake she spread out a white and orange cloth and kneeled at the bank. She prayed and poured libation asking that her Ancestors provide her guidance and clarity. Images of the past played across her mind.

For the first time in her life Neema lets go of her emotions and simply cries. She reflected on the cruelty of life. Yasha and Neema had been in love long ago. Neema felt she was very young spiritually; but not physically. Yasha was older, wiser and more experienced; or at least in Neema's eyes. When they were going through their rites, the two of them connected in a way that Neema had not felt with anyone for several lifetimes. It scared her so much that over time Neema began to distance herself from Yasha until their relationship ended.

As Neema poured and prayed, she realized that this was her pattern. She would love deeply for a moment and then become scared, distant and cold. She did this every time, especially if she felt herself loving too deeply. Neema could see that this same pattern still exists. She did it with Yasha and also with Chuma. After pouring libation until she was satisfied and crying until she was spent Neema decided to "make it straight." During her rites, she had been taught about "Maat" and the concept of righteousness, balance, truth and justice. She almost had decided not to go meet with Yasha but knew she needed to "make it straight." It will be unrighteous for all parties if she does not face the consequences of her actions.

That evening by 6:45 she and Chuma both arrive and sit outside in their cars. At seven o'clock sharp Uhuru opens her front door and motions for them to come inside. Together they get out of their cars and follow her inside the house. The peppermint scent that greets both of them in Uhuru's house puts them at ease a bit. They eat quietly over dinner, lost in their own little world of memories.

Breaking the silence, Chuma finally speaks "I love you both and want both of you to be happy. I have never seen either of you act like this and it hurts me to my core. What do we need to do to restore peace?"

Yasha sighs and then speaks. "Neema, I forgive you. We were both young and you did what you thought was best. Over the years.... despite my hurt I have never wished any ill upon you and I will not bring that energy into this situation. I love both of you as well. We were friends before we became lovers so maybe we can become friends again."

Neema sits very still. After a moment she stands up and takes her clothes off and kneels before Yasha . Yasha smiles; Chuma is perplexed. Within a few minutes Yasha reaches for Neema and lifts her off the floor. "All is forgiven." During their rite of passage both were taught that if someone causes an offense and wants to apologize -- the purest way is for them to bare their bodies and humble (prostrate) themselves to the person. This allows the person to decide their fate. Uhuru, aka Yasha, decided to accept the apology and to forgive Neema.

They finish dinner and tentatively begin to talk.   The two women explain the ritual manner in which one apologizes if an offense is made. Chuma sees this as his chance. He stands up, takes off all his clothes and kneels before both women. They allow him to stay in the prostate position for nearly five minutes before granting him forgiveness.

When he rises the two women hug Chuma. Tears of gladness and appreciation fall from their eyes. Their kisses fall upon his body and his erection rises as hard as wood. He doesn't know how to respond, so he does nothing. They continue to rub, touch, kiss and caress him. Finally, Yasha aka Uhuru speaks. "Years ago we made a vow that if we ever found a man that we couldn't be without....we would share him." May it be so.

Sage Wisdom: Cleansing Your Space

Did you ever experience or feel that the energy in your house just doesn't feel right but you can't discern... why? It may be simply that the vibratory energy of the space needs cleansing. I remember reading that everything is energy. Energy can exist in a variety of forms that our senses can detect (visual, auditory, kinesthetic, olfactory/gustatory). The purpose of cleansing your space is to move energy; replace negative or unwanted vibratory energy with positive vibratory energy. You can do this in your home, office, a public space, or even within the confines of your automobile. Here are a few tips:

First clean, tidy or straighten the area. Wait until the area is clear of guests or involve people you trust, or who have knowledge of cleansing (even if you have to teach them) and who agree with what you are doing and hope to achieve. After **cleaning** your space you can use several methods to **cleanse** your space: Sprinkling, Smudging, Blessing, Libations or Scenting. Each of these things can be done individually or combined.

Sprinkling
Items needed: Small clean bowl or cup preferably glass or silver bowls; any type is fine; it is best to use distilled or spring water (this is optimum but any clean water will work). Essential oils can be used. *see Sage Wisdom: Essential Oils

What to do: Fill a glass bowl or cup with clean water. Then offer a prayer over the water asking the Creator to provide a blessing or to provide what is needed. Peppermint oil may be used for cleansing. After the prayer is done one should walk around the areas you want cleansed or blessed. Gently sprinkle the prepared water on all surfaces until you are satisfied with the way the area feels. When finished, if there is water left, you pour it into a plant as long as there or no

---

essential oils in it. The water can also be poured outside into the earth. You can do this routinely for maintenance i.e. weekly, monthly… with prayers

Scenting
Items needed: incense or oil burner and oils
What to do: Light incense or oil burner and walk around area spreading the scent or allow it to simply burn in the area you wish to cleanse. (This can also be done with prayers.)

Blessing/Prayers
Items needed: A clear mind
What to do: Take a moment to focus your thought and intent. When your mind is clear on what you hope to achieve walk around the intended space or area and do prayers asking the Creator to put the energy you want in the space. This requires that you constantly keep in mind what you desire. It takes concentration and focus. This can be combined with one of the other cleansings

Smudging:
Items needed: Smudge stick or smudging bundle which you can purchase or make yourself. A lighter, ashtray or metal bowl is needed in which to put the burning item. (Sage is the most often used smudging property and peppermint or other uplifting herbs can also be used)

If making your own smudging bundle herbs should be completely dried out and wrapped together tightly with string before use

What to do: Holding one end of the stick/bundle of bound dried herbs light the opposite end and walk around the area allowing the smoke to surround all items or corners of the space. When you are finished you can put it out or let it continue to burn in an ashtray, metal bowl, etc.,

NISHIKE (TOUCH ME)

From across the room I saw her. She was busy handing out information to the participants of the workshop. When she looked up I caught her eye. She gave the warmest, truest, most inviting smile and nodded for me to come over (well it was more than just me but that isn't the point). When I got close she pushed papers in our hands, followed by instructions that I could not hear, then motioned for us to have a seat, right in the front. "Oooooo child, things are going to get easier." The words always made me think of her smile. That smile has gotten me through so many lonely nights, tough times and plain old boredom.

My focus was at about zero as she moved back and forth from the podium, talking, smiling, explaining, **smiling,** accepting questions, and **smiling.**
The only thing better than her smile was her lips: they were soft, full, pink, shiny, and pouty at times and they framed that...smile. I often envisioned her underneath me, mouth slightly open, smiling at me. Thanking me, enjoying me and approving of me. But I must focus on her words so that I have the talking points later.

She concludes before I can focus. I would like to thank everyone for coming out tonight. I truly appreciate your time and input. If you have any questions or would like to schedule a consultation please feel free to see me at the back of the room. We also have refreshments so please enjoy them. We will meet here next month at the same time. May *you be strong...AND LIVE LONG! The crowd responded in call and response. Everyone burst into applause then began to talk excitedly to each other.*

I waited nearly an hour to speak with her...I was patient. I allowed people to go in front of me hoping to be the last person to speak with her. Standing in front of her finally... she greeted me with a hug, and touched both sides of my face with hers. She smelled sweet like honey and tea tree; intoxication befell me. "I apologize, I know you have waited awhile to speak with me and I saw you allowing others to go first. I have to catch a train for my next seminar. But when I return I can meet with you if there is something pressing." In my mind all I could see was me pressing my lips against hers. Then she reached up and fulfilled my dream. Her smile this time was for me alone with only me in mind. I gathered my thoughts as her assistant tugged at her lappa (skirt made of wrapped African cloth) to remind her it was time to depart.

"That is not necessary. Have a safe trip and make sure you return to me... us... safely my sista." She paused for a moment. I hoped I had not offended her. Her next embrace was even warmer and longer; it said that I had not.
Of course I was at the following seminar. However, she was not. Her business partner facilitated the next training on opening a "Community Market," which was good because I actually learned something this time. I laughed to myself at how intense my feelings were for her. I was surprised when her partner touched my hand as she passed. I was asked to wait a moment while she finished a conversation.

"You must be the brother Ethereal told me about. She described you to a tee with every detail except your name...which is?" "Antoine" "Well Ndugu (kiswahili for brother) Dada (kiswahili for sister) Ethereal asked that I get this letter to you. So here you go. Asante Sana (thank you very much) for coming out again."

I did not, could not, dare open it there and melt in front of everyone. SoI decide to take it home with me to read it. I will carry her close to my heart... in this letter and indulge in her later. When I finally open it; I notice the letter carries her scent and energy. It is written on recycled paper and embodies all of her vibe.

Ndugu(Brother)
Nisimehe (I am sorry) I did not catch your name but I wanted to say asante (thank you) again for your attendance at the seminar and your patience to wait and speak with me. I could feel your energy during our last encounter and appreciate the man that you are. I hope that you enjoyed the information and that it was useful to you. I would like to invite you to my home for a reading if you are open to the idea.

Peace and Blessings,
Ethereal

I stand in disbelief and look around for the cameras and the people jumping out to tell me this was some sort of practical joke; it was not. Before I finish my story let me tell you a little about my Ethereal; no I am not a stalker. She is beautiful, not like any other woman I have encountered in life. Her spirit shines bright in every arena I have seen her in. She dances beautifully, can drink anyone under a table, is great with children and elders, she can heal with touch and doesn't take any mess from anyone. Plus she has blue black skin, long legs, perky breast, a round ass and that damn smile.

I know, I know, it seems improbable, impossible even but it is true and she is real. If I did not know better I would think all of our interactions were dreams, my imagination running amok. Now she wants me in her home. I am not sure I am ready for this. I have no game, I am just me. But I'd rather embarrass myself trying than have her know nothing of me. Our date, that's how I think of it, went very well. The divination proved to be very insightful and helped me put some things into perspective. She was honest without being abrasive; encouraging without being condescending.

When she asked me to stay for dinner I was ecstatic. We had a great time, talking and laughing, I realize how goofy and down to earth she really is. Whenever she was in town and had some "down time" she called me... that's right she would call ME to hang out.

One evening while vegging out on the couch with her I noticed the beads around her waist and she notices me noticing them. "These are my womanhood beads. I got them after I completed my initiation." I am intrigued. "You do know what that means don't you?" I want to save face so I hesitantly say, "I have a notion but enlighten me." "You have heard someone being initiated into the Yoruba spiritual system or priesthood. Right?" "Oh, yeah." Many of the forms of initiation are similar or carry the same fundamental truths."

She smiles at me again and asks. "You want to touch them?" "Not to sound naïve but is that allowed?" "Yes and no. I cannot share with you the meaning or my experiences. But, it is up to me who I allow to touch them because they are sacred to me. If I feel someone is worthy and/or in alignment with me then... Yes. Others who have been initiated can know the meaning and touch them. Besides if you're going to be touching my bare body... I figure I should formally let you touch them."

"Wait, I'm going to be touching your bare body?!!! Damn, I should not have said that aloud and definitely not sounding so excited." "Eventually, yes, I hope you will." She reaches for my hand and guides them gently across her beads. I feel a charge. I jerk my hand back slightly but she holds on to reassure me and places my hands back on them. "Wow, that's actually nice." Of course, she bestows me one of her "smiles".

"How many other people like me have you let touch them? Can you tell me the reason you cannot let people touch them." She replies, "Well it depends on what you mean by people like you, if you mean a handsome, intuitive, joyful, loving man who peaks my interest... well then just you. But if you mean uninitiated people then...just you."

She looks at me so honestly and peacefully that we both get lost in that space of connection for a moment before she continues. "As far as people touching them there are four reasons why people are not allowed to touch them: one- to protect me from their energy and whatever they have going on spiritually, two- to protect them from what I have going on spiritually; three-to not leave them open to my energies or potentially cheapen the experience for them... if they ever choose to go through the process of initiation, and four-to protect those energies on my beads. Maybe one day you will be initiated into something compatible and we can share our experiences." "Hmm? Maybe," I reply simply. After I leave her I research everything I can about initiation so I can ask her deeper questions... the next time we meet.

I will be seeing her tomorrow and I think I am more knowledge about the process of initiation. I recognize there is much that I don't understand. When I arrive at her home the door is unlocked and slightly open. As I knock on the door.... a force moves my hand to open the door. I can see her silhouette in the kitchen. She calls for me to come in and take off my shoes. She doesn't allow shoes to be worn inside her house for health and spiritual reasons. She prefers a clean environment; not wanting physical dirt and debris tracked inside the house. On a spiritual level she prefers that negative attitudes, unclean energies and harmful psychic thoughts be left outside — as well. It is simply a different type of filth. While taking off my shoes I catch a glimpse of her walking towards me completely nude. She carries two glasses in her hands. She smiles and signals for me to come into her meditation room where she does her readings.

Before I enter the room, I take off my clothes for the same reason. The last time cloth is nearby for me but I see none. She motions again for me to come in. Naked and erect I enter her sacred space and sit on the floor next to her. She lights a candle and does a prayer. I mentally prepare for a reading. She speaks in a very deep voice. "Before we engage physically I want to let you know that I am a "conduit" or "spiritual medium." I think, well I didn't read that far ahead. She continues with an explanation. "I'm not sure how much you know about that but it basically means that I am sensitive to things beyond the natural range of perception; it even means that energies can speak through me."

"Hmmm... so when you say "energies" and "speak" what do you mean?" "The universe is a vast place and things exist on more than one plane or realm of existence. We are more than just flesh, we are spirit.. energy.. that animates what is walking around that we see and touch. However as our elders have taught us.. if I cut you open I am not going to find you, the real you. I mean the real you.. what is giving you vitality and causing your breath. That energy existed before your conception and will continue after your physical death."

She pauses in her explanation. "We all have an ability to tap into that energy in ourselves, others and in the universe. For me it is just easier to do. I am able to convey what others energies want me to share." I ask, "you mean like spirit possessions and stuff like that?" She could tell I was uneasy. "There is nothing spooky about it. This is real; it isn't something out of a movie. You know how sometimes you get in a zone and you are so focused on something that things become clearer or easier to do? It is similar. I zone into a particular energy and convey its thoughts so to speak. I let the energy have a voice through me." Maybe, I am not ready for this. Where the hell is she going with this? I think to myself. "It is through that type of connection with spirits, energy and the universe that I am able to tap into that. Don't worry, I am not going to do any of that now; I just want to share more of myself with you before I take you inside of me."

By now my erection is gone but that made it come right back. She reaches out and touches my face. She smiles at me once more. She rubs her hands across her body and begins to please herself. I am not sure how to respond. Should I just watch, join in, touch myself, or do nothing? I chose to do nothing. It is better to err on the side of caution than be offensive. She touches herself until she has an orgasm. Then she asks me to lay next to her. She turns on her side and we lay face to face. She kisses my lips before reaching between her legs again but this time she presses against me and puts her leg around my body.

My erection slides easily inside of her and we start rocking in harmony. Her hands explore every inch of my body as her breaths turn into moans and her juices flow freely over my tekken. She smiles as she bursts into ecstasy again and her body demands that I do as well. Though I did not want it to be over my body complies with her demands and my warmth spills forth inside her. (**Side note**) She and I had previously shared our medical histories so we know each other's status. She smiles at me once more before wrapping a piece of cloth around herself and walking out the shrine room.

I lay there in afterglow for a bit. When I finally get up to leave the room I see my clothing waiting for me. She tells me the time that the next train is leaving. She is still very open with me but it just feels "too abrupt." My feelings are somewhat hurt but I decide not to allow it to show. I don't know why but I feel used. I experience a sense of longing. I did not want to leave so quickly after being intimate with her. She hugs me tightly and asks that I spend the night the next time I come over. I agree even though I am still processing everything.

Over the next week I have some of the most vivid dreams I ever have experienced in my life. I am more sensitive to things around me. We speak via chat and I am excited that she plans to return the following week. My excitement wanes when she asks for a rain check because she is too busy. After nearly six months of her asking for "rain checks" I stop reaching out to her. I see her smile on almost every woman's face. She is still very present in my body, mind and soul.

Sage Wisdom: Get Your Spirit in Shape

It might be time to focus on improving your spiritual, social and mental health in the same way we do our physical health? We try to eat right, exercise, drink water, etc. to stay fit and in shape, yet often we overlook our spiritual, social and mental health. Of course, you know there is no blueprint on "How to get your spirit environment and mind looking right." We won't see a horrible infomercial with actors saying "My spirit used to be out of space and dull but now look at me! My spirit is in awesome shape!!!"

,
Yet our spiritual, social and mental health is just as important as our physical health. We must exercise and nurture our minds, surroundings and spirits daily as well. As we focus on our physical health constantly, here are a few tips to make sure to "Get Your Spirit in Shape." Consider trying one or more of these kick ass spirit shaping activities and find what works best for you:

- ❖ Love YOURSELF- Look in the mirror and memorize your beauty and reflect on the many beautiful acts that define you
- ❖ Chuckle. Giggle. Cackle. Guffaw. Gut hurting laughter
- ❖ Spend time with loved ones. It always feels good...
- ❖ Do brain teasers
- ❖ Learn a new skill
- ❖ Play a game – a new game or one of your old favorites
- ❖ Pray (focusing your energy toward a spiritual thought)
- ❖ Grow plants and herbs in your homes or outside
- ❖ Unplug: try to meditate and "unplug" *(spend concentrated time without mechanical devices)*
- ❖ Reduce your carbon footprint, and most importantly
- ❖ Be good to people and do good things

When you put out positive vibes they come back to you in many forms AND improve your mental, physical, social and spiritual health as well. Let's get our spirits in shape together!!!!!!!

Neighbor

After nearly 2 weeks away from home all I could think about was taking a nice hot shower and climbing into my bed. I love the work that I do, traveling around meeting different people and studying their culture and celebrations; but I love being home more.

The taxi driver stopped in front of my home and carried my bags to the porch and I gave him a tip and a hug. I'm a hugger. It is hard to believe I don't have any mail so either my sister has been over here or the post office has held my mail again. Either way, I will deal with that later. I kick my shoes off as I enter my home and immediately strip down. Before I could get my water running, good my doorbell rings. I must have left something in the taxi; I am always forgetting something. I wrap my cloth around me and hurry to the door not even looking out.

"What did I forget this time?" I say as I open the door.
"To say thank you I suppose." My neighbor responded.
"Oh... I'm sorry I thought you were the taxi driver."
"Not in this lifetime." He replied.

I held back my smile not wanting to give him any indication that I was amused. My neighbor is a muscular, intelligent, sweet smelling, nice talking, finger sucking, good looking, man-goodness!!!!!!! BUT he's a player with different women coming in out of his house daily. He has some staples like the moaner, crier, growler and chirper which I named according to the sounds they make. I get tired of hearing his loud ass guest. At first I thought it was arousing and exciting. Now it is just annoying.

"How may I help you?"
"It is I that can help you." He said slyly.
"Look I don't want to be short with you but I am just getting back from a long trip and I would like to take a shower and lay in my bed. So what is it that you need?"

"I just wanted to let you know that I have your mail. I would suggest in the future you have someone pick it up for you so that people won't know you are gone. It isn't as safe around here as it used to be. Before I ran to the store I just wanted to let you know."

"Oh... Okay. Well thank you. I will get it after I rest for a moment and you are back from the store."
"I won't be gone long and I will be here all night."
"I bet." I let slip out. "I mean okay."

He smiled and backed off my porch looking at me until I closed the door. He's beautiful but he has high traffic. I take my time in the shower then lay down. I hear a car door slam and I get up to look out the window. *Sigh* I forgot about the screamer. That is the LAST thing I want to listen to all damn night after just getting back. Maybe I will go over my sister's house. No, I'm staying home. I will not be chased away by some boisterous sex.

I was surprised that the screamer didn't stay long. After a couple of hours of vocal exercise she got in her car and left. Shortly after she pulled off my doorbell rang. I loosely wrapped my cloth around me and headed for the door. I knew it was him. When I got to the door he had all my mail in his arms. When I reached for it my cloth fell to my waist revealing my erect nipples. I turned red from embarrassment and quickly rewrapped myself. "I'm sorry about that. I was just resting and threw this cloth on."

"You don't have to apologize about showing me such beautiful breast." I did not respond. Instead I gathered my mail and closed the door. How rude of me. The next day I picked up some mango from the market on my way home as a "thank you" for his kindness. I often smell the scent coming from his home. I hesitate knocking on his door unannounced but I tap on his window. He opened the door so quickly I jumped. And he laughed at me.

"Hey beautiful. I didn't mean to catch you off guard. I was just heading out for a bite to eat."

"I'm sorry too I didn't mean to intrude I just wanted to say thank you for keeping an eye on my mail for me. I always forget that type of thing when I am going out of town."
"You're forgetful. I often see you running back inside 2 or 3 times a morning to get things."
I chuckled.

"Would you like to come with me to get a bite to eat? I know you don't cook because you always are having something delivered to your home," He said. "Excuse you! I cook very well! It is just that with my schedule I rarely get the chance. But, sure I would love to go to a nice restaurant instead of sitting at home alone. (I don't know why I said alone) Just give me second to change out these work clothes."

I hurried into my house and threw on some jeans and my Ankh by Drumlight t-shirt. When I came back out he was moving things out the front seat of his car. I waited for him to finish and motion for me.
While we were waiting on our meals he asked "Are you celibate?" I must have made an ugly face because he nearly choked on his water. "What?! I am just asking. I never see you have company and you leave go to work and come straight home. Unless you are getting it on at work I don't see when you have time."

"I'm surprised you have time to clock my habits seeing as you have SOOOO much traffic coming in and out of your house. Not to mention being distracted by all the animal planet sounds that come from your home. Are you filming a nature series? Maybe you are a condom tester by profession. Do you take extra vitamins? "

"I like you. You are quick with the come back. Usually when I say something like that to a woman she is stunned in her track or offended. It is my ice breaker. After that the conversation just opens up."

"That is a terrible ice breaking and this one has just closed down."

I excused myself to the restroom. I laughed my ass off quietly to myself about his bold ass questions and comments. But I was not going to let him think that shit was cute. When I got back to the table the food had arrived and he was eating. He is rude as hell. I approached the table and sat down. I lowered my head and began my prayers aloud: "Great Creator, Great Mkela. Please remove any and all negativity that has been grown or put into this food in any process of the way of it making it to my plate. Please bless the hands that have prepared it and give them joy. Allow this food to nourish my mind, body and spirit. Please bless this brother and teach him some manners. Ashe."

He chuckled as I picked up my fork.
"Well that is the first time I have been checked in a prayer."
"Probably won't be the last."
"Indeed. But you never answered my question?"
"And you never answered mine?"
We were at a standstill and neither of us was ready to cave in. The rest of dinner was spent making idle conversation. Until he said.
"YOU would think I was having sex with all those women..."

I almost went clean off but I knew he was trying to bait me. So instead I said, "I really don't care what it is you are doing other than the fact that there are nights that I cannot sleep because your guest, or maybe it is you, who is making so much noise that I can't even drown out the sound. I know I am the only house near yours but you are very inconsiderate. I only haven't said anything because I respect your right to do what you want in your home and as long as you aren't harming anyone.

But in the future, when you are wondering whether I am having sex or not - instead you should wonder if you are keeping me awake."
Just in time our waiter came and I asked for the check I paid for both of our meals. Thanked him and left him at the table and walked outside to call the taxi company. It was drizzling so I stood under the awning. He came out the door and stood next to me.
"Ummm... I can take you home."
"I appreciate it but I am not going home."
Okay then I will wait with you for your ride."

We stood in silence until my taxi arrived. I thanked him again and got in. I had the driver take me to my sister's house and told her about my crazy ass neighbor. The next morning she dropped me off early to shower and get ready for work. When I walked outside there was a note on my car that said. I enjoyed you last night. Let me cook for you tonight.

I scribbled. No thank you on the note and put it on his car. All day I laughed at our exchange. I must admit I find his candidness refreshing.
Several days passed of him leaving the same note on my car and each time I refused. I noticed that his guests were not as loud and I appreciated that. I could actually sleep through them now.

I heard a knock at my door 5 minutes before it was time for me to leave. I know it is him. I sighed as I walked to the door to find a gigantic peace lily in my door with a note. "I am sorry if I have offended you. Let me make it up to you by cooking your dinner." I chuckled and sat the plant inside my door. I wrote "It took you long enough to apologize ☺ Tonight at 7pm" on a piece of paper and left it in my screen door because I knew he was watching.

I returned home around 5 I had planned to take a relaxing bath and get a catnap in but when I arrived there was another plant in my door along with a note "Can we make it 5:30?

I have an early morning." Darn now I don't have time to rest. I showered quickly and put on my shea butter blend with tea tree and lime which is my favorite then headed to his house. The door was opened so I knocked and stood on his porch waiting. "Karibu, Welcome."

He called from the back and I stepped into his home. The dark wooden stair case had Ankhs carved into it of different sizes and shapes and wrapped around the wall leading to up stairs.

There was a stained glass window with an image of Hannibal designed into it. To the right was a sun room filled with plants and herbs which smelled magnificent. Straight ahead there were several more doors. To my left and right and at the end of the hall was his kitchen and him standing over a pot.

He placed the spoon down and walked toward me smiling and reached out to hug me. I let him hug me but did not hug him back. "For you to be a hugger you sure don't hug well." "Well for a gigolo I'm sure you don't know what a good hug is."
I laughed and wrapped my arms around him. I don't have to describe how hugging a sexy ass person feels so you know I was tripping a little. He pulled back before I did and I felt a little embarrassed. "Your hugs are actually pretty good." "Yours aren't." I retorted. I don't even know why I go back and forth with him. I usually am not this way.

I followed him into his kitchen and I could smell the chili simmering in the pot *see Sage Wisdom: Aphrodisiacs * the herbs and spices filled the air and sparked my hunger. "MMMM…. That smells good. No wonder you have all the women making animal noises." "Thank you but that is not what makes them make noises, I am." I was instantly uncomfortable I didn't know where to go with it but before I could think I said "Well show me what does."

He walked from around the counter grabbed my head and lead me to his basement door. "You sure you're ready?" He smiled I grabbed the doorknob and pushed it open. He walked down the winding stairs and through some cowrie shell curtains into a room filled with crystal, herbs, and bed laying in the middle of it. "This is where all the "animal noises" come from. That bed right there, If I tell you a secret will you believe me?" he asked. I was silent. He continued.

"This room is sound proof. So if you could hear them you either had to be in here with us, imagining it or. Never mind. Are you ready to eat?" My alarms were blaring so I said "Yes. I'm starving," and we headed back upstairs. We sat on the floor in his front room, ate and talked for hours. He was very intriguing and we jousted with words all night. When there was a break in the conversation I said "No. Yes" "No. Yes. What?"

"No I am not celibate; yes I get it on at work." "Wow!!! I AM surprised." "I travel a lot for my job so I have to find ways to enjoy my time away from home. I have friends that I see each time I go out of town."
"Friendsss with an "s"." "Yes, with an "s"" "How many friends do you have?" "I have many friends but I don't sleep with all of them. How about you? I know there are at least 4 or 5 women that I have counted." "I actually AM celibate."

I laughed aloud for several moments before he began to look annoyed. "What is so hard to believe about that?" He asked "Look, we've been off to a good start. It's getting late and I have a flight to catch in the morning. Thanks for dinner, great conversation and a good laugh." I got up and walked to the front door and let myself out. "Shoot. I forgot to ask my sister to get my mail." I thought as I sat in the cab on the way home. I knew that he would have my mail and I would have to talk to him again. As we pulled up to my house I was surprised to see my mailbox stuffed with mail. I'm guessing he is done trying to impress me since it didn't go well last time.

I gathered my belongings and grabbed my pile of mail as I went into the house. After a shower and dinner I sat down to go through my mail. It was the usual bills, coupons and advertisements but there was also a handwritten envelope addressed to "The non-believer." I chuckled, as I opened it. It was a DVD with no markings on it. I did not know what to expect but I wanted to know what was on it. It started with music then him adjusting the camera to his face. Then he began to speak. "Hello non believer. I hope that you will watch this video seeing as how I took the time to make it."

He smiled for a moment then continued. "Five years ago I travel to a remote village in Malawi while I was there I got very sick and the elders of the community told me it was "spirit sickness" and that I would have to go to the bush to be healed. I didn't know what the hell that meant but I didn't care I was so sick I was willing to try anything. I cannot give you all the details but I was taken through their rites to be a healer.

It was the hardest and most fulfilling thing in my life. I was encouraged to stay there but my life, home, family, fiancé and existence was here. So I came back home. Before I came home I took a blood oath that I would not cause harm to anyone using my skills, but I didn't really think I could or would. Retrospectively, I should have gotten more information from the elders. But I didn't. He lowered his head for a moment before continuing.

"When I got home I wanted to show my finance all the things I had learned and she tried everything I asked. Let me say this some healing is done through sex and that is what we were doing together even though she didn't need it. I never even thought of the effects of doing some of those things on a healthy person.

It never crossed my mind. One day she came home from her regular doctor's visit and told me that her uterus had been ruptured, she had been bleeding internally for some time and that she could not have children.

Her doctor wanted her to undergo some surgeries and testing but she wanted me to heal her.

She still believed in me not knowing that I was the cause of her problems. I knew it was because I had abused my knowledge. She didn't blame me but I did and I vowed never to have sex again. She refused to be treated by anyone else and she passed away in her sleep one night still believing I would save her life. I shut the world out for nearly a year until she came to me in a dream and made me promise to be the healer I am supposed to be.

Which I have been but I still cannot bring myself to have sex with anyone. Those "animal noises" you hear are healing rituals that I perform on the women you see. Touch, taste, sight, sound and the rest can all be used to heal or restore someone to good health. Those women make the noises that they feel are freeing and healing. No sex. He shrugged his shoulders, smiled and stopped recording.

I must have watched it 7 times studying his voice, body language and words looking for any signs of dishonesty but I found none. I wanted to go to him and hold him and cry for his loss but I could not bring myself to do it or even see him. I avoided him for weeks until I decided to leave a plant on his door like he had once done mine. I also included a letter about how sorry I was for his loss that was gut retching to write. When he opened his door he took the letter and the plant inside but I did not hear anything from him for months.

Out of the blue he knocked on my door. When I answered the door he looked worried and asked to come in. "I just came from the doctor and they said I have "the priest disease" "Wow, what is that?" I inquired "It is called Prostatic congestion and basically means that I am not ejaculating enough. I don't know what to do, I can't take western medicine because of my rites, I can't bring myself to masturbate and I can't ignore the pain any longer. I don't even know why I came over here." He shook his head and turned to go out of the door. I grabbed his arm and lead him into my bedroom. "No sex." He said. "No sex." I said in agreement. I lit a candle and did a prayer for clarity and healing then took his clothes off and laid him on my bed. He's the first man to actually be in my bed.

I always go to my friend's houses or get a hotel room because it is always out of town. So it is a little awkward for me but at the same time I want to help him. I took off my clothes revealing my talisman. "You never told me you were a healer too." He said. I sat next to him on the bed and began to run on his arms, slowly moving my fingers across his skin until goose bumps began to form. He closed his eyes and his erection began to rise.

I covered my hand with an olive and lavender oil blend and stroked him gently focusing on the thought of eruption. He brushed his hand against my body as if he had never touched a woman and I guided his arousal with my touch. I held his member in my hand while massaging his prostate with my finger until he began to jerk and moan loudly. I thought of all the animal kingdom sounds coming from his house and chuckled. "Are you thinking of the women?"

I nodded and laughed and he laughed with me. I continued to stroke as we laughed, until his sap burst everywhere covering his body, my leg and bed. I laid next to him and held him as he basked in the feelings. He turned to me and kissed my cheek. After a moment I got up to get him a towel and he took a shower before dressing and walking to the door. Before he walked out he proposed "Once a month?" "Once a week for now," I said. So each month he cooks, we gather and I help him heal. I guess my leaving my mail was the remedy he needed.

Temple

My body is your temple; come inside and worship me

Only you can say the words and prayers that will set me free

Light my fires, pray at my altars, attend to my special needs

Give me flowers, share sacred showers and praise me on your knees

Burn incense, sing songs and honour me through dance

My ancient waters flow to cause you to fall deep into trance

Only then will I take your body, mind, soul and ride you like the wind

Explain to you my secrets from beginning to the end

Enlightenment will be yours, if to my body, you do pray

After I enjoy you fully, you must then go away

Until I call upon you again to worship me another day

Sage Wisdom: Cleansing Your Temple

Your body needs time to rest and regroup. Have you ever thought about the amount of toxins and additives that are added to all the foods we consume, whether you do it consciously or unconsciously? Your digestive track needs time to rest from trying to break down all the foods consumed into healthy sources of nutrition.

People often ask me why I consistently talk about fasting, cleansing or detoxing my body. Well, the answer is very simple: "**Because I choose to do so.**" I enjoy how my body feels when it does not have to analyze the proteins, fats, vitamins, and nutrients that it needs to break down. Do you ever wonder how confused our body might be as we consume quick, freeze-dried processed foods, dripped in salt drive-up oily fast foods, over cooked cafeteria-type foods, somewhat undercooked or raw foods, not popular because of their nutritious value?

It is also a nice way to keep your body in balance and promote wellness. Fasting and cleansing is essential for overcoming chronic diseases and rejuvenating an aging body. I enjoy the heightening, my body getting a break from working to digest food and the mental clarity it provides. IDEALLY while fasting or cleansing you would eliminate ALL toxic things including: people, ideas, situations and environment. But very few of us are living on mountain tops or beaches free of worries so you work with what you have.

Try to minimize toxicity from your body; this means those things that can make you sick – like breads, sugars, fast foods, etc., Remember to drink plenty of water, eliminate as much as possible -- which means go to the bathroom, sweat, blow your nose, go to the sauna and sweat.

Exercise calmness using meditations or some sort of focusing. Meditations and focusing exercises are the mental and "spiritual" part of the cleansing. The intent is to remove negative ideas, self-concepts and to heal our total being while we heal our bodies.

Just a gentle warning: when you cleanse it will immediately affect your senses, emotions and sensitivity. YOU WILL BE VERY HEIGHTENED!!! This can be both rewarding and challenging. You might find yourself more sensitive, emotional, tearful or you may reflect on your life choices.

As with anything that you commit to doing, if you desire to cleanse, you should do your own research. Set small goals but most importantly listen to your body. When starting a fast it is best to try a simple one and work your way up to a more advanced type of cleansing. It is also essential that you drink plenty of water and get plenty of rest during the fast; also referred to as cleansing/detoxing. Remember that your ultimate goal is healing, restoring good health and restoring healthy habits – of course one should also get more sleep. Sleep is always restorative and healing.

I will outline a few of the concepts:

Fasting: *"Period of restricted food or drink intake"*
A fast is defined as abstaining from foods, liquids or limiting food intake. It can be anywhere from several hours to several months and can range from eliminating one item from your diet to only consuming liquids.

Cleansing: *"Removal of waste products from the body, cleaning the body of harmful or dangerous things"*
A cleanse may involve consuming teas, herbs, lemon water, supplements and or foods that help to flush your system out. Hydration is one of the most important elements to ensure that waste is removed.

Detoxing: *"To abstain from or ridding the body of toxic or unhealthy substances"*
Detoxing can be done by fasting or cleansing or by simply cutting something out of your system such as sugar, drugs, cigarettes, etc. It is ridding your body of a particular thing.

Light Exercise: *"Light exercise or moderate exercise is also very beneficial because movement causes your body to push toxins out of the body faster."*
Exercise is not about pushing yourself past your limits at this time. Walking, yoga, stretching or light workouts are the best type of exercise to do during a fast/cleanse.

Please note that I am not a doctor. I am sharing with you knowledge from my personal research, experiences, trial and error and from the experiences of those close to me -- who also fast or cleanse regularly. What are the benefits? This allows the body to have a period of rest from having to digest foods; restorative abilities of the body to heal itself and optimum health.

From my experience, fasting, detoxing and cleansing each have their benefits and challenges. All have been a part of human life for spiritual, cultural, religious, health or other reasons since the beginning of time. Our bodies naturally do these things when we are sick, spiritually heightened, "in the zone", have a lot on our mind or have other things going on that take precedence. Often times our appetite decreases or we lose our desire to certain food items and crave other healthier things.

One of the reasons this happens is because our bodies need "breaks" too. When we are pulling on ourselves in other ways, the time, effort and energy it takes to prepare and consume food gets pushed to the back burner subconsciously. Have you ever "forgotten to eat" or "noticed that you had not eaten all day" or "haven't been hungry for some reason" those are some of those times. Our bodies can survive with a lot less food than we are conditioned to believe we need in western society. People all over the world survive and thrive eating a fraction of what we consume and still incorporate fasting, cleansing and detoxing.

When you eat a well-balanced diet with little to no processed foods, enjoy a lifestyle with an abundance of fresh foods, herbs and drink plenty of clean (non-polluted water) our bodies don't have to work as hard. Of course, the body does still need rest. All known spiritual or religious practices incorporate fasting, cleansing and detoxing as a method to ensure the physical body is pure, clean and open to better connect to The Creator… every single one. A combination of fasting, detoxing and cleansing is most effective for me especially when seeking a higher state of consciousness.

I enjoy the feeling, the heightening, my body getting a break from working to digest food and the mental clarity it provides. IDEALLY while fasting or cleansing you would eliminate ALL toxic things including: people, ideas, situations, environment, etc. Which is why in many cultures when you fast/cleanse/detox you don't work and you limit your contact with others. At times even silence is used. However, here we work with what we have.

I love to fast and cleanse. Everything is not for everybody... I prefer the "master cleanse" which is basically drinking "spicy lemonade" as I like to call it for 3-10 days and "going raw" which is eating only fresh fruits, vegetables, legumes and herbs. I absolutely LOVEEE fasting that way but my favorite fast is consuming raw foods. It is my favorite although I don't do it as much because of my schedule. I am tossing around doing a melon fast that was recommended by my beautiful sister. Fasting is a part of my routine. While speaking with Kita I was inspired to share information about the more heightened state of being while fasting. I enjoy all these things under "normal" circumstance BUT when I incorporate these other habits into my regiment while fasting the health benefits increase. Check it out!

When I fast and....

Exercise: I have more vigor, flexibility and oomph. I can feel my blood pumping through my veins and my muscles throbbing with nutrients. Even when I'm done my body continues to tingle.

Nature: I feel connected to EVERY living thing. The natural world whispers its ancient secrets of life to my spirit. The sun's rays warmly caresses my body bringing me closer to the cosmic maladies (my word pronounced: (m/ɛ/-l/ɑː/n-d/eɪ/s) or (mel-an-days) this is a combination of melanin & melody....Yep.

Sleep: I go into a unfathomable slumber where my body regenerates like wolverine (you better believe it). My dreams become animated paintings of delightful encounters.

Write/read: My mind is more imaginative and vibrant. I can touch, taste, smell, and feel the words as they dance around in my mind swaying to the harmonies in my head.

Meditate: I instantaneously receive clarity, focus and insight. Things make better sense and I can see every puzzle piece, where it goes, how it fits as well as I can see the bigger picture.

Music: When I listen to music I hear tones and pitches that were previously hidden behind bass, treble clefs, crescendo and melodies to be discovered by the listener.

Dance: BEST FEELING EVER!!!! Take all of the above and add a euphoric trance like state of complete bliss. That would best describe dance.

Chill: I spend more quality time with loved ones. My connection to them intensifies and I feel them more. Their jokes are funnier, their touch is intense and our bond is fortified and renewed.

Motherhood: I go into 'mommy mode'. I see my sons as the divine physical manifestation of The Creator....in physical form. I can see them in the past, present and future simultaneously. I can smell their essence, their voices and their laughter aligns my spirit.

Bathe: I slide into a hot oasis where the rushing water lulls me into a reverie of healing and comfort. My bath frees me from all earthly worries. Due to the cleansing nature of bathing every other experience I have is equally heightened. When I bathe during the first few days of the fast I get a "fasting high" that keeps me at a constant state of calm. I welcome you to try it at your own pace and see how your body embraces it.

Simple Cleanse (Basic)

You will see many of the different characters in my stories make reference to fasting, detoxing and or cleansing for spiritual, or health reasons so I decided to give a little more information about it. Again...I reiterate that you do your own research to find out what cleanse or fast works best for you. Each of our bodies responds differently to what we put in them and there is no "one size fits all" suggestion on what to do.

Breakfast –Fresh fruit, smoothie or protein drink (check the ingredients carefully because not all "protein drinks" are healthy. Stay away from ones with artificial flavors, colors or added ingredients)   It is recommended that you eat between 6am-8am or immediately after waking up.

Snack–Light snack (fruit or veggie) Eat between 10am-12pm or a few hours past breakfast

Lunch – Heaviest meal of the day (still free of fried, dairy, sugars, MSG, high fat, processed foods, etc.) – Eat between 12pm-2pm or 2 hours past your snack

Snack – Light snack (fruit or veggie) Eat between 2pm-4pm or 2 hours past your lunch

Dinner – Light meal (vegetables should be your largest portions of the meal) Eat between 4pm-6pm or 2 hours past your snack
NO meals should be consumed after 7pm (or an hour past your dinner).

DRINK PLENTY OF WATER!!!!!!
Note I recognize that we don't all have the same schedule so adjust the times to fit you but try to keep the same pacing. You can set the number of days but three days is a good start.

3- Day Detox (Basic)

1st Day
Drink **8 oz. of protein drink** (check the ingredients not all "protein drinks" are healthy. Stay away from ones with artificial flavors, colors or added ingredients), every **2 hours** for a total of 8 hours (**5 drinks**) starting no later than 8:00 am & ending by 4:00 pm (i.e. 8, 10, 12, 2 and 4pm) or (7, 9, 11, 1, and 3pm)
8 oz. of water should follow EACH drink every **2 hours** for a total of 5 8oz glasses (minimum)

At **6pm** eat a huge **garden** salad & add a protein (6oz of lean meat, **or** 2 tblsp of olive oil **or** 1/2 avocado)

2nd and 3rd Day
Every **2 hours**, eat fruit 2-3 oz. of fruit i.e., strawberries, watermelon, bananas, blueberries, cantaloupe, melon, oranges etc.
At 6pm make a huge **garden** salad and add a protein (6oz of lean meat, **or** 2 tblsp of olive oil **or** 1/2 avocado)

Do this multiple times take at least 4 days off between cycles (Be mindful of your intake during this time) you can repeat as many times as you would like

Master Cleanse (More advanced)

32 oz. of water preferably distilled (warm water if you'd like i.e. tea)
Lemon (2-2 ½)
Cayenne Pepper (desired amount for heat)
Pure Maple Syrup (Grade B is better than Grade A)
*You can also add tsp or ½ tsp of apple cider vinegar for extra cleansing properties
Drink 32oz several times a day, every time you feel hungry
You can do 3, 7, up to 21 days (You should start small and build up if you are not use to fasting).   It will cleanse your entire system.

Please note: **You cannot return to regular eating habits immediately following this cleanse**. You need to come off your fast properly to ensure that you do not experience serious stomach issues. In closing, while doing this cleanse, drink 100% orange juice for each meal (no other foods or drinks) (besides water) for at least 2 days (take more days if you feel the need to).

You know your body so do what is best for you. (I sometimes do broths or raw soups and they work fine). Then transition to eating fresh fruits & add vegetables. Resume healthy eating habits after 2-3 days of fruits & veggies.

Juicing (More advanced)

Freshly juiced-Carrot juice, other fresh fruit juice or vegetable juice
Juice organic carrots (or other vegetables) through juicer (Champion juicer is a nice one)
Drink 8 oz. every 1-2 hrs.
This can be done for 1-2 weeks or longer if you'd like. Make sure to drink PLENTY of water. If you don't have a juicer you can purchase fresh pressed juices from several health food stores.

Raw Food Diet (Advanced)

Only consume fresh fruits, legumes, seeds and vegetables over a 2-4 week period. You can also eat/drink smoothies, raw nuts, pates, etc. Ensure that you consume plenty of water the entire time. Eat often (at least every 1 – 2 hours). There are a wide variety of foods and Sage Wisdom, but you have to be willing to put in a little time.

15 day Cleanse/Detox (Advanced)

Created by Erica Strong of Adero Wellness Services

1st Day of the Cleanse

Drink cups of cleansing tea (Colon Cleanse, Smooth Move, Daily Detox), Castor Oil & Juice, Epsom Salt or Mixture to help you produce bowel movement (Recommended for you to have at least 2-3 trips to the bathroom daily)
Drink 2 glasses of water mixed with lemon (warm distilled or alkaline water is best)
Freshly Squeezed or 100% fresh pressed juices with no added sugar or other ingredients

2nd Day

Morning (2-3) Glasses of Warm Water with Lemon
Breakfast; Lunch and Dinner –Juices & Water
******Take an Evening Bath for 30 minutes

Bath to Include:
- •2-3 cups of Epsom Salt; Juice from 2 Lemons;
- •Drink 2 glasses of water right before bath
- •After bath, wrap yourself in plastic, wrap into a bed and cover yourself for at least 15-30 minutes

3rd & 4th Day

Morning (2-3) Glasses of Warm Water with Lemon
Breakfast; Lunch and Dinner –Juices & Water

5th & 6th Day

Breakfast & Lunch (Juices & Water)
Dinner
Vegetable Juice (4- Beets, 2- Celery, 4 Carrots, 1- Apple, 1- Cucumber)
Carrots & Celery (Smooth & Soup), 1 Avocado & Bunch of Spinach (Blend)

Eat Soup Slowly & Enjoy!

7th Day

Eat Fruits, Salads, & Juices

8th- 10th Day

Eat Fruits & Vegetables – Steamed 2-3 minutes

11th – 14th Day

Fruit, Salads
Vegetables (Steam Vegetables)
Introduce Small portion of any kind of Carbohydrates (Brown Rice, Baked Potato, Brown Rice Pasta)

15th Day

Continue Day 14 and slowly adopt a diet that includes more fresh fruits & vegetables, and fewer starches.

My Plan for Holistic Wellness...

The Covenant

She watches from behind the cloth that is draped over the table she is hiding under as **they** knock over tables, chairs and step on many valuable treasure – carelessly tossed on the floor. She watches as they "interrogated" her mama and hold her baba (father) down so he must watch. She watches as blood pours from her mothers wounds.

Her mother mouths these last words, "Saya baskee, Ndia" (I love you Ndia). She watches but does not cry. When it is all over her baba kneels over her mama's body and weeps in a way Ndia had never seen. She watches him looking through the tiny hole of the cloth.

It seems as if this is how she spends the next year of her life… looking through a hole in the cloth. As she and her baba travel across many lands Ndia does not speak, emote or smile. Expressionless, she stays at her baba's side, walking silently while clinging to his cloth. They find many safe houses along the way and at each one she barely eats or sleeps. She just watches and listens. It seems like years pass to the little one; to her they have travelled across the world twice.

"Ndia…" her baba said. "We are here." They approach a massive wall made of wood and martyr. He pulls out her mother's necklace and holds it in the air calling out words she does not understand. She hears the gate unlatch and then it opens to reveal a haven where even the air smells sweeter.

The village is filled with beautiful Afrikan women donned in colorful flowing cloth. She listens intently as her baba explains that this is the land her mother came from before they were joined. He repeats words that her mother taught her from very young. "Beauty is defined by how a person treats others and how much love can be seen in one's aura." Ndia looks around at the village. It is very different.

There are bells and chimes on every home and at every temple. The air seems to sing with each blowing wind. Ndia and her baba are taken to a small hut. This is the first time they have their "own place." Her baba unpacks all her belongings, she notices that his items remain packed.

The hut is immaculate and smells of honey and lotus. It has one bed inside it. There are freshly cut flowers lying on top of the covers. A crystal chime hangs from the center of the hut. Ndia crawls into the bed with the flowers. The flowers remind Ndia of her mother. For the first time since forever, she feels at peace for several moments before sleep claims her that night. She has not felt that peaceful in over a year. When she opens her eyes, Ndia realizes that her mother's precious necklace is around her neck. She immediately begins to panic.

Tears fill her eyes. She knows that her baba has also left her. She runs to the massive gates and pounds on them to open until one of the women comes to speak to her. "Little one," she said "This is your home now." Ndia sits next to the gate and stares at it wordlessly while clutching her mother's necklace. She does not cry.

Ndia sits at the gate all night and all day, watching people come and go, not speaking, not eating or moving. Many women try to talk to her, bring her food and try to comfort her but she does not respond. She only responds if someone touches her trying to move her, when that happens she flies into a fit of rage so violent that the women have no choice but to leave her alone.

"The little one is strong willed like you Nayah. Why don't you try to talk to her." The leader of the women says to her captain of the guard. Without words Nayah walks toward Ndia and stands next to her. She stands with the child in comfortable silence looking through the gate, for nearly half the day and much into the night. Finally Ndia speaks for the first time since she watched her mother slain. "Is baba coming back?" "No." Nayah responds.

Ndia asks "Can I leave?" "No," Nayah responds again. "What is your name?" the little one inquires. "Nayah." There is silence. Then Nayah speaks. "You must eat little one, your mother would want that." Nayah reaches her hand out and Ndia grabs it tightly... clinging to it the way she once held her mama's. Nayah takes Ndia to her hut. It is clean from the top to the bottom. She grows sweet smelling herbs all over. Each one is labeled and categorized. Her wall is filled with blades and arrows arranged by size. She also has beautiful silver and gold anklets and bracelets filling up her table.

"It is beautiful here, but I want to go home," Ndia says as she looks around the hut. "Your home and your village was destroyed. Your baba brought you here because he knew that you would be safe. This is your home now." Ndia did not speak again for several days. During that time she continues to follow Nayah around day and night watching everything she does. She clutches a piece of cloth given to her by Nayah and never lets it go. She sleeps in Nayah's bed. She becomes Nayah's permanent shadow.

One day Nayah is teaching archery. All of her students shoot arrows but they miss their target. Ndia tugs on Nayah's cloth and asks if she could try. Nayah hands Ndia the bow and arrow without giving her any instructions. The women stop shooting arrows. They sigh with annoyance because they know their instruction time is limited. Ndia aims her arrow and hits the target on the first try. Nayah shows no sign of approval she simply says, "Again." Ndia aims her arrow and hits the center of the target over and over without fail. Finally, Nayah is satisfied and asks Ndia to stop shooting arrows.

She turns to the women she is teaching. "Precision and consistency! That is how you win a battle." She winks at Ndia. The word spreads of Ndia's "lucky shots" and the leader hears about the incident. She sends for Nayah and her 'little shadow.' When they arrive the leader reaches out her hand to Ndia. "Come here little one." Ndia lets go of Nayah cloth for the first time and takes the elders' hand. There is something about the elder that reminds Ndia of her mother. She instantly feels comfortable.

"I heard you had great luck today in your archery lesson." Ndia shook her head hard indicating "NO." The leader raises her eyebrow and continues. "You did not have luck?" Ndia shakes her head "NO" again. "Well, what do you think it was little one?"

Ndia bravely responds, 'Skill'. There is no luck in war." The leader and Nayah smile broadly at the little warrior. "Well then," said the leader. "Let us increase your skills, since you have already been greatly impacted by this war." Ndia is excited and enthusiastic for the first time in many moons.

That evening during the council meeting Ndia sits outside the big hut, holding a piece of cloth that Nayah leaves with her, while listening to the discussion. She realizes, they are talking about her...even if she is unable to distinguish all of the speakers' voices.

The voices cross over each other. "She is too young to fight and too old to begin training..." "She has been exposed to the sickness too much not to have been affected..." "Her father brought her here for protection; not training....."

"She does not even speak..." "She does speak..." "She barely speaks and does not have any manners..." "I don't agree with this at all..." I think it is a waste of time..." "She is nothing more than Nayah's trained pet, who knows only a few tricks...."

The conversation continues until Nayah's voice rings out. It is the only voice she actually recognizes. "Her skill and ability far exceeds many of you and she has the time, discipline, capacity and desire to learn. I will teach her."

Silence engulfs the group. Another voice speaks out into the quiet. Ndia thinks it is the leader but she is not positive. "Women we are at the pinnacle of battle, the more skilled women we have in battle... the better. It takes nothing from us to let this little one join our ranks and learn our ways.

There is more chattering then a gong sounds and all the women begin to exit the hut. On the way out several of them roll their eyes at Ndia; while others smile and nod in her direction. Nayah finally appears and winks at Ndia, but she keeps walking. As much as she desires to follow Nayah; she has been instructed to wait until the leader comes out of the hut.

It seems like hours pass. Ndia sits quietly while fumbling with Nayah's cloth. She waits and thinks about everything that has happened. Finally the elder is in front of Ndia. She motions for the young female to follow her. Ndia resists the urge to grab the elders' flowing dress as she walks behind her. As they walk, the leader speaks. "You will begin your training at first light tomorrow. It will be hard training and even though you are skilled you must work hard and pull your weight.

You are facing a severe disadvantage. The other women you will be training with are older, stronger and faster. They will know more about our methods and they have been training their entire lives."

Ndia interrupts the elder. "So does that mean they will be angry when I beat them?" The leader chuckles at her audacity. "You are only competing with yourself. You can't compare yourself to them." Ndia responds again. "I know, I am better." The leader chuckles again. "I think you will do just fine... little one."

The next few years Ndia trains tirelessly. When the others rest or play she relentlessly trains harder. She receives top honors in all areas. This causes ire amongst the women. Nayah and the leader are advocates of Ndia's growing skill level; while others are adamantly against her progress. For this reason, the leader is very hard on Ndia at every level. Every time she achieves one thing she is sent to learn a new skill with very few accolades provided to her. Ndia does not resent the training. She enjoys being referred to as a "supreme warrior."

This is what she calls herself. She and Nayah grow very close. Nayah is her teacher, confidante, friend and most fierce competitor. They do everything together. But it is the leader whom Ndia views as her "mama." She is always striving to please her and make her proud. As time passes Ndia learns all the various levels of warriorship. One day out of thin air she states, "You know I will be leaving soon don't you Nayah." "Yes," Nayah responds. Will you come with me?" Ndia inquires. "No," Nayah responds. Ndia laughs aloud. "I knew you would say that." They laugh, wrestle and talk until day breaks.

Letter to My Sister

Dear Sister:

I know your schedule is busy so I will keep this short. Woman to woman I want to say I love and appreciate you. The way The Creator has manifested herself as you is more powerful and stunning than The Seven Wonders of the Ancient World. So often I forget to tell you how wonderful and meaningful you are to me and there are times when I don't show you how much I recognize your worth... I apologize for that. My spirit soars every time I see you smiling and I am enamored by your beautiful energy. Remembering your strength and endurance allows me to make it through the toughest times. Your spirit echoes through centuries of triumphs and victories. My love for you flows from the highest peaks flooding the deepest valleys.

I hold you in my arms embracing your spirit assuring you that everything in Creation will understand and honor your existence. I will see to it.

Love Always,

Your Sister
Milele

Colors of Love

White flames with Red hues,
Condensation producing dew
Purple psychic awareness
Thoughts so divine
Breaking down limitations
Without crossing lines
Black All inside me
Black All around you
Sharing green breaths… they are so few
Hardness to softness Blue back again
Fear to trust then fear again
Hearts beating fast... restrictions bend
Softness to softness the cycle ends
Greying understandings
Become crystal clear
Too far to reach…yet standing right here
Warm Orange oceans flow deep within souls
Nervous to have but can't let go
Conditions are set then broken once more
Mending wounds from long before
A terrestrial bond to a Lavender kiss
From defensive blows to healing bliss
Goosebumps form and levees shatter
At this point nothing really matters

Sage Wisdom: Colors in Healing & Stones

Stone	Color	Attributes
	Green *is known as* "Wadj"	Green is represented on hieroglyphics as "vegetation, fertility and new life"
	Red *is known as* "Khenmet"	Red is a powerful color represented on hieroglyphics as "victory, vitality and life"
	Black *is known as* "Kem"	Black is associated with the dark, afterlife and fertility"
	Blue *is known as* "Khesbedj or Irtiyu"	Blue is associated with the concepts of life and re-birth
	White *is known as* "Hedj/Shesep"	White blends all colors; it is considered the color of simple and sacred things; representative of cleanliness and purity
	Yellow *is known as* "Khenet".	Yellow represents the sun and its life-giving, regenerative properties

Ancient Kemet

From the moment of birth, we are surrounded by vibrant colors. Some are translucent...transparent... pellucid colors; they effortlessly penetrate our consciousness. Colors draw us in to heighten our senses of joy, excitement, inspiration and arousal. Other colors calm us down to bring us a sense of peace, contentment, reflective awareness and tranquility. When colors wrap themselves around our consciousness our brain conveys the hues into images which promote relaxation or stimulation.

This is not a new phenomenon – it began in Ancient Kemet. The invisible vibrations of color can bring a person back to harmony and balance using color to either relax or stimulate. In ancient times, Egyptians designed special healing temples which captured and split the sun's rays into its component colors creating light-bathing rooms used by Egyptian physicians. Within the spectrum, wave-spacing light produces the six colors of Red, Black, Blue, White, Green and Yellow that were used to affect various areas of the body.

Wadj or Green

The color green is called "Wadj-Wer" or more specifically "the Great Green" to represent the Nile River and its connection to mother earth and vegetation. In the Book of the Dead, Budge describes the deceased as a falcon with wings of green stone because the Eye of Heru amulet provides protection and healing. Many called Heru the "green God." During the mummification process many ancient priests left the heart in the person's body. A green heart scarab was placed over the actual heart to magically protect it from damage.

Red (Desr/Khenmet)

The color red is called "khenmet" or "Desr" (a much older word). The color is associated with virility, the fiery, life giving rays of the sun and also the solar aspects of kingship. In ancient Kemet the people would paint their entire bodies to connect with the vital life force of blood or virility; also the life source of the sun. Red was also the "heraldic color" of Lower Egypt, embodied by its signature *Deshret Crown* worn by royalty. Amulets made either of cornelian, a deep red stone or the Eye of Ra were worn to symbolize the virility, protective rays of the sun or kingship.

Black (Kem)

The color black is known as "Kem." The black pigment was one of the earliest pigments known to man. The color black was associated with the afterlife due to "resurrection from the dead" and "fertility" --likely due to the abundance provided by the dark, black silt of the annual flooding of the Nile (hence Kemet is known as "Black Land."

Blue (Khesbedj/Irtiyu)

Blue was not part of the earliest system(s) of color symbolism in Kemet but it has become a prestigious color. The color blue is symbolic of the heavenly realm of the sky and the life-giving properties of the Nile, with all their regenerative properties. The color symbolizes the concepts of life and re-birth.

White (Hedj/Shesep)

The color white (Hedj or Shesep) was a pigment that has been used since ancient Kemet. The color white blends all colors; it suggests omnipotence and purity. Due to its lack of color on the spectrum of light, white was also considered the color of simple and sacred things; it is representative of cleanliness and purity. Many use the color for ritual clothes. The white stone were primarily used in all the temple architecture.

Yellow (*Khenet*)

The color yellow represents the sun and its life-giving, regenerative properties. Yellow serves as a two-dimensional substitute for gold and is also symbolic of all that is eternal and imperishable.

Spiritual Colors

White blends all colors; used for purity, goodness and balance
. .

Black absorbs all light; used to reach deeper levels of the consciousness and to absorb or banish negativity.

Yellow builds confidence, encourages imagination and intelligence.

Orange attracts positive energy, desired outcomes and stimulates courage.

Pink promotes love, creates a pleasing environment and being friendly.

Red represents blood and symbolizing vitality, strength and protection.

Purple is a high vibration color used for spiritual work, psychic awareness and powerful healing.

Brown is used for balance, grounding and connection to the animals.

Blue encourages peace and tranquility.

Green is for growth, regeneration, fertility and connection to Mother Earth.

Use of Colors

- We wear specific color clothes to adjust our moods
- We eat specific food groupings based upon colors (broccoli, spinach, beets, corn)
- We envision colors while meditating
- We use colored walls/ furnishings in our home and offices to help us feel either stimulated/peace
- We use color lights with prisms-crystals for healing
- We use color candles in spiritual rituals/organized religions
- We use colors in traffic signs to indicate stop, yield, schools, construction warnings

Color... directly influences human behavior. Knowing the basic principles of using color can assist with attitude, confidence, healing, moving in daily routines, creating positive environments and living in harmony in the universe.

Mpenzi Wangu *(My Love)*

When I heard your name chanted over miles of land the vibration sent chills through my body. Each time it happened I felt closer to you longing to free you from your life and heal you of your hurts. I decided to find you no matter what it took knowing that I could offer you solace and the depth of my being. I never imagined that it would be you who saved me.

When things happened to me on my journey to you I would simply go to the star where we existed without boundaries and orbit around your warmth. There are things our bodies have taken that no one else could imagine yet when we touched those pains dissipated.

The first time we met I was behind bars and I saw you being led by me as I watched you like we all did: our champion you turned and looked at me. Your look said, "Now is not the time," so I smiled and wished you well.

As I heard your name chanted and your victory declared I asked the universe to guide you to me. I wistfully daydreamed of you hoping that my personal mission would not be in vain. I wondered what you thought of seeing me in captivity and if you knew how much I longed to heal you. I contemplated breaking away and coming to you but I knew if I just waited a little longer I could have you more fully. So I waited…

There was a bustle in "the market" as it was called and I felt you before I saw you and even though we hadn't met I felt like we belonged together. Before you approached my place of holding another did and requested me. My heart sank as I thought of never having the chance to meet you before I was taken away.

But then you turned, walked towards me pointed at me, and said "Her" then continued walking. As I was released from my holdings

I was washed and prepared for you, the women around me whispered of how blessed I was to be chosen by you, not knowing that it was I who had chosen you many moons before. I must admit a part of me quivered while wondering how rough you would be because of your battle tactics. Upon entering your chambers I felt calming warmth and followed your gesture to come closer. You asked my name, which no man who claimed me had ever done, so I stumbled over my words "My, My name? My name is..." before I could utter it you had pulled me close to you. I breathed you in as my heart pounded and my skin shivered from your touch.

Your rough hands moved across my shoulder and down my side while taking my dress off and revealing my seasoned body. I returned the gesture and pulled at your clothing until you stood bare before me. I looked at your body and traced your scars as I pressed my lips against yours. You tasted of fruit, wine and meat; a taste that I would never be able to erase from my memories. Your strong arms around my body pulled me into you as you lifted me on to your sleeping structure and hovered over me. I loved you before I even knew you and now you would love me too.

"Let me heal you" I said as my hips were raised and you thrust inside of me causing me to moisten and throb with each stroke. My legs wrapped around you and I held you tight as your thrusting brought my mind, body and soul ease. We healed each other as our bodies blended and our souls were set ablaze from the experience. Your weight on my body forced me to surrender to your every whim; yet your essence caused me pleasure beyond measure.

I belong to you now and I wanted you to have me however, wherever and whenever you wanted. You collapsed on top of

me as your body shook and I held you tightly in my arms and legs. Before I could relax and enjoy the pulsing in my body you began to thrust again, pulling my hair to reveal my neck that you bit violently leaving your mark on my skin showing that I was yours, daring others to try to touch me. I wanted you to mark me everywhere; stake your claim on my body and soul for eternity.

I felt a rising in my spirit that had been dormant for years and I spoke in tongue as aspects of me came forth wanting to experience your essence; yet you calmed me and held me tight as my others revealed themselves to you. Once I was calm you began pleasing me again this time with your head between my legs as you gripped my breast and legs. My back arched as you sent your power through me and caused me to rumble. You name fell from my lips as I rubbed your head and praised the God in you. "I belong only to you love for now and always. No one will ever have me like this." I vowed as my spirit expanded from my body. When I thought I could know no more pleasure you laid on your back and pulled me on top of you. I ran my fingers across each scar on you and asked that you tell me each story.

You filled me with your seeds and allowed the hurt to flow into my body to be transformed into our joy. You placed your hands on my hips holding me firmly against you while you pumped upwards causing my body to fold into you. Tears flowed from my soul as you made everything I had experienced worth it. I lay motionless on top of you panting and trembling and your chest became my pillow. Do you remember? Wewe ni mtu wa ndoto yangu (You are the man of my dreams).

Bad Ass Sister!

She's as fine as wine and twice as sweet
honey brown skin from head to feet.
She winks at you so angelically
yet possesses the power to part the seas.
She touches loved ones....gently
as she sings and rocks them off to sleep.
Her love is so sweet it will bring you to your knees
and capture your soul with just one squeeze.
Who is this woman, where can she be?
Is she connected, partnered or is she free?
And when she looks in the mirror what does she see?
She sees. . . a Bad Ass Sister looking back at me.

DRY

His response to my text is "DRY." I wonder what is wrong but I do not sweat it. I remember the experience of letting go with him and try to reassure myself that I have not made the same mistake as before.

I take a nice long shower to wash away the stresses of the world and reinforce my "no regrets" policy in life. Although I am not feeling the murky environment of going to a club, I need to hear the music and see the people. I text him once more and again he is D.R.Y.

I arrive on the set and am instantly pleased with the music selection by DJ Willpower & Needles of The Soulition. I came alone. I don't feel much like talking or listening for that matter. At least, I don't want to listen to words, or thought s or troubles. I want to listen just to notes, melodies and rhythms. I position myself as far to the back as I can. I close my eyes to enjoy the music more fully. Above the tones I hear a familiar sound.... his laugh. Knowing I have to be tripping, I keep my eyes closed and continue my musical journey.

I am startled by his hand on my arm. I slowly open my eyes and focus on him and stare blankly at him. Although I can see his lips are moving I can't comprehend what he is saying. Why is he here? Why did he feel the need to come and talk to me? I assume he is giving some sort of explanation but my brain will not let me perceive it. I just want to escape so I slide out of the booth and give him a brief hug before walking to the bathroom.

"Damn, there goes my peaceful night," I muse as he races around in my brain... more than I care to admit: His scent, his taste, his laughter, his grip on my..., his intense gaze before reaching ecstasy, his words, hell even his texts. I am sure it is just me; after all he hasn't changed since I let down my guards. I begin to regret every experience we had and take everything as a sign that I had made the wrong choice; although I knew I had not.

I splash water on my face before I go back out to the bar. I ask for a bottle of water and enjoy the cool feel against my lips, on my tongue going down my throat. *If I drink enough water I can flush out this feeling, replace these old feelings with new ones.* While re-grouping I am provided with additional help by the music. I head straight for the dance floor, which is my escape, my portal to freedom. I am sure the words are specifically played for me, I am the only one dancing and I love it. I am not paying attention to my surroundings until I feel him, behind me, against me.

I want to ask him what he wants and what he thinks he is doing but I cannot formulate my words properly, so I just dance. Sweat pours from my pores and soaks my clothes. I can feel the water rushing through my veins and bursting through my skin as it had the last night I allowed him in. I can feel his energy rising and he whispers "Use me" as he rubs against my body causing my juices to flow down my legs. My sweat hides my arousal as his hands slide on the outside of my pants. I manage to get lost in him again and I dance until I near climax.

I pull myself away from him and walk away quickly - only stopping to say my goodbyes to all my friends before leaving. I hear him calling behind me as I dart behind the building and get on my bike to ride like the wind home. My clothes are soaked but I lie on my couch replaying the night and open myself to the truth of the end of things. I know that I am shutting him out but I don't know how not to. I can still feel him but I will not allow myself to feel him for long. I ignore his calls and his text while I enjoy the sweet sorrow for a moment before drifting off to sleep.

Swimming

I must have drank too much because my head is swimming
I must have drank too much because my head is swimming
I must have drank too much because my head is swimming
He never asked and I never said no
He came up from behind and grabbed my waist and forced
my body to the bed
He pulled my panties down to my knees but did not touch my
shirt
He spread my legs apart and ran his member cross my ass before
pushing in

He slid in and out and in and out and in and out and in and out
and in and out
He pushed my hand away as I grasped his hips trying to control
his thrust
He told me and showed me that it was his and only he could
have me like this
He whispered vague words into my ears as I tried to hold on to
the little sanity I had left

I must have drank too much because my head is swimming
I must have drank too much because my head is swimming
I must have drank too much because my head is swimming
I resisted his words as he told me how to lay, move, touch
him…be

He said "You need to learn to listen sometimes….
before mounting me again

He looked deep into my soul and demanded that I stay here and feel him
He hurt me, made me scream, made me cry, and held my arms above my head
He pushed inside me as he pushed inside me and he would not stop
He touched my womanhood beads and held onto them claiming his right to do so
He dripped sweat on to my body and breathed heavily in my ear as he hit my "cry spot"
He smirked as he inquired: this is what you wanted, this is what you wanted, isn't it?

He came inside me
I must have drank too much because my head is swimming
I must have drank too much because my head is swimming
I must have drank too much because my head is swimming
He never asked and I never said no

My intent was to just chill with my "friend"
My legs trembled from the pressure
My mind heard the lyrics "Who gave you permission to rearrange me...certainly not me"
My body ached, my juices ran and pooled under me, under him on top of me
My thoughts sent me other places between the time he demanded I look at him

My lips opened to tell him to stop but no words came out
My world stopped and started at least a dozen times that I counted
My phone chimed in the background offering a moment of reality to seep in
He never asked and I never said no
I did not see it coming, thought it would not happen to me with him with us...
I ignored the innuendo, the look in his eyes, the desire I felt and dreams I had

I felt intensity, passion, depth, strength, determination, power and ecstasy
I blindly walked in thinking that I really knew what he was capable of
I still feel him inside of me, still taste him, and still tingle
I wanted it? I asked for it...I deserved it?
I wanted to slip through time and relive every moment to make sure it was/is real
I had my first, second, third and forth penetrating orgasm and felt cosmic love

I never asked and he never said no

RITE OF PASSAGE

My clothing is removed as I enter the room. It feels as if I am spiritually reborn, cleansed and provided new skin. I stand bare before elder women of the council while they quiz me intensely on sacred knowledge. After several hours of standing, my sisters and I are allowed to sit while the women of various ages share wisdom of their journeys.

Collectively, their stories span across a millennium. I look into their eyes as they speak, knowing that wonderment is stamped across my face. Some of them whisper their lessons; others hum while they talk. Their words are so intimate, so personal that they seem almost incomprehensible to my spirit.

After talking for hours and hours, while an intoxicating sweet smelling resin is burned, we, initiates are bound together by cloth to ritualistically start our journey. For the next several weeks we eat, sleep, breathe and exist together without words.

Our decisions are all made collectively and any disagreements are frowned upon by the elder women – usually by their silence. Anticipation fills my heart as the final day draws near. How do you know when you're ready? I know that my response to everything that I experienced is visceral.

There are no words in this language that would describe the experience. Intense is too gentle of a word. When I reflect upon all the prayers, spiritual trainings, bush lessons, sharing of sage wisdom and the women secrets; I understand more fully what it means to be Afrikan. Of course, there are the deeper rites; but I can't expose those to the uninitiated.

My heart pounds as we are each blindfolded and led into the shrine house. The blindfolds are removed when we are seated inside the shrine house. It is forbidden to know the location of the shrine houses until the female child is fully initiated into womanhood. We are not fully initiated yet so I appreciate the opportunity to look around at everything.

The first thing I notice is a temperature change. My body temperature fluctuates from hot to cold as air gently caresses my bare skin. I can actually feel both warm and cool air as it whisks around my head. There is no breeze. Inwardly, I laugh. Then, I think about all of my previous experiences, since initiation began, and how many of them did not have a rational explanation. This calms me and I stop looking for answers. Next was the scent; it was soft, subtle, comforting, natural, like honey in the wind on a spring day while children laugh in the background and flower petals hit the ground. We were separated for each of us had our own journey to take.

My journey began with darkness; I was placed into a well which was cold, damp, empty and alive. As I was sealed in the elders advised "Look into the waters until you see yourself" What the hell does that mean I can't see anything, it is pitch black and cold, so cold I am sure I would see my breath before I saw anything else. The water in which I sat seemed to move independent of my movements and crawled over my skin in ways that were impossible. After several chills ran through my body I began to remember my teaching and begin my mediations and prayers.

I thought that I must have fallen asleep because I began to warm as I was lifted out of the well by my elders. I walked toward the light, barely able to move my feet or open my eyes to the fiery light. When I finally was able to see I could not believe my eyes. I stood before myself engulfed in flames and smiling. As I reached out to touch myself I could feel the warmth of the flames and the cold of the well The walls were closing in, I told myself not to panic and to just stay calm. This is not happening.

Then I was lifted into the air and my stomach dropped as I sailed through time forwards and backwards making abrupt starts and stops. The fiery me was always in my peripheral vision with arms crossed, head high, blade across her, my, our, breast. I began to hear my name called in my head where I could not hide, block or meditate it away. "Who are you?" "Who am I?" I responded confused and disoriented. Being dizzy, cold, on fire and alone are the least of my concerns as I watched the warrior women rush towards me with their weapons drawn and rage in their eyes.

Yet I did not feel afraid. Instead I stood, tall, strong and determined. This would not be my death, this would not end my journey, and I would be victorious. As they run pass me I began to run with them. At first my legs were so heavy it was like I was running through chest high sand. The more I engaged in the battle -- the easier my steps would get until I ran along side them... with them, these great warrior women.

I can speak all their languages and understand all their commands. I feel the heat, taste the blood and sweat, hear the clash of metal, slicing of skin, tearing of flesh and breaking of bones. The feeling is intoxicating; I can feel the spinning of the earth as we fight.

"FREEEEEEEEEEEDDDDOOOOOOOOOOOOOMMMMMMMMMM!!!" I scream over and over and over and over. One by one we fall until it is just me covered in the blood of my sisters, my mothers, my daughters, my friends....me.

All the enemies are slain. Our blood soaks the ground causing life to spring forth. We destroy their entire nation. We, are the warrior women; we who refuse to let the battle come to our doorsteps; we who stand alone, we who seek out the enemies at their home and destroy them, their children, their history, culture and the thought of them; we, who are infinite. One by one our spirits rise from our bodies in a sparkling brilliance and our flesh is swallowed by the grounds below us.

"Leave no trace of them." This rings in my head as my body falls to the ground and I ascend; back to the beginning, back to The Creator...back into me.... now in the well.

I gasp for air as I return to my body and the elders pull me out like lightning and check my body. The healer mama covers me in herbs that sting as they soak into my open gashes and wounds. "Speak not of this to your sisters for they must find their own way." "Yebo (Yes), Mama." I reply with a new found strength and humility.

That night I am still feeling the great loss and carnage, I hope it is not real even though I am certain it is. That same night we all cry out in our own way as our bodies weaken and our spirits grow strong.

It seems as if sleep lasts only for five seconds before we begin to hear the songs of our mamas calling to us to awaken. I look down at my skin and it is healed but still has the paste from the herbs on it.

There is a waterfall near the compound and we all bathe under the water. The water, which does not feel like water, caresses us like hands, millions of hands covering and exploring every inch searching for weaknesses to be washed away and strengths to be nurtured.

The sun was high in the sky and beaming down to test our resolve and shed light on any darkness in our soul...Suddenly the term "**Born of fire**..". is clear to me. I have heard that phrase all of my life. I can hear the phrase whispered in the water as it cascades down my body to the ground.

When I say I can hear the water, I mean I can hear the water as it voices its thoughts and intent. Water sounds like sparkles or thousands of shards of glass moving in unison speaking of healing and cleansing. It speaks of my journey and triumph; it heals me and cools my spirit.

It isn't long before the meeting of the water and sun causes steam filled with divine images to rise from our bodies. I began to hear the battle cries again. I looked around to find myself back in the blood soaked fields of battle.

There is a calm that rides with death that is unmatched. It begins to rain and although I can no longer feel the physical properties I can feel the healing and cleansing.

Flowers and vines spring forth from the bodies of my sisters. It is a scene that seems to be in time-lapse; it was marvelous.

The wind carries our victory and freedom song to our homes with whispers of love to our children and family. I watch as the field transforms from red to green and back to red bursting with blossoming buds filled with life and color. My mama's hands on my shoulders bring me back to the waterfall..."You will have to learn to control your travels with time." She says as she wraps me in cloth.

All day my mind wanders as we dance, sing, eat, laugh, rest and learn of our sacred ways. It all seems surreal compared to the battlefield where I belong. By the time the sun begins to set I ran to my mamas and blurt out "I must go back, I must return, I must, Mama, Mama, let me go back."

 The elders calmly look upon me. One speaks "That is only one stop on your journey, if you get off at the first stop you will not know where it is that you truly belong. Complete your journey, then decide where it is you belong. Gather your sisters and meet us in the circle in fifteen minutes." "Yebo, Mama." I humbly reply. *Only the first stop, I cannot imagine what is next*.

True to their words, my other journeys were just as impactful. I drifted between various journeys connecting points and visions slowly weaving together the fullness of my existence. I clearly could see how each connected to my current existence, thoughts, desires, fears, preferences....you name it. I could see the continuum of me that was longer, and deeper than I ever imagined possible.

It is the final night/day of our crossing into full womanhood. We enter a tent that is draped in beautiful brilliant white cloth, crystals, flowers, with elaborate women warrior shields. The tents are scented with wonderful smelling incense, oils and fragrances. Dozens of other tents are filled with tables covered by foods, fruits, wines, and desserts.

This is the time we learn of our "sexual" selves and how to reach higher levels through the senses. My excitement could not be contained. I walk around in amazement looking at the beauty, touching, smelling and tasting of everything. I slowly notice that while I focus on the external things others lay quietly touching and experiencing themselves. I instantly feel uncomfortable. It is one thing to tap into your spirit through visions, travels, incantations or invocations, but to touch myself in a manner that brings it about seems improbable at best. I know if I could not achieve my goal I will remain a child in the eyes of my society and I did not want that. So I began.

I sit with my legs crossed, close my eyes and breathe deeply. I focus on my breaths... inhale, exhale, inhale, exhale, inhale, exhale, inhale, exhale, inhale, exhale, inhale, exhale, inhale. The tension begins to leave slowly and I recline on the pillow on the ground. It is soft and comforting and smells of lotus.

I start by rubbing my fingertips together, then my hands, then caressing my entire arm. I notice the feel of my skin touching and being touched. I watch as goose bumps form and know I am doing well. My nipples begin to rise so I attend to them rubbing, touching, pinching and massaging them taking note of how my body responds to each sensation. *I like gentle pinching best.* During the time I explore every inch of my body inside and out. At a point quivers rush through me and I enjoy the waves of energy that flow around the tent. I steady my movements and I can hear the moans, words and breaths of others around me.

I Pray...

"Great women of joy, pleasure and light I invoke the thought of you in the Creator and ask that you provide insight, guidance, protection, under-standing and abilities. I desire to feel divine pleasure and fulfillment.
As I embark on this journey please move through and around me heightening my senses and allowing me to feel ecstatic joy, arousal and release. Ashe."

The words I humbly pray do not convey the depth of my true feelings. I feel the woman within me becoming stronger and stronger. I began to cum and liquid squirts from between my legs in what seems like streams. I see a vast mountain range and a woman climbing up the side nearing the top. The closer she gets to the top....the more intense my orgasm becomes. When she reaches the top the sun shines on her and beams of light shoot from her, to me, and back to her causing a primal jolt of heat that spreads over my entire body.

he begins to lift off the ground... I see myself standing in beams of light and I can feel myself floating. "She" slowly spins, there is light dancing all around her until she is indistinguishable from the light. I once again look down on my physical body; this time there is no blood or carnage -- just beauty and light. Everything feels good, even my aura. I am disappointed when I hear the sistrum bell ring to call us back to the present. I would have stayed there forever.

It's hard to explain but I feel like a woman now, for the first time, I understand me and all my quirks; what makes me tick and what makes me advance. I still have an understanding that I must continue to grow and evolve. That night we all gather for our closing ceremony and make our womanhood beads to be worn. They are all unique but carry a common vibe, energy and theme. We can finally speak of our personal experiences. We chat all night until the moon bursts into flames.

We receive our final instructions about the handling of our beads and who can touch them, who we can share our experiences with and what we may experience over the next few weeks. We join hands in a circle for our closing prayer. Then into the night everyone disperses; but we are still very much connected. There are places that I looked at so many times in the past, but now realize that I will never look at things the same. There are so many significant lessons and experiences we shared that are sacred.

Everything, every place, every person has their secrets that I may never know of and I would not see just by looking at them with my eyes. The world seems foreign to me as I walk the "familiar" streets and encounter "familiar" people with new eyes. My whole world is different and strange.

Although everything is the same... I am completely different.

Simple

My heart races like stallions
My beating drum strikes like thunder
My eyes release an ocean of tears
My thoughts are fast and strong
Pumping and running through my mind

I love ellipsis

• • • • • • • •

• • • • • •

• • • • •

• • • •

• • •

• •

•

They are so....

The Sum

The desire to love, to feel love and be loved
This comes from a place that is Divine.
Does that mean that divine love is only what we should accept?

If it is... why do we allow it to hurt us so bad when we love?
Is it because we are not - Divine?

Hell no. It might be that we don't believe it. Well, not yet.
They say: beauty is only skin deep? But that just isn't true.
I have seen Beautiful African people.
Beauty that spreads from their bones to their soul
Smiles and laughs, hugs and touches, anything you can imagine
coming from them as a whole.

They... yes... they told me a long time ago and I know it to be true
that hell knows no fury like a woman's scorn.
Yet that same woman can be love, she can be the heavens reborn.
Ironically, the sum of one plus one is not simply me and you
It is all the hurt, pain, hate, joy, love and truth.

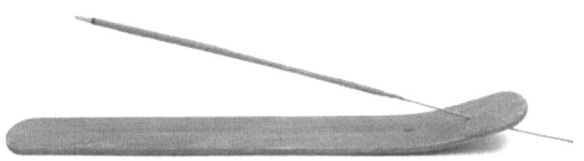

Sage Wisdom: **Incense**

Earliest Uses of Incense

Kemet and other ancient cultures soaked fragrant woods and resins in water and oil and rubbed their bodies with the liquid; this was considered one of the oldest forms of perfume. At religious and embalmment ceremonies many kinds of resins and woods were used as incense. In Cleopatra's chambers incense was burned all the time. She would customarily anoint her body with the same rare fragrant oils so anyone who entered would believe that they were near a beautiful flower.

What's your favorite incense? How do you pick a perfect scent for yourself or a loved one? Consider what you want to use the incense for then look for some non- toxic, all natural, hand rolled sticks, and an aroma that fits you or the occasion. Using incense is a form of aromatherapy like using oils. Scents range in smell, purpose and attraction.

Incense has widespread uses – and is used by all ages, colors, nationalities, races, spiritual denominations. A few commonly used incenses include: Frankincense and Myrrh, Cinnamon, Lotus, Coconut, Honeysuckle, Jasmine, Lavender.

Some of the most common uses for incense:
- Meditate or to unwind during yoga or other calming exercise
- Encourage emotional release and healing
- Soak in the tub while listening to music
- Relax with an aromatic cup of tea and a good book
- Spread good energy and joy
- Heighten sensuality and physical arousal
- Help to raise energy, adjust the energy of the area, and/or to achieve trance.
- Achieve a state of clarity, focus, and/or calm.
- Purify the air in a room
- Show respect/salute the Creator or ancestors

Common Incenses and Their Purpose

1. **Amber** transforms negative energy into positive; it is also calming, attracts loving, faithful emotions.
2. **Bayberry** -attracts money; it is also used for protection, happiness and control.
3. **Cedar** encourages the flow of energy and eliminates blockages, and toxins, physically, mentally, and emotionally.
4. **Cedarwood** -denotes strength, power and increase virility in men; it is used to push the strength outward into the world.
5. **Cinnamon** -is an aphrodisiac used to raise energy, promote psychic awareness and attract money.
6. **Citron** - aids in healing and strengthens psychic powers.
7. **Clove** -protects and cleanses the body, aids in removing negativity and is calming and comforting to emotions.
8. **Copal** -purifies, uplifts spirits, protects and attracts love.
9. **Coconut** - is good for protection.
10. **Dragons Blood** - energizes and attracts inspiration and success, protection, virility, strength and passion.
11. **Eucalyptus** –heals, purifies and protects.
12. **Frankincense** - blesses spiritual rites and helps one reach a meditative state.
13. **Frankincense-Myrrh** –blesses spiritual rites; sometimes used for funerary rites. Can be used to reach a meditative state.
14. **Gardenia** - denotes peace, love and healing.
15. **Ginger** - attracts wealth, love and heightens arousal.
16. **Honeysuckle** - strengthens memory.
17. **High John the Conqueror** - aids to overcome obstacles, achieve goals, and protect against negative energies; strengthens masculine energies.
18. **Jasmine**-promotes friendship and aids in emotional connections.
19. **Juniper**-aids in healing, calming, and protection.

20. **Lavender** -induces rest and sleep, relaxation; it is also used for healing of headaches.
21. **Lemon-** attracts joy, stimulates the mind and relieves stress.
22. **Lemongrass** - aids in developing mental clarity.
23. **Lilac** -attracts harmony into one's life.
24. **Lotus** -increases focus, mental clarity and heightened intelligence.
25. **Mint**-possesses strong healing vibrations and protective powers.
26. **Musk** – realigns one's energies and removes negative influences.
27. **Myrrh** – consecrates, purify, and blesses spiritual rites; often used with Frankincense.
28. **Musk** – encourages self-esteem, desirability and can assist in transmuting sexual love into higher emotion.
29. **Nag Champa** – aids in reaching a meditative state for spiritual enlightenment; it is primarily comprised of Sandalwood.
30. **Nutmeg** - calms the mind and it is often used for insomnia.
31. **Opium** aids sleep with visual lucid dreaming.
32. **Orange** attracts abundance and happiness through love.
33. **Patchouli** -awakens fertility and balances feminine energies.
34. **Pennyroyal** -repels negativity.
35. **Peppermint** -increases energy, heightens the vibratory level for cleansing and healing.
36. **Pine** -promotes strength, cleansing and healing.
37. **Rose** – attracts love to help one visualize desires; strengthens feminine energies.
38. **Rose Geranium** – aids in promoting courage and protection.
39. **Rosemary** - promotes restful sleep and pleasant dreams.
40. **Sage** – promotes wisdom, clarity and healing.
41. **Sandalwood** –aids in purification/blessing a spiritual altar or shrine.
42. **Strawberry** – attracts love and increases luck.
43. **Thyme** - attracts good health.
44. **Vanilla** – heightens mental thought and intelligence.
45. **Ylang Ylang –** heightens euphoria, feelings of love and harmony.

Tapping into my inner self (spirit)...

Just Friends

When it comes to "sexual freedom" I am ALLLLL in, well, in theory at least. I believe **women** and men should express themselves freely, love openly and all that good *we are the world* type stuff. BUT I keep myself rather reserved in my physical, spiritual and emotional interactions with others. In relationships I never demand that I be the "only woman." My mates have always been intimately involved with other women and occasionally other men too.

In fact, I often encourage them to seek fulfillment where they find it as long as there is love, honesty and safety (condoms, testing, good health, etc.). Some can handle this, some cannot. In terms of ME allowing myself to be completely comfortable with my desires, preferences, attractions and the like... well, not so much. But as I mature I seek my own "sexual liberation." I decide to take matters into my own hands; pun intended.

It is pretty much slapstick comedy so far but I enjoy myself and others. I even surprise myself with some of my innate talents and abilities to reach an orgasm, but that is <u>another story.</u> With all this exploring I still do not reach that deeper spiritual sexual experience or "Cosmic Cumming" as I call it that I seek. I have orgasm after orgasm but still I am not satiated. I know that this has everything to do with me -- and how open I am, since I haven't experienced the kind of depth that I seek with anyone; well not yet. I re-read the sage wisdom in books such as **"The Spirit of Intimacy," "Facing Mount Kenya," "Three Magic Words"** and "**The Divine Horsemen**." I even received a reading about the "***Magic Key***" I was missing. Of course it is very simple!

The key to reaching "spiritual enlightenment through sexual liberation" is opening yourself to the truth of the universe, accepting your destiny, your reason for manifestation, submitting to the experience and surrounding yourself with a loving, nurturing, supportive family AND environment. All this seems pretty simple, right? Wrong.

Though I had already finished my rite of passage into womanhood, studied the deeper sciences and surrounded myself with a loving family and progressive environment. This promotes a somewhat healthy view of sex, sexuality, women, men, relationships and Afrikans in this country (amerika) but is a hard thing to do. Despite the fact that I consider myself to be a very spiritual (whatever that really means) I must admit that I am influenced by some of society's views of sex, love, women, monogamy, marriage and relationships. This society's perception of "correct behavior" still colors my thoughts and actions. Most times I can rationalize my doubts and insecurities away or intuit what is the sacred MAAT view of what is true; but not always.

To add to my dilemma, many of the people that I come across don't view things – particularly sensuality and sexuality -- the same way that I do. So I find myself often closing myself off to others and their secular view of life. I find myself struggling the same way as other adults with sexuality. I struggle with how to "let go" and tap into **my** sexual spirituality or my spiritual sexuality depending on how you want to look at it. I often use the excuse that I don't want to hurt or mislead anyone but truthfully I simply don't want to be rejected or alienated for having my personal views or actions. If my partner doesn't share my views and values how can that person truly love and accept me? I wonder, do they secretly judge me? I question, are they trying to change me? I know I over think things. Do you ever do that?

I had a dream about my best friend that made me want something more. I reached out to him to hang out and catch up on life. If I could talk to anyone about this I could talk to him. So, this morning when he calls to confirm the time we are getting together I decide to see if I can reach that "*Cosmic Cumming" I've been seeking, maybe it can be done* with him.

No, I haven't actually spoken with him about us being physically intimate yet. And, yes, it may seem *weird* that I am having these thoughts about my best friend. And, no I don't know how he will react to this proposition. And, yes it is a possibility that he may reject me. But I am sure about one thing, I know that he loves and accepts me **unconditionally.** So there is no risk involved because at the end of the day, we will still be best friends. He picks me up right on time, but before we leave he sits down to talk to my family. He always does that until I have to remind him of our plans. "I didn't come here to see you," he says with a wink. As I grab my coat off the rack, he follows behind, giving dap to my brothers. He gives me his credit card while we walk to the car reminding me that it is his treat for the night. We playfully argue about whose turn it is to "fetch" (going to get the drinks all night.) Eventually, he agrees to be the "fetcher" since I am wearing my dope ass "come hither" heels. As we drive to the **Soulition event**, we contemplate eating first but then the music tugs at our spirit; so hunger is forgotten.

We pull up to **The Soulition** event and walk inside greeting everyone. We walk straight to the dance floor and begin to party. I dance for a long while until my heels begin to hurt my feet on the marble floor. *Why make a dance floor out of marble anyway?* I ask myself. I take a seat on the edge of a booth watching him continue to dance. I chuckle quietly, sipping my drink, as I watch his style of dancing. He definitely has his own style. He catches me looking at him and pauses mid-stride for a moment. I notice for the first time how attractive he really is as a man. There is always one or several beautiful, desirous women who will hang out with us for the night. This is our routine when we go out together. It is never the other way around. I never pick up men who hang out with us for the night.

 For one, I am not *that* comfortable around just any man or woman, particularly ones I just meet. Secondly, he is too over protective. He is always comically hostile towards men who are attracted to me. His tantalizing choice for the night is tall, slender, hazel brown and brightens the room with the warmest eyes ever. When he introduces her, she speaks with a slight Caribbean accent that is as beautiful as her energy. "Wow, your *sister* is really pretty. You two look alike too, she said to him." I laugh to myself. For the next hour I sit watching them and others dance while I sip my drink. I like the way the crowd sways to the, DJ Willpower314 mixes from the turntables.

As much as I want to get back on the floor I am diligently weighing my options as I plan it all out in my mind. I nearly talk myself out of approaching him with the proposal about seven times. Lost in my thoughts, I jump when he leans up against me. "Want another drink?" he shouts in my ear so he can be heard over the music. I nod yes and he disappears just as fast, then he is lost again in the crowd. I wonder how sleeping with him will affect our friendship. I know we will be okay but I question the overall affect. Will he feel uncomfortable with me later? Will it throw him off guard? I wonder if he will be able to even get aroused with me. He returns with three more drinks for me and I laugh. "What? I didn't want to have to go back through the crowd again and you KNOW you are going to ask me to go back," he says jokingly. By the time the next round of song ends I am finished. Yes, I finish all three drinks.

I can feel the tingling in my body from the alcohol coursing through it. The crowd seems to move sporadically with the beats. I know it is my inebriation and the thoughts of us that are making me miss a few things. My thoughts take me to a realization that although we are both *very **attractive** to each other*, we are not exactly **attracted** to each other. He is beyond "safe," he is family. We are best friends; since childhood. We may not see or talk to each for months but when we come back together it feels like we are right back where we left off. We have that kind of bond. Decades ago I decided that he would be "my first" when I started having sex. He refused, very lovingly of course, but without a second thought.

Our relationship has always been strictly platonic, yet very emotionally intimate. We have spent nights in each other's arms, showered together, slept naked together, and one time in college we had sex with other people in the same room. The thought of being physical with him did not cross my mind; not until last week when I had the dream.

In my dream... I *follow him up this narrow spiral staircase that seems to reach up into the universe. At one point I finally catch up to him. We look into each other's eyes, standing face to face, our bodies slightly touching. The energy between us is tantalizing, arousing and pleasing. He slowly slides his hand up my dress then simultaneously inserts his fingers into my wetness. I struggle to open his zipper but I can't concentrate. He nibbles on my lower lip... whispering words that are in a different language. Then we are in my bedroom and he is on top of me moving in and out of my depth while massaging my breasts. I wrap my legs around him and repeat his name over and over....softly. His name feels so right spilling from my lips. Above us is the universe again and the stars seem close enough to touch. As he moves faster inside me; his energy surrounds me as I approach climax.*

I woke up feeling disoriented because that is not the reality of our relationship. This is not how I see him. I was soaking wet and could feel his touch all over my body. I knew something must be up if I am dreaming about him like that so I decided to call him immediately – even though it was very early. I shared the dream with him as I sought understanding. He told me about his recent layoff from the job and his financial woes. I scolded him for not telling me and I ask him not to be a creepy creeper who lurks around in my dreams. We laughed and talked on the phone for hours. Finally we decided to get together for some much needed face time. That was the first time that it actually crossed my mind.

"You cool? He says as he nudges me, interrupting my train of thought "You seem to be off somewhere else in the middle of the club." I smile and motion for him to go back to his new friend. He grabs my arm and pulls me with him back to the dance floor as we dance for the rest of the night. As the event is ending we grab our things and head for the door. I give out hugs to all my friends as we exit the building. "This was fun!!! I really enjoyed sweating it out." As he grabs my hand, he asks me, "What now potato head?" (a personal nickname for me).

We decide to go to the vegan restaurant that is open all night. He cracks jokes about my "rabbit food" but finishes his entire meal. As the night begins to wind down he asks if I am coming over his house for more drinks... we go hard.

We arrive at his house and I notice he has several new records and books. He notices me noticing and smiles broadly. "Now that I have time off I finally have a chance to go to all those little shops I often pass by while walking. We barter -- the shops provide me goods in exchange for my technical services. He shares with me his idea about starting a new project. "I want to go live in another country and do my work from there." I can tell he is very excited about the possibility. I am really excited for him. We talk about it for a while exploring different scenarios before I decide to take a shower.

He follows me into the bathroom shaking his head ruefully. "Look... please don't make the water hell hot like you normally do when I am not around." After we shower together I slip into one of his pajama sets. He wears the bottoms and I wear the top. He pours us a glass of wine and we settle on the couch to watch a marathon of Dr. Who episodes. Of course, I analyze the faulty science behind the adventures. "You always ruin it, with your silly logic. This is science FICTION which means everything is powered by the magic," he says. Hours pass and we drift off to sleep entwined together. Yes, this is common for us over the years and no we never "slipped up" because sex was never an option for us. We always joked that we were like "best girlfriends."

The next morning when I wake up he is on the phone walking around in just his boxer briefs. I watch him in admiration. I don't think I ever noticed how sexy or how wonderfully sculpted and toned he is. It still seems weird looking at him as a woman and not as his *sister*. I brush my teeth and get a pair of his sweat pants to wear. I am still intent on having this experience of "Cosmic Cumming" with him so I suggest we have dinner tonight after finishing with our day. I even volunteer to cook.

As the day flies by the butterflies multiply in my stomach. I consider the magnitude of what I am about to do, or attempt to do with my best friend, my brother. While I shop I pick up his favorite organic liquor and grab some wine for me. Later at home, I shake my head in amazement as I choose an alluring, sexy set of underwear in his favorite color. Hell, if I am going to do this I might as well go all the way.

I reminisce on a recent discussion we had. He says I live in the present and he lives in the moment. He says I always consider all elements of my decisions causing me to *live in the present*. In contrast, he says that he always considers all the enjoyable elements which allows him to *live in the moment*. It is a running joke between us. Tonight, I plan to live in the moment but I bet he will live ironically in the present. I decide to go to his house so he will be more relaxed, that way, if things become awkward I will be able to leave and clear my mind on the way home. I try to anticipate everything.

It is a delicious meal but I can barely eat any of it because I am so nervous. Of course, he eats both his and my portions. After dinner I take off my clothes, wrap a piece of cloth around me and tell him to unwind and to bring us drinks. Since we have been friends for decades - our comfort zone is well established. So he undresses down to his briefs and brings us glasses of some drinks that he concocted.

As we sit on the couch laughing and talking I reach over and kiss his cheek. He reciprocates and hugs me in that brotherly way that is customary. I seem calm but inside I am freaking out! I decide to stop being a scary cat about the whole thing and just go for it. I un-wrap my cloth and stand in front of him showing him my new set. "Oh Lord not another strip tease practice. I thought you are done with wanting to be a dancer?" I slowly take them off and straddle him. He stops laughing. His face is one of puzzlement and intrigue at the same time but he does not move or say anything. I can feel him rising but I know this is natural and no indication of a desire for me.

He is waiting. I think he is waiting to see what I am doing before he reacts. I kiss his cheek again and again he kisses mine. However, this time he did not give me the brotherly hug that always follows. I know it is because I am straddling him naked or because we have never been at this place before. I kiss him again; this time on his lips. This is still not a big deal because we often kiss on the lips when parting. But then I gather the courage and I slide my tongue gently across his lips and reach beneath me to stroke his hardness.

"What are you doing, potato?!" He says, but his voice hitches. I continue to stroke him and rub his tekken against my wetness. He is calm but his breathing becomes unsteady. I wonder how far he is going to let me go before he stops this. I adjust him beneath me as I prepare to slide down on him. He grabs my wrists to stop me. He repeats his question. "What are you doing potato?" He is still very calm but sweat breaks out on his forehead. I simply look at him, lean in close, then I moan gently as I nibble on his ear because I know exactly what he likes. He is still calm but his breathing is a bit more labored now. I know I am crossing that invisible line. We said we should not cross. My next move erases the line..... Several days later I call him and he picks up immediately. "Hey," he says somewhat tentatively. "How are you today?"

"I feel absolutely great!" I explain to him why I chose to experience "us" like that the other night. I also share my feelings about the connection. "I am so glad you feel the same way. I didn't want things to be awkward between us after being so close to you like that. I feel like it will deepen our friendship." I listen while he continues to express himself.

"I am glad we are so close that no boundaries exist between us. Now we can be even better friends because I know that our relationship is not based on that." I agree with him. Our relationship is even deeper now that we know there is nothing "sexual" between us. Although I am a bit disappointed that we didn't "go all the way" the other night I feel better knowing that I tried. I didn't feel much like dressing up and going out but I want to dance. So I call him and suggest we go dancing for an hour then get some movies afterwards; he agrees. After dancing we go back to my place because we agree my couch is better for watching "cry-cry movies." That is what he calls them. I don't necessarily subscribe to romantic notions of love and relationships (they are based in unrealistic and immature expectations) but I do enjoy a good romance movie.

Whenever we watch he heckles the entire movie which makes it fun for both of us. After the first movie ends he asks me to come lay down with him in my bed. He says he just wants to rest. We turn off the TV and I pour myself a glass of sweet red wine and head to my bedroom. He is naked and under the cover before I can even close the door. I laugh at him. "Damn go-go gadget stripper. You aren't even wearing your boxers." I laugh so hard I almost drop my glass. Of course, he laughs at me.

I pull a book out to read and get ready for bed. "Are you going to sleep in your clothes? You know half way through the night you are going to get hot then wake ME up getting undressed." I roll my eyes but he is right. I take off my clothes, wrap cloth around me and slide under the covers with him. I lay in the bed with my back facing him so I can use the light to read.

He puts his hands on my butt and gently rubs my skin. It feels weird but I didn't think anything of it. He moves his hand down and I let it rest between my thighs. I open my legs slightly and then whisper, "You might as well put it in if you gonna be rubbing all on my cakes and shit." We both begin to laugh. We continue to laugh until he reaches over and kisses my back. Then he begins to play with my clitoris.

Hmmmm... this is different I thought to myself. He rubs with a steady stroke until I am wet. I'm thinking to myself... he turns me down the last time...I really am not sure how to respond. After that I was done with the notion of sleeping with him. I take a deep breath and calm my mind. "What are you doing?" I ask. He did not answer. He rolls me over to my back and moves down under the covers. I inhale deeply as he kisses my thighs and rubs my body. As ready as I thought I was for this... I wasn't. I grab him by his shoulders and pull him from under the covers. "What's wrong? You weren't enjoying it?" "Yes, very much." But..." "Here we go," he sighs and he becomes frustrated.

"This right here is the exact reason why I said no the other night. You are so fickle. You claim to be all free and shit then you put up all these damn blockers. You are such a hypocrite!! That is why I have never messed with you over the years. You have too many damn rules for me."

"Well now… don't hold back. Tell me how you really feel," I interject, cutting him off. His shocked face looks at me before bursting into laugher. "I guess I had been holding that in since the other night." "Yeah… I guess so." "BUT, you just don't see what I see. For YEARS I have watched you come in and out of your relationships…. playing those "can't catch me" games while controlling your own emotions. You only allow yourself to go so far then you draw the lines in the sand. AND for what you are doing it this way!!" He shouts.

"You are initiated and I am not but I have allowed myself to grow more spiritually and emotionally grounded than you have over the years. If you want your "Cosmic Cumming" you're going to have to open up. I have bit my tongue about this for awhile, trying to give you time to do and be something different in your relationships, but you haven't made any changes."

"The other night I said no because I did not want it to be rushed or a spur of the moment thing. I wanted you to be sure. And you aren't." He turns over and closes his eyes. I sit up slightly and take a sip of my wine. I ponder everything he said. After about 30 minutes I tap him on the shoulder and quietly say, "I'm ready."

…"Ready for what?" he says. "To let go," I reply. He sat up and looked me in my face to see if I am serious. He takes my glass out of my hand and sets it on the floor next to my bed. Then he pulls me close to him. We kiss like lovers for the first time. It feels sooo right. By the time the one kiss is finished I am wet and he is rock hard. He lifts me on top of him and enters me with one thrust. Then he stops moving.

He smells my hair and kisses my neck. He is still inside of me pulsating but not moving. He runs his finger through my coils. I rub his bald head and tell him I love him. He holds me even tighter and says, "You are the one. You are my soul and I have to have you in my life." His eyes fill with tears as he begins to pump inside me. The feeling of his thickness moving rhythmically inside me is incredible. My lips part but no words escape my mouth. My body speaks for me. It is confessing all my fears, hurts, passion and joy to him. I begin to moan….

I hold him so tightly in my arms… trying to pull him deeper into my soul. He places his hands under my butt and buries his head in my neck while pushing deeper and deeper inside me. I kiss him everywhere and wherever my lips touch his body – my tears follow. "I love you so much. I never thought it could feel this good." The warmth from his body covers mine. We press against each other to the beat of our hearts. There is a comfort and pleasure I feel with him that I have never felt before.

He often stops to make sure I am still comfortable in my decision. He turns me over on my stomach and wraps his big hands around my neck. I relax all my fears. It's time to do so. I trust him. My body melts into his and I feel a wave of love, protection, and synergy between us. A wave of different emotions and energy rush my body and through my soul. My clit throbs as he continues to move even more deeply... from this position. I hold him even tighter beckoning him not to stop. His sweet strokes send us both into ecstasy. My moaning is louder than the grunts he makes as we experience the ultimate "cosmic cumming." I chuckle as I replay our conversation and the most beautiful sex I have ever experienced in my life. I stroke his face as I drift off to sleep in his arms. I can't sleep because my body continues to pulsate as I long for him to be back inside me again.

I look at his sleeping face and see a man I have always loved. I begin to kiss his stomach and chest as I stroke his tekken. I hope he will be able to go again. He is erect before his consciousness is fully awake. I climb on top of him taking all of him with one motion. I move back and forth on him as he watches my expressions. He has an indulgent smile while allowing me to use him for my pleasure. He yanks me towards him so that we can kiss. He touches my body lovingly, stroking my head, my back, my legs and my shapely butt. My groans became louder as my arousal explodes. Before I know what is happening I am cumming again. My body jerks with fulfillment. He continues to move beneath me until he also comes undone. I lay next to him rubbing his head.

I listen to our heart beats as they slow down. He drifts back to sleep with me still on top of him. I am mesmerized that he is still holding me. I revel in the thought of my best friend... my brother.

Wandering

Not only does he twist my body he twists my mind past cognition to submission and back again. Want more but scared of the effect and after effects.

Will regret follow if I swallow him whole within my soul or will he just disappear and reappear in the sky, at the bar or in the recesses of my mind from time to time?

The more I hold back the deeper it goes. Cumming undone at the seams seems to be the norm so why am I surprised each, and, every, time he touches my spine. Insanity is expecting it to be different for him to be slipping.

Even though I see his beauty in moments shared and taken dares I shouldn't even be here… not physically, not spiritually, not emotionally and not actually **here** with him, truly with him.

I hear wedding rings calling in the back of my mind reminding me of the time but the tingle in my spine and desires in my mind are louder, faster, stronger, bolder, boulders on my brain causing pain of reality or maybe it's just me tripping…

Cause I'm sitting at my desk waiting on a response………

Yes.

BREATHS

She focuses on her breathing. Each breath brings new life, each moment is different. She bends and stretches and stretches her bends. Tree pose, warrior pose, downward facing dog, child pose, breathing in and out. Take deep, slow, full breaths. Concentrate on every muscle. Feel the oxygen flowing. Contract, release... and breathe.

She didn't notice the rise of her nipples through her tank top but he did. Her bending and stretching creates a rising in his core and stiffens his resolve to do a good job and execute every position perfectly. In her world there is only breath; in his world there is only her..... breathing, nipples hard, muscles relaxing... taking it all in.

Maybe today would be the day he gets to embrace her. Each day after class the members embrace and enjoy each other, since they are now fully open. Each week she smiles heading in his direction. Each week he avoids eye contact. He does not want her to meet his rising upon first encounter. But his rising is exactly what she wants to meet. She enjoys the rising, rousing pulse that flows through the room after deep slow, full breaths.

As they slide in and out of the final poses, then hug themselves, to thank their body, she stands and looks in his direction. He does not divert his eyes this time. As others quickly walk in for their embrace, the two of them slowly approach each other with a growing pull at each step. As they touch...he wraps his arms around her fully and folds into her. She pulls him in tightly pressing her face into his chest. Instinctively, his rising rises even more and instinctively she pushes her pelvic bone deeply into him. No embrace was too long or too short in this class. It just is. So they stand together intimately holding, connecting, exploring, with deep slow, full breaths filled of each other.

As a tingle shoots through their bodies... both release a deep moan that is a familiar sign of a position perfectly executed. She breaths, he breaths, then they break the embrace. Her smile is pure ecstasy. She squeezes his hand and walks away grabbing her items as she leaves.

Releasing My Personal Limitations...

_____

_____

_____

_____

_____

_____

_____

_____

_____

_____

_____

_____

Fiending

fiending n. craving, desiring, wanting, obsessing (over or about something or someone).
- Slang word

You left so fast there was no time to seduce.... Please come back.. I have something... just for you.

We don't even have to go too far, just come in a little closer and lay with me on the floor.

Or hold me up against the wall; whichever you choose. Tell me how to make you stay, what should I do?

We can do it in the car baby, I will put on my shoes...right here and throw on a dress. No need to clutch the steering wheel, I am here to impress.

Just pull around back... no one will notice if I climb on your lap. Or we can try it in the basement on top of the wash machine. I don't care where baby... just make me scream.

No need to go to the bistro, I got a love jones right here. If you're too tired baby I can just ride you in the chair.

Slap my ass, pull my hair, and make me yell that it's yours. You don't have to do much baby... just walk through that door.
It is now 2 o'clock in the morning and I'm still not making love to you. I call, but you don't answer, what the hell am I to do?

Breathing heavy, body ready all I have to stroke is this pen. Just one knock, Scott and I promise to just let you in.

You see I am fiending, fuck that, I'm begging for a touch I know is all mine. So come on baby, do your job and rest next to my spine.

I'm lying on my stomach, wet, all you have to do is put it in. Then I'll get up on my knees and from the waist I will bend.

Baby? Can you hear me calling you, asking you to cum? Cum over and help me baby add yourself to my sum.

I have this unique problem that I need you to solve. See there is me all ready and wet but no addition because you aren't here yet. Then there's a hunger so great, that only you can feed. And there is my legs wide open with nothing but dreams of you, between these thighs, when I open my eyes.

Scott? Can you feel me wrapped around your dick? I am going crazy I can barely take this shit. A cold shower didn't help, because your love is so fierce. It's like a sword or a spear through my heart... that you did pierce. Can you taste me Scott as I wrap my legs around your head. Baby, this is what I gift to you, can you hear or feel what I said. After all this time you are the one to make me moan, but this isn't right cause I am here making love all alone.

Scott? Can you see me... I have on the shoes that you love. Cum here baby and make me call to the skies high above. Yeah, I am tripping and I don't give a damn. Just fuck me, make me happy, I am yours for the taking, I am. I just can't stop at four pages. I'm still going on. Cause I can't resist your love... that is so strong.

Okay... I give up. Don't cum! I can do it all by myself. Who needs you anyway with all of this wealth? I don't need you to undress me with only your eyes. I can make my own self wet just by parting my thighs.

I don't need you to taste sweet in my mouth. And I damn sure don't need you to wear my shapely ass out. I don't need to feel you behind me firmly gripping my hips. I definitely don't need to hear my name on your lips. I already came twice without your unique touch. Yeah, I fantasized about you... but not really THAT much. I don't need your *tks* talking shit, saying exactly what I want you to say....
phone rings

Hello... What?!!! You are on your way??

A Lott Moore

I watch you on your journey from a distance
Answering questions, fixing chaotic scenarios and echoing your
triumphs from mountain peaks
I never speak, nor do I show my face

I keep up with your progress through your friends, family and your
words
If you are excitement, I guess I am serenity
To me, your words are heartbeats... breaths... blood
You keep me alive and wanting, taking, demanding more, more, a
Lott Moore.

Soulmates? I wouldn't go that far
Intricate fragments of each other's thoughts, ideas, goals, triumphs
and essence
Yet we never have to say thank you or share our thoughts

You caress me with your ideas, arouse me with your thoughts and
make love to me with your words
And I feel such heat from your brain

Allow me... to... put your brain on ice
Massage away your troubles
Comfort you with mine
I never imagined that there could be another to put
passion, love, lust, rage, trust... even themselves between the lines

But you do
And still I long for you to give me Moore
Moore of you
Moore of me
A Lott Moore

Opening of the Year

To celebrate the New Year which marked 6260 AFK (after founding of Kemet) we gathered, ate, drank, sang, danced and told stories of Sepdet and the flooding of the Nile. The call and response: For as long as the sun shines... *And the water flows....* **Forever...** *Forever....* **Harambee.... Harambeeeeeeeeeee......** **echoed across the airs.**

In the middle of the compound is where the festivities took place with the entire community; however only the initiated were privy to the deeper meaning of the symbols, songs, dances, activities and masquerades. The closing prayer and libation was done as the sun sets. I saw **HIM** from a distance for the first time in years.

Over the course of the next several weeks the arousal, intensity and heat of the "dog days of summer" rose following the solstice. I could feel the universe stirring and I wondered what this new season would bring to my life. While bartering at the market I ran into **HIM** and he complimented me on how beautifully I had danced at the Festival a few weeks ago when he asked me to dinner.

I remained distant in my thoughts and vibe, so I would not pull him in or be pulled by him; but that did not deter him. His persistence and our history whittled away at my reservations. I agreed to have dinner with him.

Let me tell you a little about our history. When we met over a decade ago, I was going through my initiation into being a medium. We only had passing interactions within our society. For almost two years we would see each other at different events but never interacted directly. Inevitably, because of the nature of our work we ended up working together providing programs, classes and workshops to "underprivileged youth" which is when my deep attraction to him began to grow. I greatly respected his love for the youth, intelligence and quiet intensity.

I believe that how you treat, love, respond to and care for your people is a direct reflection of how you will interact with those you have physical intimacies with so I was very interested. He was a man I desired to know more fully but since my main focus was the evolution and improvement of the state of the world, I took no time for frivolous things that did not help me towards my ultimate goal: the complete and total liberation of Afrikan people all over the world.

Our work together was brief yet it helped to foster and cultivate many programs. For me, it whet my appetite for him. Unfortunately after helping to establish a "Freedom School" and working solely with it, I lost direct contact with him for a while. While organizing an event that I needed local presenters; he was recommended from several different sources.

I hadn't had any real interactions with him for years but my attraction for him never faded. After confirming he was actively still engaged in youth development, I put the word out that I was looking for him. Within a matter of days he contacted me and we set up a meeting. I was happy to see that his vibe, energy and commitment was still the same.

He still wanted to bring about change... that was truly refreshing. We combed through all the details to make sure we did not forget any aspect. By the time we finished all the planning the Autumn Equinox was rolling around so I invited him over to observe it with me. I explained the Equinox to him. I told him during the Equinox the time of the year when the day and night are the exact same length to mark a "crossing." This is a good time to reflect, plan and make movement for the upcoming season or to simply enjoy the subtleties of the shift.

He accepted and asked if he needed to bring or do anything. "Wear light colored clothing and come with an open mind. If you have any divination systems that you use and would like to bring them, feel free. This is a favorable time to seek guidance from the invisible world," I told him. When he arrives 10 minutes early in all white with his Meter Neter divination cards in hand... I must say again that I am impressed. I begin by lighting the charcoal and offering a salute to the Great Creator, ancestors, forces within nature and special friends and guides. He follows suit, then we light the multi-colored candles together and asks for blessings.

I asked was there anything specific he wanted to divine about personally. He pulled out his deck, did a salute and asked several questions about how to better impact our community, improve his station in life and manifest those things he was working towards.

We closed our session giving thanks to the Creator with an offering of frankincense & myrrh incense. I have a new and even deeper respect for this brother. "I am not trying to pry but I thought you were Christian." He replies, "I am but I am also open to learn, explore and accept other people's beliefs as long as there is no conflict in divergent perspectives. "I take it you are not?" "No, I am not. Of course I believe in some of the principles but I study the more ancient sciences and practices." We talked for hours. It was so refreshing.

During our conversation he spoke of some of the skills he has been able to hone over the years. Of course we spent a great deal of time talking about him reaching a heightened spiritual level through "tantric sex" and how he often was called upon for his "talents." I had often thought of him in that manner and was obviously intrigued about his humility, yet confident demeanor.

At the time I had been looking for a brother I felt I could connect with, in that manner without pretenses, games or baggage. This usually accompanies dealing with a person who isn't initiated into the sciences or an African system of study. I did not want to "settle down" but I desire that level of sacredness, openness and intimacy. So I took a leap of faith and asked him, "Will you have sex with me?" His response was genuine. "Wow, you just jumped right out there with that o sure, well okay." There was no need for further discussion -- Now we just need to plan it.

When I arrive at his house I ask him if he is okay with me doing a prayer and sprinkling his room to cleanse the energy? I am serious about the sexual act being sacred and meaningful. I am clear this is a deep brother in harmony with all aspects of himself and one who has connection with the universal forces. I am not clear about how this will translate in a sexual experience.

It is years since I am even open to the concept of sharing myself with a man in this manner but it is not uncomfortable for him to be the one. I previously took my shower. After my prayers I take off my clothes and lay down in his bed to wait on him. After he showers, he lights candles and turns on some music then joins me. Initially we talk about happenings in our respective lives. Soon we begin to explore each others' bodies. I did not realize how much I had missed being touched or how arousing and pleasurable it feels.

His scent is soft, clean, subtle yet prominent. His large coarse hands touch every inch of my body. I allow my sounds to guide him and follow his cues in return. Before long we are completely enraptured in each other. The room grows hotter and hotter with every gesture and we merge closer with every movement. At this point we can no longer tell where he begins and I end. The experience can only be compared to the fulfillment I felt during my initiation rites.

Over that next year we cross many boundaries and limitations with each other. Nothing is taboo for us to say, discuss or do. We enjoy this bond until I suddenly stop calling or responding to his calls or texts.

This brings me back to the present. After all of that history I have not seen him in nearly three years. So, when I say my decision to have dinner with him is "complicated" this is an understatement. I dreamt about him the night before our date. I am anxious about our connection being strong but I believe in keeping things in perspective.

I want to go to a restaurant, rather than us staying at home but because of the life changes I adopted recently -- all spiritual -- it is now more challenging for me to find people who can prepare my food without it having some sort of adverse affect on me or them. So I prepare a meal for both of us at my home.

"You realize this is my first time eating your food. Right?" "No it is not the first time. Remember when we were working on the teen programs? I cooked during that time and you ate my cooking several times; then again that time when we celebrated the Equinox together. " "Man that was a long time ago, you have a good memory" "Thanks, I remember those things I want to retain fairly easily."

As he ate the delicious meal, the dreaded subject came up. "So what happened to you awhile back when you just disappeared on me?" I sighed, wondering how to convey this to him. Let me start by first apologizing for disappearing without an explanation. Physically you and I seem very compatible. We had gone to extreme highs and I appreciated all that we shared. We reached heights I thought I would never reach sexually. But one day I woke up and knew I needed something more meaningful."

"So you ran because you started to get feelings?" "Just the opposite," I clarified. "I "ran" because there were none." His confused look encouraged me to explain further. "I wanted more and it would have been unfair of me to seek that from you when we already had an understanding about how things would be between us. What we were sharing was very fulfilling, pleasing, enjoyable, etc. etc. etc., **physically**." "But what I needed was the divine aspects of it. This is something I was not getting or giving. I was not allowing the spiritual aspect of our lovemaking to be expressed....something so divine and momentous. I wanted something more for you as well. I felt that you were limited by giving just the physical without the celestial aspect of it because I was not willing to contribute to that aspect. I did not know how to change that or if you would even be open to it."

"The only thing that was clear to me was that I could not continue our interaction without making significant changes." I figured since you were still involved with other sisters you would have no issue with having one less woman to connect with sexually. Plus I did not want to be exposed to all the energies of the other sisters you were involved with physically. I had to walk away for my own development, growth and peace of mind."

"I can understand that, he said graciously. By doing it that way you took away something that was feeding me in a way that I had not been fed before and an opportunity for me to experience something different than the physical. You also took away MY choice in the matter by not sharing your concerns. That was a little selfish and short sighted." I breathed deeply as the reality of what he felt touched my spirit. He continued, "You opened me up, introduced me to a new way of thinking, being, doing things then you just walked away because YOU wanted more. Did you ever stop to think maybe I wanted more also? Maybe I wanted something deeper, a stronger connection, and a more meaningful relationship.

You knew that I was tired of being in that stage of my life also. Outside of the physical I thought we were friends. I think I deserved better than that." "I agree, I was wrong and I truly apologize," I conceded. There was silence for a long while. We eventually loosened up and began to catch up on the past years. It only took a few hours before we seemed to be where we left off.

"Will you sleep with me?" he randomly interjects in the conversation. And before I could say no he explains all the reasons that he still wants to engage: a desire for something he has not been able to find, us being closer and feeling The Creator through me. I didn't know what to say. I had already been unrighteous in my treatment of him; his reasons are logical. I consent and begin to take my clothes off.

"**No**, not now, not yet," he laughs. I would like more time with you and I am very tired. I want you to be comfortable and fully in agreement with the decision." We end our evening amicably. Afterwards, I ran myself a lavender bath and slide into the memories of us. He visits me in my dreams and expertly explores my body. By the time I awaken I want him more than ever before. He is late for our next date so I call him several times. I leave two messages but he does not respond. At one point in the evening I wonder if he is trying to teach me a lesson. When I finally decide to call it a night, my phone rings.

His voice is very apologetic. "I am very sorry I missed our date. I was unable to contact you before now... I have been caught up with an emergency with one of the youth that I mentor and his family." I could feel his anxiety as he continues. "He was jailed for statutory rape and I have been trying to work his situation out all day." I purchase the flowers, several oils, organic fruits and vegetables, aloe vera, a white 100% cotton wrap, and wild rice. Praying over the food, I offer for us to reschedule for later in the evening but he adamantly refuses.

He says, "he needs to relax." We agree to spend the night together another day and I will still cook for us. While at the store purchasing food... I see there is a fresh shipment of white carnations and feel he might benefit from an aura cleansing bath. I think about how the evening would go tonight. When he calls to inform me he is 10 minutes away I begin to run his bath water. By the time he arrives dinner is prepared, the house is immaculate, the oils for his massage are mixed and ready; the bath water is at a perfect temperature.

He removes his shoes and jacket upon entering my house. "Follow me" I instruct him. As we head up the stairs we both can feel the energy rise. "Take off your clothes please." Although he did not know what might happen we still trust each other – even after all these years. With no hesitation he obliges. I open the door to the bathroom to reveal lit white candles, towels, carnations and a fuzzy white rug.

The room is steamy and inviting. I motion for him to get into the tub. As he slips into the water I take off my wrap and replace it with a sheer white lappa revealing my womanhood beads that I rarely remove. (The only time I ever remove is when we used to have intercourse. I studiously avoid getting other people's energy on them. The sight of my beads creates nostalgia for him; both comforting and uncomfortable.

The water cascades up to his upper abdomen and it smells of carnations and faintly of lotus. Capturing one of the seven carnations floating in the water I begin to wash his head and pray. I have performed this aura cleansing bath ritual on numerous occasions for others, and knew he would be appreciative. His tensions, hurts and frustrations melt away as the bath progresses. Most of his stress levels are completely gone by the time I drain the water and wrap him in the cotton cloth. I take the used petals outside so they can be buried. While I am outside, I ask him to lay down on my bed. He lays down on the purple throw on my bed.

I walk back into the room and sit on the floor next to him rubbing oil into his skin and focus my prayers on asking the Creator to bring him peace, joy, light, and protection. I complete the massage and prayer. He sleeps for a long while. After he wakes we head downstairs to eat. Over dinner we speak about the past good times and the success of the bath.

"I really needed that! Just when I think I have you all figured out you spring something new on me," he smiles appreciatively while speaking. After dinner he cleans the kitchen and we play awari for many hours. I continually beat him until he gives up. "I quit." He laughs "Of course you do, I'm unbeatable!" I say confidently.

Later that evening as I prepare for bed he tries to leave. "Hapana!! You are not leaving and undoing all the work I did with the bath. And yes, it is ALL about me!" I was jokingly -- not joking. For the rest of the night we talk, joke and read to each other until we fall off to sleep. The next morning when he awakes I was already gone.

I left a note by the bed that said:

> Habari?
> Breakfast is on the stove, I am meeting with a
> lawyer and judge now to resolve your mentees
> issue. I will be back by noon. I know… I am
> great…and modest too ☺ Enjoy your morning and
> relax! That is an order.

When I returned home he had prepared lunch and cleaned up. I was extremely grateful because I was tired and hungry. "So what happened?!" he blurted out. "I am good, thank you for asking." I joke with him, "It has been resolved and the young man will be released this afternoon to his mother. As we ate lunch I explain the terms and conditions outlined by the judge.

Since they were both minors when they began their sexual relationship, it was obvious that the female's aunt, who filed the charges, was very angry that he would not bend to her whim after they had a child together. She explains that at this point the two of them are engaged and the young man has no priors so all charges were dropped pending counseling. The young lady in question will actually turn 18 within the next year.

One of the stipulations is they do have to wait until she is 18 for them to have sexual intercourse. You could see her dimple, as she states, "So YOU have to make sure they stick to that clause or the deal is null and void."

The other court stipulations include: him performing community service, attending counseling sessions and parenting classes each week. He thanks me emphatically.

Don't thank me yet I owe them… so you owe me BIG TIME! You will pay; you will pay dearly and repeatedly!" At first he thinks I am serious but then my eyes show my amusement. I reach out to jab him in the chest but decide to pull my finger back when he suddenly grabs my arm, throws me over his back and runs upstairs with me laughing almost hysterically.

He lays me on my stomach and initiates a massage. I smile but say, "no thanks." "What, are you scared to be open to me or do you think I don't know what I am doing?" he asks? "Honestly, it's a little of both. In addition I don't think you can handle me now. If you open me up in that manner I am not sure what may come forth. I am not sure what you believe in, in regards to energy work but when I am open I can be raw or very gentle it just depends on what you spark. I don't play with that... nor would I set you up like that."

 It takes him a moment to process my words.   Then he quietly speaks. "I already know this is about you and I know that you have held back during all our encounters. I have studied many practices and I'm a lot more aware than you give me credit for. You are not the only one who knows the mystics... the secrets."

Many of my concerns are lifted, not by his words, but the feeling of truth and power behind them. Looking deeply into his eyes I decide to trust myself in ways I have not before. I begin to strip out of my clothes, lay down and prepare to fully open up to his ministrations. The oil he already has prepared is a mixture of olive oil, lavender and patchouli. He lists the ingredients: three drops of lavender oil, one drop of patchouli oil and two drops of olive gingerly blended together. He was conscience not to touch my waist beads.

The energy flowing between us heightened our awareness on a level deeper than anything we felt together before. Combining the spiritual with the physical is definitely a new experience for both of us that we plan to explore completely. Having completed the massage he lays down next to me and I begin to strum my fingers across his tekken causing it to jump with anticipation.

I guide his hand across my breast, and trail it down my stomach to my beads "You can touch them." His pupils widen with surprise and excitement as his hand moves across them. There is an immediate surge of energy, awareness, heat and cold that flashes over him. I am able to feel his divinity.

This is the point when our true blending begins. My juices drench the bed, run down both my legs and drips all over him. His hardness is bigger and longer than I have ever seen it. There is some fear on both of our parts by what we feel but it is not enough to stop the train of energy that is set into motion.

His tongue meets my parted lips to reveal a warm sweetness that is intoxicating. It feels like the room is spinning out of control. My only stability is his touch. As he delves deeper into me we lose all sense of time, space and reason. The world around us shifts and fades in and out of existence. We feel the intensity of his and my touch in waves, surges, pulses and rushes of arousal that stream freely within, around and between us.

At the point of deeper insertion the pleasure ascends to new heights. His in and out causes me to come undone. It is impossible for either of us to lessen the effect of our blending.

As our bodies suspend above the bed we switch positions like hieroglyphs telling the ancient story of the stars being created. As he cups my hips, he lifts me and digs his tekken with more precision... deeper and deeper. He clutches my body to his, like a spider to a web, holding me tighter, as drops of sweat fall upwards hitting the ceiling. Inside my eyelids, I see us drifting physically down towards the bed. My legs wrap around his waist tightly as he lifts me off the bed and sets me on the dresser to continue exploring hues and colors of ecstasy. The candles hit the floor, the crystal base clink and fall aside extinguishing the wick and darkness floods the room.

"Tell me what you see." He opened his eyes and stared into my face which was blurry at first then seemed to disappear. "Can you see me, do you know who I am?" I grabbed the back of his neck as he continued pushing, thrusting, sliding and expanding inside of me. "I know who you are, I see your colors," was his simple, yet complex reply.

Our moaning, groaning, breathing, slurping, sucking, licking, clapping and humming is so beautiful it feels musical. He begins to tap my soul and we rock together... feeling the eruption rising... rising and rising. I can feel his heightening and he can feel mine. We listen to each other's thoughts and in unison we cum. As the orgasm rushes through us, the release is so powerful all the muscles in our bodies convulse violently. We are both too weak to move. He rests still inside me and we pass out for an indeterminate time.

I feel the tenderness of my body as he pulls out and lifts me off the dresser. I clear my throat "Well now, that was umm…interesting to say the least." He does not respond. He bends over to pick up things off the floor and scrapes candle wax off of the floor.

When the room is straightened he walks over to the bed where I lay stupefied, still trembling. He begins to kiss my body. I can tell he is still zoned out but I allow him to continue. His tongue traces my areola and glides over my nipples as they harden. My clit throbs as the saliva from his tongue covers my skin. Being completely unaware of the possibility of experiencing such pleasure through touch alone causes me to let down more of my guards. The pulsing energy is so intense it is uncomfortable. I fidget on top of the covers trying to mitigate the sensations.

He continues to kiss me, rub my nipples between his fingers and nibble on my skin. He intensifies his efforts by licking and biting me on different parts of my body. I thought I would burst in a matter of minutes. The tingling spreads across my body and he places his hands above my clit, presses hard sending waves of energy through my core and into me. My body contracts and relaxes as I continue to orgasm at his command. By the eighth consecutive one I finally push him away. His tekken is hard and the pull to feel him inside me is great. But my mind drifts…

I can't take this; I don't understand what he is doing to me. I should not be allowing this to happen. He should not be able to tap into me like this. This is not what I wanted, I didn't know it would be like this; it's too much I'm over stimulated. Over stimulated? Is that even possible? Should I enjoy it this much? Does he enjoy it? I can't believe I came from him kissing on my breast. This is crazy. I can't share this with him. I should have never let him touch my beads, or given him the bath or let him massage me...

My thoughts trail off as I realize how much I am tripping. I recognize that this is what I have prayed for and desired. I knew that The Creator was providing me what I asked for through this man. I need to trust myself so that I can move to the next level. During our time together, before we had reached physical heights that I did not think were possible, I always reserved a piece of myself that I did not ever share with my former lovers unless they were initiated.

The thought of him tapping into my spirit like he once tapped into my body terrifies me. I did not want to be devoted to him. There is no doubt in my mind that our connection goes deeper than the present but I am clear that we are not meant to be in a "romantic" relationship... as it is viewed in this society. I know if I let go I would love him….yet I did and that is when our relationship begins.

Sage Wisdom: Libation

Throughout **"Confessions of a Sage Woman"** several people have acknowledged the Creator, their connection to the Great Force and/or to their family or to our historic Ancestor through the sacred act of pouring libation.

Libation is found throughout the world...not as a religious act but as a spiritual and cultural act. I mean this to say that it is not tied to a certain doctrine, church, denomination or faith. Brutha's on the corner pour libation straight out their beer cans to "give something back." Elders on the continent, in the same spirit pour libation to "give something back."

Libation is a ritual to acknowledge gratitude for all the blessings that we receive, for our family members (Ancestors) who are still very tied to us in thoughts and prayers and increase/deepens our connection to The Great Creator in all aspects of life.

The way it was explained to me was simple: "pouring libation" serves as a salute, prayer, acknowledgement, appreciation and much more. The significance of this ritual transcends across time/space occupied by the African experience of life.

Honored Elder Myron K. Buchanan pouring libations at Utani

History of Libation

Ayi Kwei Armah, Author of Two Thousand Seasons, gives her perspective of the importance of libation: "[t]his legend explains the rise of a propitiatory custom found everywhere on the African continent: libation, the pouring of alcohol, water or other drinks as offerings to ancestors and divinities." (Armah, 2006, p. 207).

Libation is an immensely important part of African culture. In fact, the ritual is a marker of African identity because it is used at many African rites ceremonies - to name a few: infant naming ceremonies, puberty rite of passage ceremonies, weddings, elder rites, burial rites, etc. Its persistence across place and places, time and times, exemplifies much about the origin of all Africans, their relation to each other and about cultural transmission in general.

Honored Elder Myron K. Buchanan preparing to pour libation at opening of Halima and Jason McWilliams' Arusi (wedding)

Pour libation as follows:

Water – is an offering considered as a "purifier." One can pour water outdoors directly into the earth; water can also be poured indoors into a large plant. Sometimes water is poured ceremonially into a large bowl or calabash while prayers or salutes are done aloud or silently.

Water has universal uses and can be used for any type of offering. Spring or Mineral is best because of the natural elements but any clean water can be used after being prayed over.

Wine/Gin/Rum – are offerings considered as "spirits" because of the distillation process of transforming fruit or grain into the alcohol. Also "spirits" are said to begin evaporating immediately so as soon as the pouring begins some of it is transformed into energy. Ghanaian Chieftan/Master Drummer Nana Cornelius "CK" Kweku Ganyo would always say "Libations are for here (to the earth) and also for here (to the body) "meaning we pour libations to the earth and drink parts of it to connect us to our Ancestors."

It is part of the tradition to share with the spirits drinking and pouring interchangeably. This rite has been passed down for generations and is still prevalent in African societies. Each liquor carries its own vibe and energy so different ones can be poured at different times. Please take some time and research the energy of each type to see what is best to be used for what you are seeking.

Oils – Libations using scented oil is often rites that symbolize transitions in life i.e., marriage, naming ceremonies, womanhood rites, manhood rites, elder rites, and funerary. Traditionally, spiritual heads, religious heads, heads of households or elders will pour libation during transitions of life or death using essential oil and water to mark items for ceremony or for a tomb of the dead. Sometimes oil is also used directly on the physical body to invoke the energy. Oils – particularly Frankincense and Myrrh or Peppermint - may also be added to water after the water has been prepared to be poured as previously mentioned.

Conjur2

"I don't know how I let you talk me into this just because you had a dream about some Usher looking dude who had sex with you."

"It was not a dream!! Shut up and concentrate."

As before, the ritual requires the use of charcoal, frankincense & myrrh, and white candles to beckon the energy.

The two women begin to chant: *"We ask that you come, Be Here With Us at this time and place. Come. Brother of the light. Be here at this place at this time with us. We say welcome to you. We are open. Karibu!* She clinks the glass together, it jingles like bells, and then she pours a libation of gin into the bowl asking that a doorway be open. The two of them sit on the floor bare bodied with African cloth draped across them.

Again, they repeat the chant: *"Come to us brother of the light. Be here at this place at this time with us. We are open. We ask that you come, Be Here with us at this time and place. Come. Brother of the light. We say welcome to you. Karibu!"*

The room begins to feel suffocatingly hot; their eyes, their skin, and the walls of the room get hot. The charcoal burns a deeper red and begins to hiss. Before they can see him, they hear his breathing.

She looks at him with wide, big eyes. She realizes that this energy is very old, very ancient. She tries to prepare for what is to come. Little did she know there is no preparation for some energies that are invoked. The room goes dark and then, a powerful surge of pure, raw, magnificent maleness surrounds them. The energy sends intense heat down their backs touching them from behind -- all spectrum of light and color erupts behind their eyes. One single thought pops up in their mind…. ***it's just like the first time.*** The friend who was talked into the ritual was so petrified she refused to look directly at him. As she listens to her own racing heartbeat and examines this force, she struggles to maintain her composure.

He does not physically move but they can feel his energy surround them both. His body covers both of them completely. He parts her legs aggressively. They can feel his huge member ascending each of their open legs simultaneously . . . While her friend exhales, she inhales…. He is more than they anticipated. They did not expect *HIM* to be this primal and are unprepared for the reality of their heightened arousal and pleasure. Their bodies are confined by the entity and they experience sensations on many different planes of existence and reality.

The energy flows in and out of their bodies simultaneously; deeper, faster, slower, riveting and joyfully separating their bodies from their minds. All you can hear is deep moans, heavy breathing and light bells jingling until there is a tumultuous peak pounding throughout time. Then the energy speaks to them; causing them both to black out. When they awaken he is gone. They lay next to each other in the bed silently holding hands and replaying the night in their minds.

"Tomorrow?" Raba asks
"Yes. Tomorrow." Nafisa replies

Pendulum of Love

I am dealing with the back and forth
of water and earth, stagnation and movement
As I ebb and flow, like the tides.

Constantly changing, constantly staying the same
Only the sand knows of my true nature
When I will leave and when I will come again
Sometimes gentle, sometimes a tsunami; always wet....

Only I can move the sand, massively changing all that was;
And keeping all that is needed
Then there is the moon that pulls me stronger and harder
causing my cresting, changing my flow.
Me and the moon have moved in harmony
since the beginning of time... before the sand formed

The moon and I are one
But the moon can't touch me the way the sand does
and the sand can't pull me like the moon.
Therefore I need both.
But they don't like to share...

So I swing like a pendulum between heaven and earth
celestial and terrestrial. Tangible and intangible
The pendulum of love
Every now and again there's an eclipse,
that's when I belong only to the sand.

Embracing My Beliefs on Sex & Intimacy.....

Enlightenment

She had the baddest body I'd ever seen. She was about 5'6 probably 190-200 lbs, early 40's with two sons and her own restaurant. The thing I liked the most was that she had a greenhouse attached to her restaurant and grew her own herbs, spices and vegetables. Oh and she's married. I was invited by a friend to her 44th Earthday celebration which was in the beginning of August, the hot as hell month in St Louis.

The invite did not do justice to the event:

Come on out and commune with us as we celebrate
The power of 44.
Wholistic! Enjoyment and great fun!
Come ready to enjoy and reach new heights
August 8, 2021
TEACH Community Park and Garden
Sponsored by PEEC & TEACH

The street was blocked at both ends and I parked nearly three blocks away. While walking to the event, I imagined approaching her and giving her my well wishes. She and her husband had a publicly "open" relationship but she had chosen not to share herself with another man, which was horrible news for all us men because she was "foine." As I got closer I could see the multicolored tents that spanned the entire park.

Their booths were color coded: Blue-relaxation; yellow-joy/inspiration; red-power/strength; green-natural foods; white-divination/spirit healing; black-sciences/initiation.

The entire Afrikan community seemed to be present at the celebration providing information, samples, foods, materials, books, and lessons. In the center of the tents was the meeting area where there was body painting, drumming, dancing, water fountains, masquerades, a juice and raw food bar, storytelling, henna tattooing, and arts and crafts. She sat in the middle of the garden gathering herbs. The sun kissed her shoulders as she moved her locs to the side and kneeled as if speaking to the plants. She touched them, smelled them, smiled and then picked the ones she wanted. I imagined their uses. Everyone was so welcoming and loving, everyone spoke and offered their skills or products, all free of charge.

No one was trying to only make money or to promote themselves. They wanted to just enjoy and share; it was a tremendous feeling. The children ran about freely eating, playing, laughing, learning and just being kids. If watoto (children) were called out or got out of line they were handled by any and every adult that was close at hand. The watoto were loved and raised by the entire community. They had recreated many of our traditional ways and propagated them in all aspects of life.

I visited as many booths as I could before approaching her. She was well versed and spoke to all kinds of people about the things she felt very passionate about. If you were not ready to fully commit to a subject she was not the person to talk to. I decided to get a reading after speaking to her. If there was bad news, it would have to wait.

I met many new people and learned a lot in the few hours I was there. I enjoyed the men's society area best. They were cool level minded brothers that ranged in ages from 15-90. Her husband was among them and took a liking to me for some reason. It could have been that we could pass for brothers in terms of height, built, stature, features and style.

I listened very intently as the Men's Society and the manhood training process was explained to me. It was nothing too deep just the basics but I was intrigued. One of the brothers invited me to a party later that evening at their house; it was for adults and by invitation only. "You may want to learn as much as you can today we will be discussing and using some of the things this evening. Are you married or involved with someone? If so, they are invited too. We just ask that you RSVP by 7pm and inform one of the brothers about any dietary restrictions.

We look forward to hosting you this evening." He spoke as if he knew that I would be there. "I appreciate it brother and look forward to it. I am not in a relationship but I may bring a close friend of mine. She enjoys this kind of stuff." I hoped I did not offend him with my words. "Ok that would be great. We will have food, drinks, dancing, loving, and all kinds of fun. You will have a wonderful time. It is by invitation only and you must have this to get in." He reached inside his pocket and pulled out a flat piece of hematite and handed it to me. "Don't lose it or you can't get in; there are no exceptions. That's boss's orders."

He motioned with his head to her preparing some sort of concoction with the herbs she had gathered. "I'll let her know about you. Please visit the booths and enjoy yourself. Oh by the way some of our guest may be nude this evening. I hope that is not a deterrent for you" "Not at all. I look forward to it." I visited several more booths soaking up as much information and positive energy as I could. I decided it was time to meet her. I began to approach her since she was now seated on a blanket laughing and telling stories to the children. I sat amongst the children also listening intently to her stories while anticipating the fun.

When the story was over and the last little child ran off I walked over to her. "Habari Gani? " she smirked when she heard me use the greeting. I could not tell if she was pleased or laughing at me. "Nzuri Sana Ndugu. Sifa Ote Une Watu Weusi I laughed aloud. "I'm sorry but " Habari Gani?" that's all the Kiswahili that I know." She laughed too. "Well it is a start. Thank you for coming out, I hope you are enjoying yourself." "More than you could imagine. Your husband invited me to your later gathering." She took in a breath and sighed deeply. I was not sure how to respond.

"Is there a problem with me coming?" She smiled politely and excused herself. I watched as she walked with determination through the crowd. Her husband saw her coming and darted behind a friend. I could not tell if she was serious or playing; either way he knew not to cross her.

She finally gave in and began to laugh when he danced around her making faces and swaying his hips. They concluded their conversation with a kiss and he patted her ass while she walked away.

She swatted his hand and winked. I decided to go to the divination booth and get a reading so I could say I had actually visited each area. I'm skeptical at my best moments and extremely pessimistic at my worst. So I was prepared to be unimpressed. I've had "readings" before and it was so vague the information they gave could have been for me or my next door neighbor. However, everything at the fair so far seemed so natural, for some reason, I have yet to put my finger on. I entered the tent, took a seat on the floor and waited my turn. I was surprised that I was called in next even though there were several people in front of me.

The people already waiting simply smiled and nodded as I went inside before them and they assured me it was okay. "Karibu, welcome come in and have a seat. We have been waiting for you all day" the diviner said. I looked around searching for this "we" but saw no one who fit the description. "How much is this going to cost me?" He was amused at my question, "Information is free but if you are so inclined you may give some money to the children outside." Of course, I smiled at his simple answer. He took out some cards and cowry and asked, "..so what do you seek?" *What do I seek? If it wasn't for her I would not even be here.* I thought to myself... The "Diviner" said, "That is a dangerous game you play: Deception and greed, lies and lust. It can only bring harm." "What kind of mumbo jumbo is that?" I instantly realized how ignorant and insulting that must have sounded. So, I regrouped and said, " Uhm... What does that mean?" I prepared myself for some vague elusive answer. "He threw the cowry on the table several times before speaking "You pretend to befriend him but you covet his wife." I was sure they were in cahoots and playing games but my arrogance would not allow me to ask him or leave. "Okay? So what do you suggest I do?" I asked cynically. "Change your mind." He said plainly. "Change my mind about what?" I asked again. "About her, him, and yourself."

Now I was thoroughly annoyed and confused. I contemplate seeking more information then I remembered my grandmother words, *"Boy you always come with you cup full asking for more to drink. Empty your cup first."* Before I could ask another question he continued "Your grandmother is with us. She is glad you remember her words."

He continued, "You are a good man; you just want something you do not understand. Their kindness is not an open invitation. If you want to be the one man she chooses other than her husband then you must be worthy of being her husband." *Damn he is all up in my shit.* "If she is to be with you she must love you first. Her husband knows this and that is why he chose you for her." *Chose me for her?* "She WILL accept you and love you. So ask yourself what you are truly seeking and if in fact not for keeps you may want to change your mind." *Well that wasn't vague and elusive at all.* I wanted to believe that it was a set-up but my heart told me otherwise.

When I got home I had a lot to consider. Should I even go? What Do I really want? Am I ready for someone to love me and to love them back? How do I really feel about sharing her? What does her husband want from me and why me? I called my friend who invited me to the festivities earlier and asked her to go to the after party. I was surprised she was already planning on going; she seemed surprised that I had been invited.

I told her about what was said to me during the reading and she was silent for a long while. "Well then, I guess you better dress to impress." "The Creator works in all things. Don't sweat it! I just enjoy the night and whatever happens, it happens." "You are absolutely no help at all!" I told her. We laughed together and hung up. I called her when I was ready to go.

She wore an almost sheer red, purple and gold dress that hit her curves just right. I almost forgot that she was my friend. "You look nice I said as she got in the car." She just smiled. We talked on the way there and I asked her everything I possibly could about them, their marriage, their lives and beliefs. She answered all questions as honestly as she could. By the time I arrived I thought I had a pretty good understanding. We knocked on the door and one of the brothers from the men's society answered the door.

He looked deeply into our eyes, though I don't know what he was looking for but he extended a basket. I remembered the stone and searched my pocket for my "golden ticket." Then I placed the stone inside the basket and followed my friend into the house. Before we were fully inside we were stopped again and smudged with herbal Sage.

I felt overdressed immediately when I finally got inside. More than half the people were naked and some others simply wore cloth loosely tied around their body. Everyone interacted as if it was normal. "Umm, don't you think your should have warned me?" I whispered to my friend as I nudged her. She ignored me and continued to introduce me. After several minutes I was comfortable and did not trip off any of the nudity. Then, I saw her. She was completely naked and carrying a tray of fruit. If I did not know any better I would say she was excited to see me but I did not want to flatter myself. Not far behind was her husband waving for me to come over. "I'm glad you could make it man!

Are you enjoying yourself so far?" Not waiting for an answer he continued, "Food is in the kitchen", he said while pointing in one direction. "There is a hot tub and towels outside in the back. They are playing cards in the basement and some people are getting massages upstairs." He smiled at me and walked off to greet another guest. I scanned the room and was surprised to see the "Diviner" present at the gathering. Before I could turn and walk away he made eye contact so I had to go and speak. To my surprise he made no mention of our earlier discussion so I said, "About earlier..." I was cut off. "I'm not working now and neither should you be. It is up to you what you do with that information." He gave me a brotha hug and walked off.

"Would you like something to eat?" She was back holding a tray to her side. I turned behind me and couldn't help scanning her entire body "That's funny," she said. "What's funny?" I asked. "I have been naked at these gatherings for countless years, but this is the first time I actually felt naked." I was so damn embarrassed. "It's okay. I'm actually flattered. Dare I ask you what you want?" I smiled and reply "I am okay and I apologize, all this takes some getting used to."

She picked a peeled mango slice off the tray and pressed it against my lips. As I parted them she slid the piece of fruit into my mouth; she wiped her fingers on my lips. She breathed deeply like she was releasing and tilted her head to the side looking for something. I chewed it slowly and swallowed. I kept my eyes focused on her. She smiled and I reciprocated. "Well... since you seem to be more comfortable now can you take this tray into the kitchen for me?" I took it from her making sure to slide my hand across her hand. Her nipples instantly became erect. She chuckled deeply and placed her hands on her hips. I did not know whether to stand and stare at her or retreat to the kitchen. *To the kitchen it is!!!*

I met a number of good people over the evening. All of them were very welcoming. As the night went on I understood that if you were invited and made it through the front door – the couple must have seen something good in you. Over a five year period, I was the only new person who had been invited. Well, apparently the only one who had not had some sort of "spiritual training or initiation." As the night went on I began to notice people getting a little bit *friendlier*. This did not bother me.. it was just interesting. I went to the backyard and noticed someone nude swimming under the water. I watched intently until I realized that it was her. "Beautiful, isn't she?" her husband asked when he walked on the deck. I did not know how to respond; or if I should. He rested his hand on my shoulder.

As if in a trance I walked through the house down the steps and out the door. I took off my clothes and lay down next to her. She said nothing and did not even acknowledge my presence. I reached out and ran my hand across hers and she let me. I fell asleep laying in the grass and when I woke up she was gone. I wondered how long I had slept and what she might have thought about my actions; I wondered if I had crossed a line. I grabbed my clothing and quickly dressed. When I returned to the house everyone was gone but myself and the diviner. I thought, Damn! I really messed up. I held my head down and headed for the door.

"Only children and cowards run away. Which are you?" he posed the question. "Neither." With that one word I had proven myself worthy and also committed myself to staying. I walked to where he was sitting and sat down next to him. "I guess it is not a bunch of bells and whistles." I tried to joke. "I have never been tested like this in my life. Why is this happening to me?" "Why not?" he stated plainly. "Would you rather someone else have this experience, this opportunity? Would you walk away and never know what could be? Or should be? Would you pass on an opportunity that could change your life forever?"

As I pondered his words, the husband and wife appeared hand in hand and joined us. She immediately began speaking, "You already know the two of us have what some describe as an "open relationship." My husband feels that I should explore myself with a man outside of our relationship. I have not done so. Finally, I cons *Ancestors* approve; then I would pursue them. My husband has done his part. He has found you.... Before we move forward, I want to know from you, if this is something you are open to."

I thought long and hard. I had no idea what "it" might entail, how things would turn out, how it would affect me or their relationship. I knew nothing except my entire being was saying 'yes'. Since I have such a skeptical view of the world....saying 'yes' is a rarity. "What would I have to do?" They all laughed heartily. They seemed relieved by my question. "Very wise to ask," said the diviner.

"Do you remember earlier...when I said you would have to change your mind?" His words rang true. But I had no idea what the hell his statement meant. She interjected, "You would have to get to know me... and I would have to get to know you...you would have to study....the Oracle would need to give a favorable response about you and..." I busted out laughing and so did the other two men, she did not. "No offense but can we take one task at a time," I asked, even while still laughing. "Fine. Let's look at what *the Oracle* has to say."

The "Diviner" pulled out his tools, did a prayer and began casting the cowry shells. After several moments he spoke. "It states, that he is ready and at a good place but you are not T'Shea." Her expression told it all; she was not surprised. "I will be." It was more than an answer, it was also a commitment.

Over months, I met with her husband and other men of their society and learned ancient ways, customs, traditions, beliefs, practices and about their lifestyle. I read several books and studied African philosophy that further expanded my knowledge and clarified African spirituality. I adapted my lifestyle to reflect my new perspectives. I began to have a clearer sense of "identity" and "connection" to the universe, the Creator and my people than I had ever experienced before.

A year passed and I forgot the initial reason for my studies, readings, diet changes, deep discussions and cleansing rituals. I forgot this was about her. It was not hard to adapt to their thoughts and way of life. It felt natural to me. I thoroughly enjoyed the bond that had cemented between myself and the brothers in the society and was humbled by the man I was becoming. I often met with the diviner to make sure I was on track and even began to dabble in the "sciences" myself. I was allowed to attend the men's festival, the equinox and solstices rituals. I had even had several cleansings and other rites to help with my spiritual alignment.

My connection to the Creator was stronger than any other time in my life. I spoke with the elders about being initiated into their deeper sciences and was welcomed. It was explained that the brotherhood would decide if, when and how that might happen. My heightened awareness of the universe had already begun. I received notice that she wanted to see me. I wondered why she had asked me to come over.

What a difference a year makes. I was very comfortable in her presence when we met. She gave me a hug and we sat on the grass. Her first words were very quiet. "I never thought I would share myself with another man... of course I believe in the so-called notion of "open relationships" because love is infinite and cannot be contained in any one vessel or form. However, I could not wrap my mind around sharing something so deeply with someone I did not know, nor did I see getting to know someone in that capacity while devoted to my husband. But... and yes there is a huge but, you have wedged yourself between my wall and my spirit. Initially, you slipped between the lines of arousal and annoyance, then over time your presence and actions stayed completely on the arousal side. I knew when I had the last dream about you... it was time to go to the next level."

All I could think after she finished speaking was, "Wow!" I thought I would immediately jump at the chance to be with her but my reaction was reserved. I was deeply humbled by her words. She continued, "so... how has your journey been?" "Good." I replied. "Now, I believe I am ready for you." During my year of studies the two of us had spent considerable time getting to know each other. So, it wasn't like this conversation was out of the blue. She continued... "You have learned our ways thus learning me. I have watched you grow; thus learning you. Good things are said about you on all fronts."

Expectantly, I stood up without even knowing my motives. I was silent for a few moments, then I excused myself with as much dignity as I could muster. Then I walked away. Even I did not understand the internal conflict that I was experiencing. I could not put a voice to my issues. I called the "Diviner" and asked to meet with him. When I arrived he smiled gently at me. His first words were, "I see you have changed your mind.." I laughed aloud and understood what the Oracle said the first time we met at her party.

Love Is

I do not know how to tell him, but I can't deny my feelings. I don't want to "be with him;" I just want to be able to show my love for and with him. I'm afraid he will not understand. I feel free around him; all my silly quirks are accepted - not exploited. He does not play on my gullibility nor does he judge me based on my "wild ways." The thoughts of our conversations make me smile and he talks to my body in a language that common men do not even know exists.

We meet at the usual time, I am trying to play it cool but the churning in my stomach won't let me. And he knows something is up, the look in his eyes tells me to go ahead spit it out. As a gesture of good faith I offer him a massage, plus it really turns me on. He places himself between my legs, a feeling so familiar that my body instantly responds. We both chuckle as I shift positions and begin caressing his shoulders.

My mind wanders as I play every scenario of how this could go, what he would say, how I would feel, how things would be and I lose myself in the thought of us, the possibilities and even our past. Memories of us in a past life surface and for the first time I let them flow; not suppressing the images or feelings. If I am to let him go I must let us go and exist in the cosmos where we belong.

I found comfort in knowing I can always love and cherish the thought of him in the universe, that part of him that no other woman has access to, those moments, encounters and exchanges that are unique to our evolution. He always falls asleep when I rub his neck. Summer rain begins to hit the window and moisten the seal. He excuses himself to close the window and I catch a glimpse of his spirit as the breeze blows a cool mist in. I breathe deeply, walk towards him and stand next to him as I look out the window; in turn he wraps his arms around me and presses his face against mine.

At this moment...despite all the restrictions, falsities, struggles and fears we exist as one... and... it... is... peaceful, beautiful, fulfilling, loving, comforting, inspiring, expansive, arousing, nurturing...and powerful. "You know, when we started spending time getting to know each other I never thought it would go down this road. I was convinced that the fantasy I had created about you was much better than the reality. I was wrong.

In a fantasy there is no unexpected, no room for surprise or growth, no room for the perfect moments that spring from mistakes, the comfort that you can only have after being uncomfortable, the silly times that are called upon in rough times to resuscitate the light or the sly smiles that spread across my face as I recall our intimate moments. But I digress.

I came into this expecting to never care too deeply; never let my guards down, never to lose perspective on us. I am not trying to be with you or lose myself in us. I guess what I am trying to say is: It's over. I don't want to love you and you don't want to be loved. I can't be who I am and have an intimate relationship with someone I can't allow myself to love."

I paused for a moment and allowed my words to land on every item in his house. He made no sound. His energy did not shift or even stir. He kept his arms around me and stared blankly into the night watching it rain. I felt the need to continue. "We both have someone that we love and have chosen to be with. And for me it has to be either or; either I'm just fucking you or I am growing deeper in love with you. Our views on love are different. Love to me doesn't mean I want to be with you; it means that I want to be able to show it outwardly, express it to you and not feel like it is going to cause you to get the wrong idea or feel anything other than loved.

I love too deeply to feel like I can't show it. I am not looking for anything from you as you already know. But I am looking for a relationship where I can be "me" fully, and divinely. So before I allow myself to love you I have to pull back." He continued to stand motionless... even when I tried to pull away from his embrace. There was no real struggle, it was just clear to him and me, that I was not going anywhere. Not yet, not now. After nearly an hour of embracing and watching the rain, he spoke.

"Well it seems like you have made up your mind and I'm not one to try to convince anyone to do anything they don't want to do... no point in that." I was motionless and still....just as he had been before when I was speaking. When he began to remove his arms from around me, I held them in place and we stood a moment longer before we released each other.

He was quiet for a moment longer and then he voiced a question. "Can you at least finish my massage before you fall in love?" We laughed and returned to the chair. I rubbed his shoulders feeling peace and resolve with my decision. So use to his touch it took me a moment before I realized his lips ran across my inner thigh.

Damn it! Why did I wear this dress? I thought. Inside my head my decision was absolute but my body and spirit had another arrangement. His warm tongue hit my panties and quickly moved them aside to slide right inside my core. His warmth and intent filled my womanness completely. Yeah, I still welcomed him. I know what you are thinking. I should stop him, tell him no, tell him to get up and leave.

There's the risk that we will be right back in that same place but you sit here with his head between **your** legs, his energy in the air and **your** spirit open and **YOU** tell him to stop- because I can't do it -- well I won't. My depth throbs and beats for him, asking him to come closer, get wet, be covered and explode deep within. I gently wrap my legs around his head trying to still show some reserve; but I have none. When his fingers enter me I hug his head and he looks deep into my spirit then pulls me closer. My legs drop on either side of him and I rock forward for him to go even deeper.

"I want to be inside you but I don't want you to…" I do not let him finish. I place my lips against his, grab his belt and begin to tug at it until it is on the ground; followed by his pants, my dress, his shirt, and then my bra. He seems much more gentle tonight and the heat from our bodies causes the mirror on his dresser to blur. He is going so deep into my soul I… can… not …breath…

I can only wait for him to give me breath with his light. The heels of my feet gently bounce off his back as we travel through thoughts of us. He is staring into my soul as he unfolds inside me and although I want to stop I feel a tingling start in my stomach, then spread across my body and I feel a flooding inside my walls that push against him to be released.

 "I can see your energy," he smiles as he continues his sway. My teeth biting my lips only provide temporary sanity as I lose myself in him. His face begins to darken and I know I am between worlds, from the ceiling I can see, feel and taste us. He throws his head back as he nears release and peers right at me as if he knows I am here now.

"Come back to me," he mouths and I crash back into my body as if yanked from the cosmos. My body slightly jerks as I reenter it and he diligently works on climbing back inside me. I push him back and turn over burying my head in the scent of us on his covers. Now moving slowly he pushes and moves like a serpent until my grumbling tells him exactly where to be and how to be there. He rests his head on my back as he knocks on my doors causing the flood to return and get stronger. He pulls out partially and I erupt all over him before he returns for more treasure.

We ebb and flow, flooding and squirting, moaning and screaming, laughing and crying for eons before I collapse on my stomach. He falls on top of me still pumping and I reach back to control his stroke but he moves my hands wanting to be as close to me as possible. I share in his pleasure, pain, joy, hurt, fears and victories. I am breathless - *I can't breathe… got to cum, I can't cum… got to breathe* echoed in my head as I took my last breath and came.

Transcendence

My love for him transcends: Time, space,
commitments, limitations, stereotypes, labels,
circumstance, truth and boundaries
If I were specific we would be: Stolen moments, quick
glances, hot nights and cold days, secret conversations
that hold volumes of us, nothing more than friends
With him I am: Myself, fulfilled, goofy and clumsy,
confident, regal, honest, free, divine
Our time together is: well spent.

Eruption

Eruption...
dormant for years
Something stirs deep within
subtle rumblings become deep waves.
Foundations shake
layers are cracked
and broken apart.
Mantles burst open
to expose an
Eruption…
Lava rising up
shooting out
slowing, crawling down.

Dormant pendant des années…
Quelque chose remue profondément en dedans
vagues profondes devenues subtiles.
Secousse de bases
les couches sont criquées et cassées à part.
Éclat de manteaux ouvert pour exposer
Éruption…
Lave se levant vers le haut
tir dehors
ralentissant le rampement en bas de…

Sage Wisdom: **Herbal Teas and Infusions**

Herbal Teas

Many people tend to consider any leaves that get added to hot water as "tea" but technically this is not correct. You can't just add hot water to any organic garden herb leaves, sticks, or roots to make a glass of "herbal tea."

For an herbal blend to be considered a real "tea" it must come from the plant *camellia sinensis*. This is the plant from which all "true teas" originate. The only "true teas" are **Green**, **Black**, **White** and **Oolong**.

Green Tea

Green Tea May be the most popular of all true teas enjoyed in the US due in part to health factors and herbal benefits. Green tea is filled with "catechin." an **antioxidant** that prevents cell damage when the tea is not heavily processed. Green tea has been shown to improve **blood flow, lower cholesterol** and block the formation of plaques that are often linked to **Alzheimer's disease.**

Black Tea

Black tea is infused with **caffeine** and a small stimulating substance called theophylline. Both can speed up your **heart rate** and make you feel more **alert.** The health benefits of black tea is: reduction in the risks of high cholesterol, diarrhea, tooth decay, low-concentration levels, digestive problems, poor blood circulation, high blood pressure and asthma.

White Tea

White tea is the rarest of the teas because it undergoes the least amount of processing; actually none at all. The process is simply to allow the leaves to wither and sun-dry. The health benefit of white tea is: weight reduction, reduction in the risk of cancer, reduction in cardiovascular disorder, improvement in oral health, protection of the skin from the harmful effects of UV light, decrease in plasma glucose levels.

Note: The main difference between black, green and white tea is the way that it is processed. During the processing stage, black tea is fermented and oxidized, which gives it the unique color, flavor, and health benefit. Green tea and white tea are not fermented.

Oolong Tea

The origins of **oolong tea** date back almost 400 years, when it found wide usage in China. **Oolong tea** is naturally rich in antioxidants, contains vital vitamins and minerals such as calcium, manganese, copper, carotene, selenium, potassium, Vitamin A, B, C, E, K, folic acid, niacin amide and other detoxifying alkaloids. The health benefits are: controlling metabolism of fat in the body, reducing obesity; antioxidant to remove free radicals in the body, reduce inflammation that causes eczema, strengthen bone density, control diabetes, improve mental health performance, protect against teeth decay and cancerous cells.

Herbal Infusions

All other liquids that we commonly call "teas" are types of herbal infusions. Though they can often be used in the same manner, teas and infusions have slightly different properties. Now… just because we know that it is not a "tea" doesn't mean the hot brew isn't infused with loads of regenerative and healing properties.

The use of "herbal infusions" in both traditional and non-traditional forms date back over 10,000 years. Popularity of drinking a hot cup of peppermint, lavender, chamomile or rosehips has grown over the years because drinking herbal infusions usually works slowly with minimal toxic side effects.

More than a quarter of all drugs used today contain active ingredients derived from ancient plants. A few of the most popular ones are: chamomile, Echinacea, goldenseal, ginseng, St. John's Wort, peppermint, saw palmetto and rosehips.

- o **Peppermint** is *the* most popular herbal infusion enjoyed for all time. Dried peppermint leaves have even been found in several Kemetian pyramids carbon dating back to 1,000 BC. The smooth minty taste relieves stomach upsets, indigestion, nausea, heartburn, muscle relaxant, skin cleanser, diarrhea, headaches, mild memory loss and irritable bowel syndrome.

- o **Chamomile** is probably the second popular herb of all time. It is frequently used as a mild sedative to calm nerves, reduce anxiety, treat hysteria, nightmares, insomnia and other sleep problems. It is also used as a digestive relaxant to treat various gastrointestinal disturbances including indigestion, diarrhea, anorexia, motion sickness, nausea, and vomiting.

- Echinacea is a herb frequently used to fight off colds or cold symptoms but it has a much wider usage. It can also be used to boost metabolism, support the immune system, fight against many infections including urinary tract infections, vaginal yeast infections, genital herpes, bloodstream infections (septicemia), gum disease, tonsillitis, streptococcus infections, syphilis, typhoid, malaria, and diphtheria.

- Ginkgo is used for a variety of purposes including to improve circulation, caused by poor blood flow in the body, including leg pain when walking or the painful response to cold, especially in the fingers and toes. It is also used for headaches, ringing in the ears, vertigo, difficulty in concentrating, mood disturbances, hearing disorders and improving brain activity such as memory loss.

- Ginseng is recommended as an herbal remedy for people who are frequently fatigued, weak, stressed, and affected by repeated colds and flu. Capable of protecting the body from physical and mental stress, Ginseng is an adaptogen which helps bodily functions return back to normal. This is why many people refer to Ginseng as a natural energy-boost.

- St. John's Wort is growing in popularity as an herbal supplement used for anxiety, tiredness, a loss of appetite and trouble sleeping. In recent years it is used often to treat mild to moderate depression.

- Spearmint can relieve a wide range of ailments, including nausea, hiccups, flatulence, motion sickness, irritable bowel syndrome and tends to increase bile production in the stomach and aid digestion. This is the historical reason for the after-dinner mint!

- Goldenseal is an ancient herb that was used by Native Americans for skin disorders, digestive complaints and even as a cancer remedy. Today, it is recognized as a powerful herbal antibiotic and immune system enhancer because it acts as a steroid and anti-inflammatory aid. It is effective against all kinds of bacterial infection, as it stimulates the immune system to quickly identify and destroy pathogens. It is also a tonic to the mucous membranes for its ability to clear up congestion in the sinuses and respiratory tract infections.

- **Licorice** was an important part of Kemetian culture as it has energy-giving properties that are still recognized in recorded battles. Licorice is great for cold and respiratory problems as it works as an expectorant by promoting mucous drainage and providing a soothing lubrication of the respiratory tract. It is also used to enhance physical and mental vigor, stimulate the adrenal gland, ease stress and to promote a feeling of euphoria. Specifically for women, licorice is a natural source of estrogen that can regulate the menstrual cycle and be affective in alleviating the painful symptoms of menstrual cramps and menopause.

- **Lavender** is very aromatic; it is one of the most versatile herbs known to humanity. The health benefit of lavender is far reaching and extends to the gastrointestinal system. It aids in the treatment of stomach problem, colic, bowel infection, flatulence, migraines, colic, loss of appetite, toothache, acne, nausea, vomiting and nervousness. It is also commonly known as a mood stabilizer and used for the treatment of depression and insomnia.

- **Hibiscus** is a thick, red flower that originates in Kemet that is rich with Vitamin C. It is known as a laxative, diuretic and anti-bacterial. Hibiscus is a good choice when you have a cold or flu. Hibiscus tea is rich in antioxidants; it can protect the liver, stimulate the appetite, help reduce fevers, soothe coughs and help repair the skin.

Embracing My Beliefs on Healing.....

_____

_____

_____

_____

_____

_____

_____

_____

_____

_____

_____

_____

Luna (Part 1)

I had never picked up a Farmer's Almanac my entire life. Now, I check it monthly. When I first moved in, I meet all my immediate neighbors; all but one. Sunny days or rainy nights, I would find myself searching for "that" one. My other neighbors, well I don't think they feel the same enthusiasm about her that I do. They shun her because of her "alternative lifestyle and weird practices." But I love what she does. One day I will be woman enough to simply knock on her door and invite her over. But for tonight, I'll just watch.

On a night of the full moon, I pull out all my sacred items. I lay them on a white sheet, outside on my deck, to be bathed in the glow of the great feminine (moon). I equally love the sun and the moon. But watching her dance naked in the moon is my preferred thing to experience. It's kind of ironic that her actual name is Luna. I am not sure if it is her real name or just what she is called. She has a greenhouse in the back, solar paneling and several barrels where she captures rain water for drinking and bathing I assume. She has a gathering at her home several times a year or so with people that seem just as interesting as she is. I'm guessing she's in her 40s maybe 50s; it's hard to tell because "Black don't crack." She looks young but has a wise old soul.

Periodically she leaves fresh herbs, fruits or vegetables on each of our door steps. Though no one ever sees her do it, we all know it's her. Once I place flowers on her porch with a thank you note. The next day I had peach preserves waiting for me when I return home. I've knocked on her door, but she never answers. Some say she is anti-social. But I don't think so. I've seen how she greets people at her parties and how she talks to the plants in her greenhouse. Once I caught her fussing at a squirrel for eating her vegetables. It is weird because the squirrel seems to listen. It sat quietly on a branch until she finished speaking, and then scurries off.

It is refreshing to see her lifestyle. From what I can tell she lives totally off what she grows on her land and barters her trades. I haven't quite figured her out. She lives in her house where she has lived longer than any other neighbors. No one is really sure how long she's been here. We have a relatively new community. All the houses in the neighbor-hood are less than 15 years old. Much of the land in the surrounding area is still under construction. The community did lay dormant for decades. Past mayors siphoned the money into wealthier neighbor-hoods. Her house is one of the last remaining original homes on the block. It is nearly 100 years old. She occasionally fixes the exterior. It astonishes me how many life skills she displays at such a young age, such as gardening, shelter building, water purification, cooking; those are just a few of the ones I know.

I sit looking out my window waiting for her approach. As I watch her move about the yard, I wonder so many things about her. I question why she sets food out at the bottom of her tree -- once a week. I question the people who visit her every three months and wonder who they might be. I question what exactly these people do when they gather? I question why she is always naked outside; in the sun, in the rain, under the full moon? I question how she is able to leave things for us without anyone seeing her and why? I question if she knows that I watch her – almost daily. I question if she maybe watches me too? I question what is the music and sounds I hear coming from her home early in the mornings? I question why I am so drawn to her? I have so many questions to ask of her.

I decide to join her tonight when she dances naked under the moon instead of watching her. Well, I am not sure if I will dance naked with her but I will definitely speak to her. As the sun begins to set there is a churning in my stomach from both excitement and fear. I hope she doesn't find ME strange or weird. Night falls and I begin to drift off to sleep as I wait for her. I am startled awake by the sound of a door closing as she re-enters her house. I think DAMN! How did I miss her? How did I miss my chance of walking this path with her? Now I will have to wait an entire month for my chance again.

I try several times knocking on her door throughout the next day, but she never answers. I leave several gifts of friendship with sincere notes of my admiration for her on her doorstep when I leave out. She accepts my gifts and in exchange leaves gifts for me - but never replies. I decide to try a different approach. I travel to city hall to research the city's archives about her home. I am truly excited! Just as I thought, her home is over a century old. However, it looks almost like it did when it was originally built. Originally it sat on a plot of land covering half the block with a small farm.

Over the years, her family sold portions of the land to other families. It seems no other family was able to sustain the land. Over time, as families lost their homes, the city seized the land for a 20-year development plan. The only thing that stands in the city's way is her family. According to articles and clippings about her family, her grandmother or great aunt (who from news clippings looks just like her) was strong-willed.

Whoever the relative might be they tirelessly fought to keep their house and land. Eventually the city stops trying to build on the land and it becomes a historical landmark, but the rest of the neighborhood is starved out. Yet here, she remains. I admire the women in her family and her even more because of their legacy. I made copies of all the information and returned home. The full moon is only a couple of nights away. I leave her a note saying:

Hello Neighbor:
I have some interesting information I found out about your house and family. I really would like to meet you one day soon. Feel free to stop by anytime.... I am here.
With love and excitement,
Your Neighbor

I think to myself that maybe the "love" part might be a bit much. I simply could not stop myself from writing it. I pour myself a glass of juice, read for a little bit, then I go peacefully to sleep. In my dream, I see myself in a long hallway and she is at the end of it. The ground is clay and covers my feet with red dust. There is a lot of activity around us but sound is muffled. She reaches out to me and I race towards her but we never get any closer. I hear a crash behind me and suddenly turn. She is right behind me. She has snake eyes and jagged claws. She smiles at me revealing sharp feline teeth. She lunges at me. The movement startles me awake and my nightstand keeps me from falling out the bed from my dream. I wake up breathing heavily. It seems so real. I hop out of bed to grab me a cup of water. My sheets are covered in red clay dust and I look down at my feet; they are also covered in the dust.

I begin to panic. I try to wake myself up. I must still be dreaming. I rush to the bathroom and splash water on my face. I now know I am awake. The clay is still on me. I move to the shower while images from my dreams continue to flash in my head. I rationalize there must be a reason for this. Unknowingly, did I step somewhere where there might be red clay before going to bed? I figure that is how it ended up on my sheets. I am unnerved. I think I am going crazy **again**. As a youngster, I was medicated because I would allegedly "hallucinate" hearing voices or seeing things in my room. My mother would always encourage me to "be true to myself." She allowed me to believe in myself without feeling crazy. It wasn't until years later I realized it was because she was crazy too.

My mother seemed so perfect to me. She shared amazing stories about the spirit world and the universe. I did not know, people believed she was crazy. Then one day they snatched her away from me. She was institutionalized and I was sent to live with my aunt. My aunt was very loving but she didn't believe I was seeing what I told her. She told me to never speak of the "the deranged stories my mother told me." Because she never believed me, my Aunt had me psychologically evaluated. I am also medicated so I will not turn out like my mother. Initially, the medicine does not work but eventually it works. Since then I am fine. The thought of going through those same experiences again or ending up like my mother terrifies me. I call my therapist and schedule an appointment so it does not happen.

For the next several days I avoid even looking at Luna's house. Whatever it is that prompts my obsession with her causes me a great deal of fear. My therapist assures me I am not "going crazy again." He tells me that one dream is not cause for alarm. Of course, I did not tell him about the clay on my feet. I knew it was nothing more than a hallucination. He also assures me that even my experiences as a child, or the things that happened to my mother will not automatically lead to my having mental problems. I feel much better leaving my session with the therapist but still decide not to focus on my neighbor anytime soon.

We reach the night that it is a full moon again. I know she is out there dancing around naked acting like a lunatic. My admiration for her turns to disdain; even though I know it is false. I decide to blame her rather than be at risk of insanity myself. Since the dream I am taking sleeping supplements which suppress my dreaming – well they did until tonight. On this night I have the same exact dream. This time I am prepared so when she lunges at me I deftly move aside. She disappears and I wake up. I am relieved until I see her standing over my bed with those beautiful brown-violet reptilian eyes. She stands quietly and curiously as she watches me. I fall out of my bed and wake up for real.

I take off from work for a few days deciding to just relax while getting things done around the house. I clean my home and find myself humming a tune my mother used to sing to me. I only realize at that moment I normally block out most things about my mother. This trepidation about me going crazy brings fresh memories rushing back. She used to sing to me every morning. My mother use to grow herbs in our windows. She used to let me run naked outside and perform moon rituals. Then it hits me for the first time that these are some of the reasons why I am so obsessed with this woman.

She reminds me of my mother. All those years of medicated treatment fades away and my love for my mother returns. I sob uncontrollably for hours and hours. The saddest thing about this is how close I am to my mother, how much like her I really am. I wonder if the same thing ever happened to my mother – will similar things happen to me? I decide to call my aunt and spend some quality time with her. I ruefully think: b*eing around her will keep me sane*. We meet for lunch. I tell my aunt about my dreams, about my obsession with my neighbor and the memories coming back. She seems worried, even more than myself. I ask her why she is worried. She tells me to come over to her house that evening so she can show me something.

I take myself to a movie, then dinner to let time pass before I meet up with my aunt again. I definitely am not going home. When I arrive at my aunt's house she offers me fresh baked pie. I think back on all the times we had pie when there was something *heavy* to talk about with me. Growing up, we always enjoyed fresh baked pie when subjects such as my period, sex, death, drugs and definitely if we talk about my mother. At first I did not notice, but her gaze prompts me to look at a tattered scrap book on the table. I can feel in my spirit this book is for me. Hesitantly, I reach for it and begin going through it.

On the first page is a picture of my mother while she is pregnant with me. She looks so happy with the brightest smile on her face. I remember the story she use to tell me about my father who was *one of the immortals*. She tells me my dad did not want any harm to come our way so he left. He did not want people to recognize that he was not aging. I smile inwardly because I remember the story. I remember believing the story, not just as a child but well into my teens. I secretly wished it to be true. I laugh to myself as I turn the page. Next I see a letter that my mother writes to me the day before I am born.

My dearest love,
Tomorrow you will cross planes into this world. Things will be different here. But my love for you is forever. It will never change. Thank you for choosing me as your vessel...your mother. I have nourished you in my body for the past four months **(Wait… What ...did she say four months? I wasn't a preemie she really is crazy).** *In the time we have been together you have taught me more about love than I learned in my entire 22 years on this planet. When the immortals return for you,*
please give them my love. I will be...
Remember that you are special and you will help to heal the world. With my entire being, I love you.

Your Mommy

As crazy as the letter sounds it brings fresh tears to my eyes. She was a perfect mother to me. I mean, other than her being crazy and all. I turn the page and then drop the book. When I pick it up I take a deep breath and turn it over. I think I am hallucinating again. Before I have time to think about it, I throw the book and my aunt runs into the room. She sits down next to me and tries to calm me down. I repeat over and over again: "I am not crazy, I am not crazy, I am not crazy." I rock back and forth reassuring myself that I am okay. My aunt picks up the book and opens it to the page I am on. "You're not crazy," she states flatly, as she holds my hands.

"Is this your neighbor?" she asks. I am unable to speak. I nod my head "Yes." My aunt looks shocked. "All these years I did not believe your mother. I believed she was making the stories up. But when you told me of what happened to you with the clay and dreams I knew your mother's stories were true. In the past, your mother described the exact same dream. She told it over and over. It is the place when she started to lose it. Your mother felt she was haunted by this woman." I shiver in my bones.

We turn the page together and the next page is the hallway from my dreams. When the figures in the picture start to move we both drop the book. I feel like I am in some "D" rated horror movie. I am not going to be a victim. I refuse! I wonder if I stay at my aunt's house or maybe look for a new home...will that work? Whatever my neighbor may or may not be, she will not get me. She can have that house and all my things. My sanity is more important.

There is a part of me that wants to burn my house down. Why should I sell it to someone else? Would she bring harm to me? Why is she being so nice to everyone and always giving us gifts? Would she bring harm to us? Then I think... what if she isn't really being nice. What if she is trying to poison us all...or worse?

I laugh to myself. I sound crazier than before I thought I was crazy. There HAS to be a reasonable explanation for all of this. I have studied other cultures and "otherwordly" stuff. Still, even though it is different, it is easily explained. I probably remember my mother talking about that dream. Maybe it is just now resurfacing. My neighbor seems familiar but I did not see her up close. Any picture could look similar to her. I am thinking the clay in my bed is something I did not notice. I must have walked through the clay at some time. I decide to put myself at ease by going to talk to her. I am going to sit on her doorstep until she answers the doorbell, comes out to speak to me or calls the police.

The next morning I make myself a smoothie and head home, but I stop at her house. I bang on the door for almost an hour straight without her answering the door. I sit next to her door and wait. Some of my other neighbors pass by and wave at me; some give me an awkward smile as they pass. I do not care what they think. I need to have peace of mind.

As the day passes I continue to sit on her porch. Eventually I fall asleep leaning against her door. My phone rings and I nearly jump out of my skin. It is a phone number I do not recognize. I press ignore and figure it is the wrong number. After the third time it rings I answer. "What do you want?" a voice says politely. "I believe you called me. Why are you asking what I want?"

"Why are you here?" the voice asks. "I think you may have a wrong number." "No, I have the right number. Why are you at my door?" I freeze with fear. Then I hear the door unlock. It slowly opens and I see her beautiful brown-violet eyes. I stumble to get up and she reaches her arm out to me. I jump and wake up. I am still sitting on her doorstep. I realize then my phone is at my house. I laugh to myself. For the hell of it, I knock one more time before heading home.

There is a box on my doorstep. Without thinking about it, I pick it up and walk into my house. I shower, eat a snack and then lay down. I hear my phone ringing but I can't find it. I look all over my room. I stop to listen but it stops ringing before I can locate my phone. A few moments later it starts ringing again. I get up and follow the sound. The ringing is coming from inside the box. I open the package and my phone is within --still ringing. I again think, "What is going on?" I hesitantly pick my phone up. "Hello?" There is no one there.

I call my aunt and explain I am coming back over. She welcomes me immediately. I stay with my aunt for three months, only going home to get more clothes or to check my mail. Things seem to go back to normal for me. I have no weird dreams, I receive no weird phones calls and I have no thoughts about her. I meet a really nice man and spend a great deal of time with him. He is a good person and we enjoy spending time together. He and I meet in such an interesting way.

I reminisce about that day. One day, when I did stopped by my house, a little dog pulled away from his leash and scrambled to my door step. I opened the door and the puppy came inside. The man calls for his puppy and steps up on my porch. He whistled and then his puppy came back out. We laughed and talked a while before exchanging phone numbers. He invited me over for dinner. I gave my aunt all of his information and headed to his house. He lived in a refurbished old home with a lot of antique African artifacts.

"Wow! Where did you get all of this? Did you inherit it?" He laughs a bit. "Something like that." I figure he doesn't want to talk about it. We eat dinner and drink red wine. I feel a slight buzz from the alcohol. I realize that it is getting late. I look up to the sky and notice a full moon. It is the first time I allow myself to pay attention to the moon... since my nightmares began. I think of everything that has happened over the last few weeks. "You may know this but I am thinking of selling my house. I think I decided to do it the day I met you." "Really? Why?" I pause for a moment.

"Well... I am a little concerned about one of my neighbors." "Is someone bothering you?" "Yes, well, no. It's complicated." "We have all night. And we have almost a full bottle of wine." His words put me at ease. I am vague in answering. "One of my neighbors is a little different. I began to imagine the worst." "Who...Luna? She's harmless." "Wait how do YOU know who I am talking about? How do you know HER?"

He laughs at me. "EVERYONE knows Luna." "Has anyone ever met her?" He laughs again. "I'm sure SOMEONE has met her." I told him a little more about my feelings but I leave out that I think I am going crazy. After a moment he grabs my hand and we head outside the house. "Where are we going?" I ask. "It's a surprise."

Before my mind can wrap itself around the truth, I already know. I can feel the fear rising up inside me. When we pull up to her house I almost have a panic attack. But I try to remain calm. "She is not going to answer. I have knocked on her door several times." He holds my hand firmly as we step on to her porch. He rings the doorbell and the door unlatches, after a few short minutes, Luna opens the door and I squeeze his hand.

"Hello Luna," he says warmly. "My friend here would like to meet you." "She must be very shy," Luna says. When I hear her words I realize my eyes are closed tight. I opened them and gaze into her warm dark brown-violet orbs. Then I sigh in relief. There are no snake eyes, no claws, no sharp teeth. I am so relieved I give her a big hug. "She's friendly too," she adds. She welcomes us into her home. It seems twice as big inside....

To be continued....

SEEiNG ME

It took me a long time to say I was rap... I was raped. Even saying it now is a struggle. Rape seems like such a violent act -- such a foreign concept. Not something you are exposed to before you can walk well. The rapist is always depicted as someone in a dark alley, looking shifty and criminal. The victim is never really a victim because something she did caused the rape, such as walking down a dark alley, drinking too much, being alone with a man, etc. But wait... men and boys are raped too but we ignore those altogether for the most part. The rapist is this person, who through no fault of their own, violently assaults someone and that female HAD to provoke them in some way.

As a young woman I viewed my childhood through a rose colored lens. There were things that happened that "I never really talked about because they don't matter now." But I was no victim. I have been successful. I did not turn into a statistic, well not a bad one. I got my doctorate by the time I was 27 and I have worked in the community with youth teaching life skills for over a decade. So my being raped and molested as a little girl never mattered. Well... not really. Sure occasionally it crossed my mind that someone sat me in front of a TV to watch porn before I could talk but hey that was not the worst thing that could have happened. My life has been good.

Maybe it did take me years to not secretly cringe every time someone touched my body but many people have quirks. I remembered questioning the term "Daddy issues" as it referred to abused women. "Daddy issues?" Is that how society sums up years of indecent advances, rape, molestation, and abuse? We package it up nicely as a complex that the victim has. So then does that mean the abuser has "daughter issues," or maybe "child issues?"

That saying never made any sense to me. But then again I was on the receiving end of it so it was always different looking down the barrel of a gun. My first "sexual experience" reeked of cigarettes and liquor. I didn't know it was sexual. I just knew children were expected to do what adults told us to do. I was a child and he was an adult. It didn't feel right but at two years old how do you express that. Crying just made it worse so I learned early not to cry. Crying hurts... literally.

I was lucky; I "got out early." Well, it was not before my wounds were made but at least in time for them to heal, right? I "lost my virginity" at nine-years-old technically. But at what point does your "innocence" actually leave you. At what point do you become guilty of being too young? How long have I been guilty of sex? When I "lost my virginity" to my 17 years old "alleged boyfriend" he was a "trusted" friend of the family. He was the best friend of my babysitters boyfriend. He thought I was "sexy"... I was nine. I didn't cry or fight. Thankfully I learned at an early age to just "let it happen and go with it."

Over time I realized the sickness and cramping in my stomach was the sign that the "worst part" was over. Is that what they mean when they say "pain is pleasure?" All my friends knew this feeling. We traded tips on coping and getting through it like other children traded baseball cards. We were part of a secret club. The "fast tailed girl" club that you were thrust into with or without your consent, knowledge or understanding.

We considered ourselves little adults in our own way. We were exposed to adult things and forced to make adult decisions. I guess it was unfortunate that our minds were not as ready to handle the responsibility as our bodies; maybe it was the other way around. At any rate I made it! Some of my friends made it too. For the most part, I have been happily married for some time.

I have daughters of my own and they have not been molested. It was not going to happen to them. I would never let it happen to them. I would definitely know. I could tell. I would just know. I won't allow it! Right?

When they were very young I constantly questioned them about anyone abusing their "innocence." I eventually realized that I may have gone too far - that I was abusing it inadvertently. Fortunately for them I am basically healed. Many of those issues are no longer an issue for me.

And their father has been a wonderful man. You've heard the phrase Daddy's girls... Well, our girls **do not** have "Daddy issues."

I was not a "Daddy's girl". Instead, I had "Daddy issues" as many other women do. You can tell which ones of us had "Daddy's issues" by our actions. Our actions reflect the pain we once experienced. We are going to refer to these women as "THEY." We all know who "THEY" are, don't we? "THEY" are women who "wear their emotions on their sleeves." Sometimes "THEY" were unnaturally angry, suspicious, fearful, controlling and expressionless. Sometimes, "THEY" were in long term committed relationships; but "THEY" did not trust easily.

But not ME… No one would never know about me.... You would not know; and that is how I like it. I don't have "Daddy issues," I don't "hate all men." I'm not a "hoe, slut or freak." I'm not like those "women who can't keep a man." Nope, I am just fine.

So where is my happiness? Where is my pleasure? Why do I still have to "talk myself through sex." I'm not talking about occasionally, often, but every time. Why do compliments about my body make me tighten up or uncomfortable? Why do I stay busy so I won't have to be intimate with him or myself? Why don't I "seem like a regular rape victim?" How come nobody "would have ever guessed that happened to me?" You know why... don't you? I'm so "well adjusted" to have been through what I have been through.

Between the Sheets

I ran my fingers down spines looking for answers to questions.... not thinking. Finding myself spiraling through words I was pulled in and stayed there, until I read every line, pictured every scene, felt every emotion~ between the lines. In the margins, drawn, scribbled and written were the answers I needed, wanted, desired and called forth.

Your truth.. is now.. our truth, dare I say my truth. It made me want more, to go deeper, feel more, fill more and be felt more. Images of women danced in my head...wanting to know them, see them, but most importantly to be them, between rows of sheets and multiple spines coming multiple times across the lines. I wonder if I saw her would I know her, could she see in my eyes what was in the mind. Would she know that I know how smoothly she flows, rather glides, across the stages at different phases of your life?

But then I saw reflections of me and traces of we. Still not knowing what was unfolding as I unfolded the pages. I love you popped in my mind for a very short time caught up in the lines. But I digress, so I move back to the stress of emotions pressed into small places. I had a dream that went like this and one that ended like that. Damn telepathy at its best could not be more accurate in how it was or will be for me but it's not me. It is we; every woman, every scene, every emotion in every way, like a well authored play it got me to sway and bend and buckle with just a couple of rhymes.

And I lie to myself about the knowledge of wealth or wealth of knowledge that is before me, it could be me... but it isn't... which makes it hot in my head from the doubt that is shed by still having my composure without the exposure of being spread eagle, wide open, naked, bare and vulnerable between the sheets.

Contradictions

This morning I saw the sunset as the sun began to rise

Last night I began to awaken as I slowly closed my eyes

The birds sang as they sat silently in their nest

I find myself gasping for air as I take long deep breaths

I have changed everything about me while remaining the same

The day became night and the moon burst into flames

These are the contradictions in life that I see

Like you being in love but it not being with me

I Want To Know...

I want to know your name
Not what your mama calls you
But what is called out when bodies touch, sweat pours, hips move
and legs part
I want to feel you inside of me touching my heart with the tip of
your excitement
Moaning, groaning, throbbing, exploding cumming into my essence

I want you to want me sooo.. bad that I can taste you
I lick, kiss and taste every inch of your soul sucking the love right
out of you
I want to raise my hips and arch my back to receive the wisdom of
your years as you run into the depths of my emotions and come out
drenched in my spirit.
I want to try every angle of love, every time, every place, and
experience that which is taboo.

The ups and downs, ins and outs, of making, creating, building and
bringing forth
I want you to fill every orifice of my body with long, strong and hot
imagination
I want to feel you breathe down the back of my neck and become a
blanket warming and covering you
I want to see my name fall from your lips when I bend over and grab
the key to our journey

Bathe Me In Your Light

As part of my releasing my fears and boundaries I agree to let a friend bathe me. It sounds simple enough but I always have reservations about opening myself up to someone. I see it as a weakness…. for myself not others. I love to give massages, bathe and pamper others but do not desire it for myself. Weeeeelllll that is not true either, I desire having it done. However, I did not desire opening myself up to receive a bath from someone other than those I had to do during my spiritual rites. But something about her asking prompts me to say yes before my mind can catch up to refuse.

So, here I am pulling up to her house. I have my own towel, soap, body oil, candles and incense. I like to be prepared. I don't know why I am still sitting outside or why I am so nervous. It feels like a ritual to me even though I know it isn't one. I can see her looking out of her blinds so I have to go through with this now. I sigh to myself as I gather all my belongings and I decide to leave the candles and incense in the car. I do not want to seem like I have to always be in control. I chuckle as I walk up to her door becoming more and more nervous as I approach.

I talk quietly to myself to build up my confidence. She opens the door and reaches for my hand. I cross the threshold and she holds my hand and kisses my cheek. She is smiling as she prods if we are still doing the bath? It's almost like she knows I am contemplating changing my mind. I smile inwardly and assure her that we are good. I take off my shoes and follow her upstairs. Her house is huge but modest. She lives alone and it shows by the empty rooms and neglected hallways that she's very masculine in that regard.

When we arrive in her bedroom she inquires how I like my water? She asks if I have any sensitivity to products, fragrance or essential oils. I like her attention to detail. She disappears into the dimly lit hall and I can faintly hear as she moves around in the bathroom. This is my first time going upstairs in her house. We usually sit in the sunroom and talk or watch movies downstairs. I guess our friendship is going to the "next level." I laugh to myself at my corny joke.

While she prepares the water I wrap my mind around the thought that I am about to let her bathe me. I try to prepare my mind. I am very nervous. I don't know whether to stand and wait for her to return, sit down and take off my clothes or simply to leave. My heart quickens as I decide to take off my clothes. Half way through undressing she returns. It doesn't appear that she is surprised that I am still here but I know she probably is.

Her calmness is contagious; it spreads across me and steadies me. She grabs candles off her night stand and returns to the bathroom. I continue to slowly undress. The anticipation is unbelievable. After I am completely bare I wrap myself in African cloth. I finally decide to sit on the edge of her bed. I wait. I feel the energy from the altar in her room; it is powerfully arousing and moistens my imagination. The whole time she remains in the bathroom.

The water stops running and I know it is time. She appears in the doorway and holds her hand out to me. I take it and follow her into the bathroom. Inside the bathroom sits a huge size Jacuzzi. She reaches for my wrap but I begin to untie it myself. Old habits die hard. I let it fall to the floor and take a deep breath. When I release my breath, I allow all concerns to dissipate.

Without hesitation I step into the water. The temperature is perfect. The smell is intoxicating. It smells of rose, lilac, lotus and lavender and the oils are having their intended effect on me. Closing the door she turns off the light and gets on her knees next to the tub. As she begins to scoop water on my legs and thighs I feel my growing arousal.

This moment is the one I dreaded for so long. I did not realize I am sitting straight up in the tub, tense and stiff, until she touches my shoulder. I take five deep breaths and force myself to relax into the warmth of the water. She chuckles and says, "I was waiting for you to completely relax." I close my eyes and she squeezes water from the washcloth onto my face and neck. I tense up for a moment, then I let go of more reservations. I feel more and more arousal...I resist the overwhelming urge to reach for her and pull her close to me. I imagine her sliding her fingers over my body, this arousing me and causing my tekken to harden and my nipples to rise. I watch her aura change colors in the darkness.

After a little while she puts the washcloth down and begins to use her bare hands. They are soft and small despite years of hard work. I am not prepared for her gentle touch, nor am I prepared for her ability to comfort and secure me. My mind drifts again as I think about the security that lies in a black woman's touch even for atypical "blend" like me. She takes my feet out of the water and begins to massage them deeply. An awareness shoots through my body and wakes it completely up.

After massaging both my feet she slowly moves her hand upwards. I open my legs hoping her fingers will stroke my warm hardness. She does not disappoint. Her lips hesitantly meet mine as she continues to explore my limits. I am frantic to touch her. I pull her shirt over her head. I need to feel her skin against mine. I need her breast to be against my chest and I need to feel her heartbeat. I think about pulling her into the bath with me. It crosses my mind but instead I relax my thoughts and enjoy all the sensations. The voices in my mind remind me that I did ask for this experience. I wanted to experience this as a blend – from a woman - so I should simply open myself up more to fully enjoy it. Her fingertips dance on my sensitive head to a cadence that is sultry, sassy and firm.

It does not take long before I am singing aloud in ecstasy to the cadence of her fingers moving up and down on my shaft. Panting heavily I try to catch my breath and open my eyes, just as her lips move from my lips to that special place under my cheek. She then places a warm soft kiss on my forehead before placing a towel on the side of the tub. "Take as long as you desire," she says. Before I come down from my high she moves to the sink, washes her hands, and walks unceremoniously out of the door. After she walks out the door, I slide down into the scented water and drift away in my mind.

Women don't realize how sensitive we are underneath it all. Decades of having to be tough, strong, manly and guarded wears on our spirits. We long to be held, pampered with love and nurtured like anyone else yet we don't have the luxury of showing it. Even as a twin spirit, mostly I show my masculine aspects. But tonight I allowed her into to my sacred desires and I will be forever changed for the better. This sister has gotten under my skin in such a profound intoxicating way.

Sage Wisdom: Essential Oils

Kemet is the birth place of ancient medicine, perfumes, and pharmaceuticals. Over 6,000 years ago, healers in Kemet performed massages with essential oils and created skin care tinctures and plant based cosmetics. Plants were also used to create aromatic fragrances, oils, balsams, and resins for embalming techniques and religious ceremonies.

According to the book, "Sticks, Stones, Roots and Bones, Stephanie Rose Burn, the definition of essential oils is: "Essential oils are the essence of plants, usually created by steam distillation or cold pressing." They offer a quick and relatively easy way of using aroma to create healing environments. Sometimes the essential oils come directly from plants, plant parts such as seeds, bark, leaves, stems, roots, flowers, or the fruit.

Today, there is a growing market of health conscious individuals and families seeking a natural, holistic way to heal the body and spirit.

Warnings

As a general rule about essential oils - always do your own research before using essential oils for healing. Generally it is recommended that essential oils not be taken internally. Also pregnant, or nursing women and children under six should use essential oils that have been greatly diluted.

What are the benefits essential oils provide?

1. The oils are regenerating, oxygenating, and immune defense properties of plants.
2. The oils are lipid soluble making them capable of penetrating cells of the body within 20 minutes.
3. They contain oxygen molecules which help to transport nutrients directly to the human cells; this stimulates the immune system.
4. The oils are very powerful antioxidants which prevent fungus, and prevent oxidation in the cells.
5. All essential oils are anti-bacterial, anti-cancerous, anti-fungal, anti-infectious, anti-microbial, anti-tumoral, anti-parasitic, anti-viral, and antiseptic.
6. The oils simultaneously restore balance to the body.
7. Essential oils are aromatic. When diffused, they provide air purification by:
   o increasing atmospheric oxygen
   o increasing ozone and negative ions in the area, which inhibits bacterial growth
   o destroying odors from mold, cigarettes, and animals
   o filling the air with a fresh aromatic scent
8. The oils help promote emotional, physical, and spiritual healing.
9. Essential oils are bio-electrical and can quickly raise the frequency of the human body restoring it to a normal, healthy level.

A Short History of Medicine

"... I have an earache."
2000 B.C.: "Here, eat this root."
1000 B.C.: "That root is heathen. Say this prayer."
1850 A.D.: "That prayer is superstition. Drink this potion."
1940 A.D.: "That potion is snake oil. Swallow this pill."
1985 A.D.: "That pill is ineffective. Take this antibiotic."
2000 A.D.: "That antibiotic has side effects. Here, take this root!"

Author unknown

Common Essential Oils,
Uses & Aromatherapy Benefits

Allspice Berry - **benefits**: warming, cheering, comforting, nurturing.

Anise - **benefits**: cheering, mildly euphoric.

Basil, Sweet – **benefits**: clarifying, uplifting, energizing, refreshing.

Bay - **benefits:** clarifying, warming.

Bergamot - **benefits**: uplifting, inspiring, confidence-building.

Cassia Bark -. **benefits**: comforting, energizing, warming.

Cedar, Atlas – **benefits**: stabilizing, centering, strengthening.

Chamomile –**benefits**: calming, relaxing, soothing.

Cinnamon Bark –**benefits**: comforting, warming.

Citronella - **benefits:** purifying, vitalizing.

Clary Sage - **benefits**: centering, euphoric, visualizing.

Clove Bud - **benefits**: warming, comforting.

Cypress - **benefits:** purifying, balancing.

Eucalyptus - **benefits**: purifying, invigorating.

Frankincense - **benefits**: calming, visualizing, meditative.

Geranium - **benefits**: soothing, mood-lifting, balancing.

Ginger - **benefits:** warming, strengthening, anchoring.

Grapefruit - **benefits:** refreshing, cheering.

Hyssop - **benefits**: refreshing, purifying.

Jasmine Absolute - **benefits:** calming, relaxing, sensual, romantic.

Juniper Berry - **benefits**: supportive, restoring.

Lavender - **benefits**: balancing, soothing, calming, relaxing, healing.

Lemon -**benefits**: uplifting, refreshing, cheering.

Lemongrass - **benefits:** vitalizing, cleansing.

Lime - **benefits:** refreshing, cheering.

Marjoram, Sweet - **benefits:** warming, balancing.

Myrrh - benefits: centering, visualizing, meditative.

Neroli - benefits: calming, soothing, sensual.

Orange, Mandarin - benefits: uplifting, cheering, sensual.

Orange, Sweet benefits: cheering, refreshing, uplifting.

Patchouli -. benefits: romantic, soothing, sensual.

Peppermint -. benefits: vitalizing, refreshing, cooling.

Peru Balsam - benefits: anchoring, strengthening.

Pine - benefits: refreshing, invigorating.

Rose Absolute -. benefits: romantic, uplifting.

Rosemary - benefits: clarifying, invigorating.

Rosewood - benefits: gently strengthening, calming.

Sandalwood - benefits: relaxing, centering, sensual.

Spearmint -benefits: refreshing, cooling, vitalizing.

Spruce -. benefits: clarifying, vitalizing.

Tangerine - benefits: cheering, uplifting.

Tea Tree - benefits: cleansing, purifying, uplifting.

Thyme, Red - benefits: cleansing, purifying, energizing.

Vanilla - benefits: calming, comforting, balancing.

Vetiver- benefits: supportive, grounding.

Wintergreen- benefits: refreshing, bracing, invigorating.

Ylang Ylang- benefits: sensual, euphoric.

Abuse

My bruised, abused and broken body was flung to the side of the road; I suppose left for dead. But I stubbornly refused to die, in this horrible way, at this place and time; without him. How could I? Most of my memories included him, getting in trouble with and because of him, going camping and to family reunions with him, going to dances together because neither of us wanted "a real date," bailing each other out of trouble and so much more.

As I dragged one leg, walking in a zig zag path down the middle of the road, I refused to think about what happened; instead I forced myself to think about him. I wrapped thoughts of him around me and how all my friends talked 'bout how cute he was and those who actually were "lucky" enough, by his account, to fall deeply in love with him. My thoughts of him....kept me going... kept me walking, bearing immense pain and a shit load of rage.

Then I heard the water tower clock bell toll. At first, I thought I was walk-dreaming. I couldn't believe it. I knew exactly where I was. I don't know if it was our bond, the Creator, or simply chance that made them leave me near enough to his home. I knew I could make it! I could make it there. While growing up, we always joked about how every place in the city was measured by distance from the clock tower. Although we never actually set foot inside it, we used it to calculate the distance everywhere, by the sound of the bells.

Simultaneously, I almost laughed and cried at the irony of it all. How this childhood game has now become a lifesaving tool. I limped closer and closer to his home, dragging myself down the street in the dark of night. At this point I could no longer feel the pain; just intense throbbing and heat. Maybe I'm in shock. I don't know. I have nothing to compare this extreme "absence" or "lack of feelings" to in this lifetime. I never cried out, not even once. I kept this chant going in my head, even when they threatened to leave me dead. Over and over again, I silently chanted: "My body you can take, even try to make me break, but you can't bend my will, my strength, or my resolve ...never!"

I reached his home and instantly felt profound relief. I could not drag myself up his front stairs. It was enough to simply sit down and rest. I rested on the steps for a while before I tried the stairs again. It took nearly 10 minutes to climb the five steps that I had so often skipped, hopped, walked or jumped down. I propped myself against his door and knocked three times; this time softer than I always did. There have been times when he takes his time coming to the door just because he knows it's me but I prayed silently that tonight would not be one of those. Then doubt began to set in:

What if he is not here? What if he has company? What if he did not hear me? What if...? I heard the first lock unlatch as if he were fumbling to open it. It just dawned on me that it was the middle of the night and I never come over here at this time of night unless something is very wrong.

As the door flew open I stepped back a little out of surprise, and then fell painfully towards him exhausted and tormented. He caught me and picked me up quickly like I was his child. He did it so quickly it made me dizzy. He kicked the door closed with such force that the entire house shook. "Who did this to you?" He said in such a quiet, fierce, intimidating tone that I instantly feared for the lives of my attackers. I'm sure my entire body was covered in cuts, lacerations, dark splotchy bruises and even more fractures. My left eye was completely swollen shut but I could see the tears in his eyes through my right eye – it was just beginning to swell. Finally able to rest... before I could respond, I passed out.

The whispers are what woke me. I heard the hushed conversations of his ancestors, some who knew me, some did not; all of them were enraged. I could see his blurred figure in front of his shrine doing prayers and casting cowry. I could not make out much that was being said until everything went silent and a voice plainly said: "If you leave her, she will die."

He pulled out his chest and looked through it intently pulling out bottle after bottle of oils until there was three that he wanted; he also grabbed a pouch of what I assumed to be herbs. I wanted so badly to reach for him as he walked out the door towards the bathroom but my arms were too heavy. The next thing I heard was water flowing.

The water seemed to run forever before he came back in and kneeled by my side. I thought I had been unconscious for hours but the sun still had not risen. Every pore of my body still reeked of their sweat, their urine, their semen and my blood. Yes, I was covered head to toe, with my own blood...fresh and dried blood. What's left of my dress was stuck to my body so he had to be very careful while he pulled it off.

I wanted to be embarrassed that I had no underwear on, but I was too damn tired to care. My modesty had been ripped off earlier in the evening – with some of my skin. He gently picked me up, carried me into the bathroom and placed me into the water. It was probably lukewarm, as he had been advised to prepare during divination, but it still burned my skin like blue-hot fire.

For the first time, since they grabbed me, I allowed my body and mind to actually "feel" and let out a visceral scream so loud that it even scared me. He did not even flinch. I continued to scream uncontrolled, unrestrained and uninhibited. I couldn't stop screaming. I screamed for all the time I wanted to but did not earlier as they raped and tortured me. I screamed out my hate, hurt, rage, frustration, fear, anger, pride, determination and disappointment. I dug my nails into his skin, like he was my attacker....and he let me.

After what seemed like an eternity, he gently pried my fingernails from his skin and began to take his clothes off. He slid into the tub behind me and started cleaning me by washing out my hair. As soon as the water hit my face I began to whimper loudly. It awakened my senses that I had buried deeply during the assault. I could feel everything now. What they did and when they did those awful things to me. I watched like it was a movie from above.... as I pictured them desecrating my body. I had shut myself down so deeply that they tossed me physically around like I was a broken rag doll.

They commented on how I was lifeless, not even worth the time; but they did not stop the assault. Here, now, in his arms I felt them inside me, I could feel them inside my head, inside my spirit, inside my soul.....something alive and sullied. I could even hear my flesh tearing and feel their fists pounding on my face, my stomach, my legs, my hips, my kidneys and on my womb.

I could feel the warmth of their urine as they took turns pissing on me, I could hear my bones popping as they hit me with boards, sticks, bottles, brooms and anything else that was close. I could smell their stench as they rammed inside of me one after another, I could feel my womb burning and bleeding. I had removed myself from the experience during the ordeal. I was detached and small inside myself; but he released the images with his gentle touch. I could feel his arms around me, holding me tight to anchor me. I had not realized that I had begun to thrash around in the tub.

His soothing words finally reached my consciousness. I don't know how long that took. When I calmed down, he pulled the stopper and let the water go down the drain I watched in amazement as the bloody, dirty, rotten, water disappeared leaving us bare in the tub. He adjusted the water and began filling the tub again with clean water.

The water seemed warmer this time. He grabbed the oils that were nearby and poured some in the water with us. I realized this was the second time he had refilled the tub and remember the Oracle saying: "Once to cleanse the body, twice to cleanse the mind, thrice is for the spirit and the last time." A third time he refilled the bathtub. But I can no longer tell what is physically happening. He used his hands to pour water over my head and body.

The stinging and burning was beginning to go away. My lips were still swollen but I could at least feel them now. My throat hurt from where multiple hands choked me, holding upright to continue beating and raping me. I don't know how long we lay there. I drifted in and out of consciousness, in and out of reality, in and out of pain, until he stood up and wrapped a towel around his waist lifting me in his arms again.

He took me to his shrine and lay me down on his pillows. He lit a white candle and jasmine incense to promote healing and cleansing. Then he did a prayer, sprinkled me with a concoction that smelled of herbs and Florida water. I lay deathly still on some pillows and he covered me up. I felt a warmth, comfort and calmness that I had not felt in years. I was captivated by the flickering flame of the candle on his shrine. I kept staring at it. He busied himself, pulling the covers off his bed and then he collected my dress. I heard him ripping my tattered dress into shreds and watched him throw it into the fireplace. Both of us stared at it while the fire set it ablaze.

When I woke up the next time, I looked at everything from painfully swollen, bloodied eyelids. The first thing my eyes focused on was his red and yellow aura. I would recognize it anywhere. Tears leaked through my eyelids. I couldn't believe I had actually made it to him. I was safe…. SAFE… at least for now…the concept had a different meaning now but…. He came closer and I could feel his presence looking at me with more than his eyes. He had a tray of soup and fresh herbs for me. "How long have I been here?" were the words I finally choked out. When he spoke he did not look at me. "Almost eight hours."

I was in disbelief. The time seemed so much longer… days even from the moment I arrived on his doorstep. There was so much I wanted to say to him, but all I could do was reach for him. He took my hand and lay down behind me, holding me so tightly it hurt. But compared to the pain I had felt this day, this was comforting and kept me grounded.

I was awakened this time by male voices. The voices sounded vaguely familiar but I was disoriented, so I panicked. I thought my time with him was only a dream, and I was still where my body and soul had split. The agony of thinking I was ripped from him caused me to cry out for the first time. I was not crying because of what they had done; but because my time with him was only a dream. I could hear footsteps running towards me.

All I could think of was "kill or be killed." I could see only blood everywhere; I had no idea where I was. The door flung open…It was him! In shock I dropped to my knees on the floor and began to cry. I had lost touch with reality. "I thought you were a dream and I was really back with them. I was ready to die. I thought I had been separated from you." I thought… as I hiccupped through my tears. He stopped me saying "Don't talk like that….you are safe, don't cry, it will be okay, be at peace. I was just talking to my brothers so that they could keep watch over you while I went out." I was too emotional to share the depth of my despair so I simply nodded. Then I whispered,

"Don't leave me alone, please." His body language told me that he heard me.

He spoke again "I called your mother and she is coming over. I could not stop her. Nor could I allow her to worry, not knowing where you were." I did not respond. I was now conscious of time and it had not even been a full day since they were inside and on top of me. Hunger hit me for the first time and I longed to be free of all my pain. This all seemed like some kind of crazy shit you hear about happening to somebody else. I don't like imposing on others. I regretted them not killing me. I regretted not killing them. I regretted being raped and tortured because my skin was black. I regretted every "nigger or nigger bitch" that spurted from their lips. I regretted taking that road home. Most of all, I regretted him seeing me like this. I regretted him having to experience my pain with me. The doorbell rang and his brothers, who apparently were still there, answered the door.

I heard my mother's voice. "Where's my baby?" Her beautiful deep cadence brought fresh tears to my eyes; but these are tears of joy... these tears free my spirit...they place a salve on my heart. "I am in my thirties and my mother still calls me her baby."

My mother walked into the room and gave him a big hug. She's smiling and crying her appreciation and thanks. It's a rare sight. She wiped her eyes after a moment and then hugs him. It lets him know it is "njema" (Swahili for "fine" or "good") for him to leave. My mother is a strong beautiful Afrikan woman who understood that the last thing I needed was a pity-party. She knew that I needed her strength and not her tears. He stuck his head in to look at me for just a moment...to make sure I was okay. I nodded and murmured "ndio" (meaning "yes" in Swahili). So he departed.

My mother sat me between her legs and began to comb my hair. This brought back wonderful childhood memories. I smiled at his thought-fullness; he recognized I needed my mother. My mother stayed all day. She cornrowed my hair, made me eat, prayed over me, got me up to walk outside to feel the sun rays. She sang to me. "You know your Baba (meaning father in Swahili) could not come and see you like this. He sends his love and will be over when you are doing a little better. You know men are much more sensitive than they let on. She had joy in her voice, knowing that I would be fine now. I was more centered now that I had spent the day with her.

He still had not returned by the time she was leaving. I began to panic internally. I could not bear being alone. I felt secure in his house. But I still walked around checking all the windows; often jumping at unexpected noises. His brothers were still outside on the porch, keeping watch just in case I needed anything. Still tired and spent I laid in his bed enjoying his particular scent which I would forever associate with safety. Finally, I heard his gentle knock on his bedroom door to let me know it was him before entering.

I was excited to see him until I noticed that he was covered in blood. I got off the bed as fast as I could and ran to him. Before I could ask him anything he said "It's not my blood." He had the look of rage in his eyes. He had never killed a man before but I was clear that he had gotten them all. I began to pull his blood soaked clothes off of him; I felt a warming that was cold-blooded. I desired to lick the blood from his face but resisted the overwhelming urge. He was almost gone into the recesses of his own mind as I guided him to the shower. I got in with him and washed him as he had done to me, not so many hours ago. Afterwards, we didn't talk but instead settled down in his bed. I held him as close as my pain would allow. It was an uneasy solace.

Time came and went. We fell into an easy pattern that friends almost always do. While lying next to me one evening he placed his hand on my stomach. "Do you still hurt?" he asked. "My body still hurts but my spirit is well." I know that is really what he needed to know. Over the next month I stayed with him, my mother came over often but today was the first time my father would be coming with her. When my father came in he hugged me tightly, then he held me at arms-length from him, looking me over from top to bottom.

We hardly said much to each other, we just spent time together. My father quietly rose from his seat when he heard the key turn in the door. He greeted him cautiously and subtly nodded toward the kitchen. The two of them went into the kitchen to talk while I strained to listen but their words were all jumbled.

All I could make out were a few of their words: bodies, fire, buried, retribution. I was surprised, for only a split second that my father was in on their "disappearance." After, they returned to the room, we casually had chakula (meaning "food" in Swahili) together before my parents had to leave. As we lay together in the quiet of the night, reflecting on the day, I decide that it is time to voice my thoughts. "I will be going home tomorrow. I am grateful for everything you have done for me, for us, but I don't want to take up any more of your time. I also know you have been putting off your business to take care of me. And, I think I am finally ready to be alone."

The next day....He walks in to my house helping me to check every window and door. He put away my clothes that had been at his house. As he prepares to leave, a panic rises up in me, and halts me in my steps. He can immediately feel the shift in me. "Would you like me to stay?" He asks. I smile and take a deep breath. After talking about my feelings, I let him leave but ask him to come back later that evening. Again, he knocks before using his key but this time I was in the tub trying to relax.

He walks in the bathroom and pulls his manhood out to pee without hesitation. I can feel the heat exuding from his body. We speak of our day; and I can tell he is tired. His body is tense so I decided to massage him. I sit on him, rubbing his body while noticing his scars, each of which I know where they come from and how he got them; all but one. "When did you get this?" He was quiet and I remember seeing it as I washed away the blood from him. "Oh, never mind, I know." When he turns over so I can rub his chest; he is erect. I adjust myself just above his manhood and continued my massage.

Looking down at him, I am enraptured by his piercing stare. His eyes never leave mine. He slowly begins to raise his head until we are face to face. It only takes a moment before we are breathing the same air. I kiss him lightly first. I can't help it. The draw is too strong to ignore. We both knew it was not because of the trauma but the love that binds us together. He wraps his arms tightly around my waist immobilizing me while he slides his tekken inside me.

I moan instantly as his heat and mass takes me by surprise, he is very slow and gentle in his upward thrust. I wondered how my body would respond to intimacy after my recent experience. Obviously, the body has a short memory span of psychological and physical pain. Pleasure overtakes bad memories. All I can feel is this beautiful man below me; no thoughts of the blood, pain and torture pops into the mind. I press my forehead against his and begin to move rhythmically with him. He grasps my hips guiding me to the bed and climbs on top of me reposition my legs with his. Our lovemaking is slow building but very heated, intense, and more physical. He knows exactly what to do, where to move, when to slow down or speed up, he is in tune with my body and my spirit.

My breathing is labored as I try to adjust to the feelings of ecstasy. He bites my body everywhere before wrapping his hand around my neck. His eyes glaze over and I feel an energy rush that passes through my body, starting at my toes and slowly moving upward to envelope me in a jolt of pleasure.

It is so intense it is painful. I gasp for air as my consciousness jumps out my body and merges into his. The physical no longer exists as we dance among the stars and chase meteors. My body convulses as he pulls out and places me on top of him putting his hands back around my neck. His hand around my neck is so arousing I can't think. I am not frightened by him because I know he won't hurt me but I am slightly alarmed by his intensity. I am more frightened of him not being inside of me. "We are one." I hear the words deep within me.

"I want to fill you up with my joy." He speaks these words aloud with a slight accent, which I know he hasn't voiced before. As he speaks he grows in magnitude. He now seems enormous, giant like, swollen and full of light. Soft lips caress mine and I can't express how his tenderness affects me. We share more kisses. He deepens the kisses. I comply willingly to open myself, feeding a fire which starts behind my eyes and lights everything in its path, including the embers.

I didn't mean for it to happen but he is touching my soul, my true spirit, my essence. My eyes become unfocused and I grab his head. The deep voice with the accent growls deeply in his throat. It sends him into an ecstatic rage -- pumping harder, slamming against me with a virility that is rare and cosmic. As he begins cumming inside me it drives me over an explosive edge.

For less than a minute he is still, before beginning his movements again. Searching for reality I looked deeply in his eyes only to find me there. My name falls from his lips as tears flow from my body. I can feel my body healing with every one of his deliberate strokes.

I begin to speak softly to him. I am sure that my words do not convey the connection and immense pleasure I am feeling. Hours pass...we both have orgasmed numerous times. I ask him if he needs to rest and his reply mirrors my own. "I can't stop. I don't want to stop." I look around and realize we are in another realm and the only thing that is familiar to us -- is each other.

How Will I Release My Pain.......

Sage Wisdom: *Healing Baths*

Spiritual baths are a way of psychically changing or impacting a person energy, spirit, or body. Most Spiritual baths use herbs, essences and spices to heal, restore and rejuvenate a person. The intent is to remove unwanted energies and rid oneself of negative vibrations. While normal baths are taken for the purposes of cleanliness and hygiene, spiritual baths are taken to restore balance and harmony in our lives. There are many different spiritual baths that can be tailored to one's specific needs.

General Preparation

ω Pick the bath of your choice based on your intent. Gather and prepare all items and ingredients needed for it.

ω Make sure that all the bathing accessories that you use are clean and dirt-free. To ensure that you are as clean, do not forget to take your normal bath/shower with soap, shampoo and water. Wash your hair and body and rid yourself of physical dirt.

ω Put the herbs/ingredients for the bath in hot water in a container (pot, bowl, small tub). Let the water absorb the essence of the herbs as you take your normal daily bath/shower.

ω When you are ready for the bath add the warm water redolent with herbs to your bucket of bath water or the tub if you have one. Use a mug or your cupped hands to pour the water over your head and body.

ω As you bathe, consciously remind yourself of the aim of taking the spiritual bath and trust the process to accomplish its purpose.

ω Use prayers/affirmations to ask for what you desire while taking or assisting someone with a bath; this is the key to obtaining one's goals.

ω *If possible do not use a towel to dry yourself after you finish bathing. Instead drape a robe, cloth or any other comfortable clothing around yourself and let the body dry naturally. This is known as air-dry in spiritual bath traditions.*

ω *If your hair is long, you don't want to sweat it out or if you have a tendency to catch colds easily, wrap a towel over your head but do not towel dry your face or body.*

ω *It is best to wait 24 hours before taking another bath. If this is not possible, at least wait 12 hours before your next bath.*

For most baths simply filling the tub with hot water, oils, crystal or herbs of your choice based on the intent and allowing the person to be covered in the water is all that it will take. The property of the item used will determine the use of the bath. Using a bathtub when it comes to these baths is a wonderful experience however you can also use a bucket, bowl, small tub or mug with the same powerful results.

7 Carnation Rejuvenation

Purpose: *With all we experience we often feel drained, sapped or tired. This bath revives and refreshes your energy and it also cleanses your aura (energy around your body)*

Items needed: *At least 7 white carnations (it is better to have more although only 7 are needed); 3 ounces of lavender; 1 sprig of rosemary; 1 sprig of basil (1 sprig of fresh peppermint can also be used)*

What to do: *Add the ingredients except the carnations to the bath water. Scrub yourself from head to toe with one blossom until the petals begin to fall apart. Pour a couple of mugs of bath water over your head and scrub yourself again with another white carnation.*

Do this with all the other carnations and the bath water until all the blossoms and the water are used up. This bath will thoroughly cleanse your aura and wash away all negative influences. A strainer of some kind can be placed to prevent clogging in the bathroom. Do remember to pick up the petals and leaves and put them in the garbage or bury them after you are done. Clean the bathtub regularly.

Aphrodisiac

Purpose: *Stress is the major cause of many woes — sometimes it even extends itself into the bedroom. If you feel your libido is lacking in "umph" then it might be good to enjoy a naturalist bath filled with aroma-filled flowers and herbs. This is one of the best cures to heighten your desires and raise your energy so you can connect with your loved one(s).*

Items needed: *A handful of the following ingredients: Rosemary, Rose Petals, Jasmine Flowers and Thyme.*

What to do: *Add all the fresh ingredients to the bath water while the bath is running. Do a prayer asking for heightening of your energy, awareness of the psychic energy of attraction and opening your spirit to fun, joy and arousal. Gently rub the flowers and herbs across your skin and visualize your desires. This bath will energize your aura and center your desires and intent. Do remember to pick up the herbs and flowers afterwards and put them in the garbage after you are done. Clean the bathtub regularly.*

Removing Negativity

Purpose: *With all the negative physical and psychic energy that surrounds us, sometimes it leaves us feeling agitated and disconnected from our spirit. This bath is to remove negative influences.*

Items needed: *Sea Salt and Baking Soda (also called Bicarbonate of Soda).*

What to do: *Take a clean measuring jar and add:*
Two cups of water that has been boiled and allowed to cool
One tablespoon of Sea Salt
Add ¼ of a cup of Baking Soda to your bath.

Stir well
Add the contents to a half-full bathtub. You should bathe three times for five minutes at a time. At the same time you should offer up a prayer for release from whatever is holding you back. This is a bath, if taken regularly, will lead to a marked improvement in your confidence, allow you to feel better and you will be more prepared to deal with life's challenges.

August 17th

Tonight I decide to wear my long flowing red sun dress. Red usually makes me feel brave, vibrant, passionate and aroused. But tonight I feel like a target for a raging bull ready to strike with all his power. The light of the moon shines brightly around me, calming my spirit and swaying my soul, like the tides of the calmest point of the Ubangi River. We sit on the patio drinking wine and laughing. The air seems so clean and crisp.

I contemplate the alcohol that is running through my body. I assure myself that it is organic and not harmful. I usually don't drink but tonight is the exception to the rule. He is touching my leg lightly under the table and the anticipation is welling up inside me. All this week I have prepared for today. But can you really prepare to face your fears? His touch is becoming more pronounced on my thighs and I can tell he is aroused. I have not touched him back tonight, I've resisted every urge to caress him other than the "hello hug" which I kept real short.

"Come here" he says as he tugs at my arm. I want to resist but then again I don't. I stand up and walk to his side of the table and a gentle breeze blows up my dress. *This is nice.* When I near him he grabs my legs and rubs his hands up and down them. I stand in front of him as he explores my lower body. He looks up at me and smiles deviously as he places his lips on the outside of my panties under my dress. I slightly rub his shoulders but the fear is rushing up inside me. He stands and pulls me close to him. The closeness seems more intense than normal. His scent eases my mind and I slip into the memory of us.

Last week during our conversation about trust, fears, control and self-imposed limitations he asks me if I ever let anyone tie me up. I am so against the thought of that EVER happening. I am offended that he even asked me so I did not answer the question. Instead I pose the same question back to him. He shares several of his past experiences with me. As the conversation continues he asks me if I trust anyone enough to let them tie me up. I never consider it a trust thing until his question is posed. Upon reflection I realize I am not comfortable with it. "No." I can't fathom what someone could do with me if I am tied up. What could they do with me that they can't do with my hands untied?

Maybe it is about trust. Most of the people I have been with know me better than to bring that up. If they do; they do it jokingly. Well, I take it as a joke at least. He seems determined to "address this trust issue." He seems determined about this matter. He thinks I should allow him to tie me up.... to demonstrate deepest levels of trust. You know me.... if someone challenges me on something I always take the challenge. Sigh....

His erection pokes against my stomach before he lifts me off the ground and wraps my legs around his waist. I want him to slide in and thrust until he is satisfied; that would be ideal. Instead he carries me into his bedroom as I hold onto him tightly. My fear surmounts when I look around to see scarves and ties laid out on his bed, neatly in a row. He moves them to the side with one hand as he lays me down on the bed. My heart is beating in my throat. Now I understand better the cartoons with the large pounding heart beating out of the main character's chest. They are both frightened and excited.   All those years of thinking people were exaggerating about this "trust act" and now it is happening to me.   He pulls my panties down… I ease up thinking that maybe I have proved my point and he won't see the need to go through with tying me up, or maybe he has changed his mind.

He pauses for a moment; I am not sure what he is thinking. He reaches next to me and grabs one of the ties and wraps it around my wrist as he kisses my lips. My breaths become heavy and full of doubt. So I concentrate and began taking deep slow, full breaths; concentrating on every muscle; feeling the oxygen flow; contracting, releasing…. breathing. He hoists my hands above my head and secures them on his bed post. As he tightens it, I tense up yet I still become slightly moist, my arousal is filled with fear and this is new for me.

If there is ever a time to panic this is it. "I am not going to hurt you." He whispers in my ear. Pain is not what worries me. I am more worried about losing control of myself. I secretly still hold onto the belief that pleasure is unnecessary. It is something I should resist. I am fine with giving pleasure and allowing others to succumb to it. I am an observer; I enjoy watching their reactions.

Of course I enjoyed tying people up but that is different. However, to willingly allow someone to do the same to me is an entirely different thing. I am trying to remember why I even agreed to being tied up. I manage to get through my entire life without doing it. When it is being done to me… it's different. He spread my legs open and places his tongue on my throbbing clit before he pushes it inside me. I can hear him lightly sucking and slurping but I can't move my hands. His body lays heavy on my legs.

He positions himself as if he will be taking his time. He laps at my clit like it's a pop sickle; all the while increasing my flowing juices. I exhale and inhale with each flick of his tongue. I want to rub his head and at the same time I desperately want to push his head away from me. I struggle with the ties and try to loosen them. I know that he will not stop until... I don't have any idea when he will stop.

How much fucking pleasure does he want me to experience? How long can he go? How wet will this bed get? I want to run... but the quivering in my body wants me to stay. He lifts his head and pulls me by my hips towards him. I am pleasantly surprised that he momentarily stops. Then he takes off his pants and reveals his swollen tekken. He uses some of the juices from his face (Yes I was THAT wet) and slides his hand up and down his shaft. Whenever we have sex I control how deeply he goes, the speed, the position...

Damn I AM controlling and do have issues with trust. I've always thought that not letting others too close to me is for their protection. But deep down inside it's been from my own fear of not being loved or accepted. Memories imprinted in my spirit of betrayal and hurt from other existences are as real to me as his touch on my skin.

I wonder if this experience will gain him entrance into me, in a way that I did not desire or intend. His tying me up binds my fears and I must relinquish control of everything. I gasp as he plunges inside me. I can feel my juices run down my buttocks. He is fully erect and taking his time.

I want to tense up but the sensations are too strong and they are causing me to surrender to this pleasure. Me? Surrender? Me? Allowing someone else to be in control of **my** pleasure? I want to be indignant. I try to focus on my regular thoughts. It is **my** job to please me, to take care of me, to keep myself in check.

With each stroke I grow closer to ecstasy and further away from fear. I am so wet that he continuously slips outs and has to reinsert himself. He is going slowly and not too deep. He is just inserting the tip, but with each moment he goes a little faster and slightly deeper. My legs wrap around him and he moves closer to me pushing down my fears, loosening my doubt, connecting with my spirit. My muscles tighten around him as I near climax. I began to thrust against him. With each of his thrusts, I forget about the past, the hurt and the promises I made to myself to never be emotionally compromised. I forget that I promised never to let anyone else in. I forget not to cum, not to enjoy it, not to open myself… I forget so many things.

He pulls out and places his tekken on my lips and I lick my sweet juices off of him. He holds my chin and I willingly take him down my throat. His silken tekken is like warm jasmine tea. His body jerks and I smile knowing that I had won this round. He always talks about how competitive I am with him. Unfortunately, he doesn't understand that I only compete with myself.

I am plagued by past lives' memories. The memories replay in my head as warnings to never repeat the same mistakes. I should never love that much, never enjoy that much, never get off track. He adjusts my ties and raises my ass in the air resting my hips on his chest. His tongue moistens my fault as he opens my cheeks. The fear comes back even as the juices flow down my legs. I think of all the things that he could do that I would never allow.

I long for them all. For the first time, I want to be free from my own limitations. Excitement rises in me as I think of all the fake orgasms I have screamed through. I even wonder if I will know the difference for myself.

Side note: I fake orgasm ALL the time.. I mean like EVERY time. Those that I don't completely fake are greatly exaggerated. It's not that I don't enjoy sex I don't desire to have orgasms. Sometimes I don't even technically fake it, I just say and do what the person enjoys and they assume I am cumming. I just let them believe it. I experience "crygasm" you know when you have an emotional release during sex but it doesn't feel like a complete orgasm. I think many women do this. Sometimes we restrict ourselves so much that our only option is to cry during/after sex. It's a release. Or maybe I cum and just don't know it because it isn't the mind blowing super release that only happens when I am alone.

Although what I am feeling now is different than all those false experiences. My adrenaline is in full blast and I can feel a warm flush coming over me.

I am so caught up in reflecting about orgasms that I forget to resist the one building inside of me. Now, it is too late. I have pulled at the ties so hard at this point that they are beginning to come loose. Now, I don't want to be free. I want to experience something that is not re-fried and re-manufactured from my imagination. I don't want to control it, I want to break the vows I made to my heart to never feel again. My spirit flows free in my body. My heart pounds in my chest. He continues to move and work me over. I don't think he has any intentions of stopping.

There is a power in losing control that I did not realize exists. I am embarking on discovering that power.

"How many licks does it take to get to the center of centuries of limitations? Nobody will ever know." I giggle to myself at these thoughts. He asks me what is funny. Before I can answer he repositions himself and slides inside me deeply. The energy surge makes me pull the ties apart as I hold him tightly and move in harmony with him. "That's it," he says. "Use me." "Trust me. He says, "Is this what you have been resisting?" He asks over and over again. My conscious mind isn't functioning; I have no rational thoughts. I am pushed back to a time where he is by my side, quietly erasing memories and centuries of pain. Instead my mind focuses on the sensations rushing through my body and the feeling of his manhood going in and out of me.

I focus on the sound of my heart, pounding in my chest, and the feeling of sweat bursting through my skin as I explode with multiple orgasms, and orgasmic spasms. He holds me tightly while my body shudders. I hold on while experiencing wave after wave of energy and pleasure coursing through my entire being. The best way I can describe this feeling is by closing my eyes for a moment, imagining warmth from the sun, and at the same time a cool breeze kissing your skin. "I just wanted to you be free from your own fears. I just wanted you to give yourself to me fully just once," he confesses, as he holds me against his body.

I cry and laugh at the same time, as centuries of tears, that I once held back, break free from my spirit. I have kept myself and all that I came to be – in this existence locked away. Now it is unfettered, I am free.

Sage Wisdom: *Sacred Spaces*

Ancestral Shrine for Keisha E.S. Redding

Life is filed with sacred places. Places that hold special interest, energies or conjures memories. These sacred places provide life a place of refuge, recollection and inspiration.

Such is the case with sacred shrines and altars. Shrines are especially designed places that hold significant items or themselves are locations of important events or happenings. ***They become sacred, meaning hallowed or considered important, because of the significance of the item held at that location and/or because of the events that took place there.***

Because of the significance of the item housed at that location or the importance of what happened at the location it is enshrined there for future generations to partake, be in communion with, learn, recollect and be uplifted.

Altars are the close relatives of shrines. They provide a surface or area for offerings to shrines and/or where ceremonial items are placed for use at shrines. In time altars themselves can become a sacred shrine but most are kept as support for shrines.

Shrines span the gamut of looks and elaboration. It can be from a simple stone where a significant and important act took place to the elaborate ones designed to capture a special energy. Shrines can be natural items never changed by human hands and/or human made sacred structures created to impart a feeling, or through the combination of related items, capture a particular spirit and force.

Sacred places themselves can be enshrined or shrines can be built at the significant location to enhance the feeling and memory of what took place there. Humanity, so far, has seen no limitation in the construction of shrines and therefore have a variety of different types and sizes.

Today shrines have taken to forms of memorials designed to cause one to remember or learn a significant event or person, and those used for the invocation of special forces and energies. Whatever your need sacred places/shrines are a natural creative development of the spirit of humanity. Enjoy.

Lines

The lines on his neck are straight curves,
long and lean. Veins pulsing leading to a
swollen head, becoming bigger.

"What did you think was going to happen?"
as hands slide across asses and puff puff
passes the high from head to head.

Instead of skin on skin there are lips on pipes,
chocolate intoxication without penetration.
as hands slide across asses and puff puff
passes the high from head to head
Brown skin lays as music plays and minds
sway softly slipping into slumber so that wonders
don't become blunders.
as hands slide across asses and puff puff
passes the high from head to head
Yet, the warm moist imagination will not be ignored
as hands slide across asses and puff puff passes
the high from head to head

Something new....

Happy

I'm supposed to be happy. I've the perfect life, free from drama, free from abuse, free from worries, free from strife.
I'm supposed to be happy. I've the perfect career, full of benefits, full of vacations, full of advancement, full of resources.
I'm supposed to be happy. I've the perfect vibe, beauty plentiful, style plentiful, joy plentiful, drive plentiful.

I'm supposed to be happy. I've the perfect interactions, creative liaisons, creative relationships, creative experiences, creative mystery.

I'm supposed to be happy. But... I've the perfect pain, heavy burden, heavy guilt, heavy sorrow, heavy strain.

I'm supposed to be happy. So... I've perfect insomniac nights, crying silently, crying passively, crying internally, crying in plain sight.

I'm supposed to be happy. Yet... I've perfect self hate, I'm a horrible person, I'm a horrible friend, I'm a horrible mate.

I'm supposed to be happy. So...I've created a perfect story... void of truth, void of emotion, void of depth, void of me.

I'm supposed to be happy...

I've the perfect....rhyme at the perfect time.

"Be Good"

Hey love, I came across this song I want you to hear. When I heard it I could not stop listening to it.
What is it about?
I want you to just listen to it first. Is that okay?

I smile at the excited expression on his face. He is such a beautiful man. It really doesn't matter what the song is about, I just love he wants to share these moments with me. I sit in my favorite chair while taking the red Afrikan tie-dyed cloth that is wrapped twice around my bust and place it under my knees. I prop my legs across his legs as he scans through the list of songs. Teasingly, he blocks my view as I try to peer over his shoulder to see the artist and title. I am sure I probably have heard it before. As he presses play I hop up and walk to the kitchen to get a cup of water. The song is paused while I get my glass of water.

I can hear it from here, go ahead and play it.
Nope. I want your full attention. I can wait.

I fill my glass with water and then fill a glass for him. As I walk back to the chair he takes off his shirt and relaxes a bit more in the chair before I place my feet back in his lap. He presses play. As I listen to the rhythm and the words I find myself lost in thought. There are so many images and scenarios flashing through my mind. Images of afrikan men walking in chains, linked together by humiliation and pain, downtrodden but still very proud. I see him. I see my male children. I see their male children. I see generations of male afrikan children.... all caged.

I didn't realize until I could see the concern in his eyes that tears are pouring down my face. His copper large hand reaches for my face and wipes the tears away. Still looking deeply disturbed, he gestures that he is going to turn the music off. But I touch his shoulder and shake my head "no". I mouth the word, "Hapana" and motion for him to play it again. He pushes the button to replay the music.

Each word brings another tear, each thought takes me to a place that I rarely allow myself to go. I wonder where my mind might drift to if there are no words to focus on across the lyrics. At least with the words playing I have something to keep me grounded in my body. I listen to the song three more times before I can muster up the nerves to let him turn it off. When the music stops, we sit in silence.

After several moments in silence, I pull my legs from his lap, stand up and walk to him. I kiss him on his cheek and go outside to listen to the seasonal cicada. Their whishing in my ear drowns out the sorrow that wells up in my spirit. It is enough for deep reflection. I didn't realize he joined me until I felt his hand on my shoulder. It causes fresh tears to flow again.

Sooooo.... I take it you like the song.

I burst into laughter while still sobbing quietly. I look a mess but he pulls me to him and holds me close. I never want to ever let him go. I want to keep him forever safe in my arms so that he never has to experience what is played in the "Be Good" lyrics. I kiss his face and smile. I can sense that he is getting concerned about me. I want to release him from his angst but I can't formulate clear thoughts in my head. I definitely can't convey the wave of emotions that I am feeling.

I wish I could explain what I'm feeling, Love.

He smiles but it doesn't reach his eyes. He gently kisses my forehead and the tears begin to flow again. He lifts me off the ground and carries me to the futon. Then he sits down with me straddling him.

Whatever it is, you need to get it out.

I bury my face into his neck and embrace him tightly around the neck. I continue to hold him while he whispers soothing words in my ear. When I finally release him, he goes upstairs and comes back down with a deep blue natural woven cloth that is wrapped around his waist. The cloth is knotted in the front, as is traditionally worn by Afrikan men. He has an assortment of items in his big hands. He is carrying a box of tissue, some drawing paper, water color pencils, a bottle of "relax" essential oil, the oil burner and matches. He places the box of tissue on the table next to the futon, pours the essential oil in the burner, lights the candle, hands me all my drawing supplies and walks away. From the other room, I can see him turn the song back on and place it on repeat.

For a moment I can't think at all. I want so much to have him inside of me. I want him to plug up the pain. As I picture it, I chuckle to myself, and try to block out my aroused state. Warm sensations pass through my body...and I hear the voices of my male ancestors.

"Tell our story" they echo.

I scribble on page after page. I startle myself by crumbling up several pages and then I start all over again. The song continues to play. I listen to it for hours. Time becomes meaningless. He is in bed by this point. As I let my spirit speak, I get up and grab my oversized paper and lay it on the table. I breathe in the calming oils surrounding me... I breathe in the words..... I breathe in the colors that the words evoke.....I let my hand move freely across the paper. Every detail, each color, each face is clear and vivid to me.

As my tears hit the paper, the water colors spread across the page adding life and energy to the figures. One by one, the images spring to life in my mind onto the paper. The more I draw, the less the tears flow. Finally I am done. I hang the picture on the wall and step back to take it all in....
I stare at the faces of hundreds upon hundreds of Afrikan men; they stare back at me. I hear his footsteps approach and I go to him and embrace him tightly. I tell him to close his eyes and lead him back to the picture.

Don't open them yet.

I leave him standing in front of the drawing with his eyes closed. I bring him a chair to sit down in front of the picture. I guide him to the chair and he sits down.

Open your eyes

He gazes upon my tear soaked creation which depicts many generations of Afrikan men in a cage showing their suffering at the hands of oppression. In the middle of this picture he sits with our son.

This is what I see. All the centuries of abuse and castration

I press play, the lyrics roll out:

Be good is her name and I sing
My lion's song and brush my mane
She would if she could
So she pulled my lion's tail and caused me pain
She said "lions are made for cages
just to look at in delight
you dare not let 'em walk around
cause they might just bite"
does she know what she does
when she dances around my cage and says her name
 be good, be good
 be good is her name
I trim my lion's claws and I
and I cut my mane
and I would if I could
but that woman treats me the same

she said "lions are made for cages
just to look at in delight
you dare not let 'em walk around
cause they might just bite"

does she know what she does
when she dances round my cage

be good is her name
I sing my lion's song
brush my mane

and she would
if she could
so she pulled my lion's tail
and cause me pain

she said lions are made for cages
just to look at in delight
you dare not let 'em walk around
'cause they might just bite

does she know what she does
when she dances around my cage?

be good
is her name
I trim my lion's claw
and I cut my mane

and I would if I could
but beee.. good
treats me the same

she said lions are made for cages
just to look at in delight
you dare let' em walk around
'cause they might just bite

does she know what she does
when she dances around my cage?
she dances around my cage
does she knoooow?
does she knooooooow?
be good
be good
be good
be good

"Be Good" song written/recorded by Gregory Porter -American jazz
vocalist, songwriter and actor

Confessions About My Self (Who am I?)

Luna (Part 2)

After all of that worrying and stressing I feel so silly about the whole ordeal but I am glad it is over. I am even more grateful that I finally, finally, got to meet her. Luna is simply amazing. She is everything I thought before my nightmares got the best of me. She is kind, loving, funny, exciting, passionate, beautiful….

My admiration comes back even stronger than before. We talk for about twenty minutes. When I finally look at my phone I see several missed calls from my aunt. I call her back. "Where have you been?" She scolds. "I was going to dinner with my friend, remember? "That was yesterday!!!! I have been calling you all morning. I was worried sick."

"YESTERDAY?!!!! Again, I think, "What is going on?" We are visiting a friend. We have only been here a little while." "Here, where is here?" "I tell her and she laughs quietly. "Ohhhh... well I can see how you might lose track of time. Does this mean you are moving back home?" "Yes, ma'am." We finish our conversation and I return to look for my friend and Luna. I don't see either of them. I can hear voices in a distance so I follow the sound. I walk through the house until I see the hallway, the same one in my dream. I feel the terror rising again.

I try to convince myself to wake up. There is whispering in my ear. I am startled when my name is called. It is my special friend. He looks puzzled as he sees my face frozen with fear. "Are you okay love?" Luna asks. "Yes, I think I'm just tired. I think we should go." "I enjoy having you visit. Come back anytime. Please remember to ring the bell because I can't hear you knock on the door from most parts of the house." I manage a fake smile as I walk out her front door.

Over the next week I slowly move my clothes and things back into my house. I am at ease again. My friend and I speak almost daily but we never speak about that night. If I wasn't so sure we visited Luna I would swear it was another one of my hallucinations. I decide to check my theory and go ring Luna's doorbell. After a few short moments I hear her voice call out "Coming!" I waited patiently. My heart races as she unlatches her door. For a split second I flash back to the snake eyes and claws. She welcomes me with a smile. "Welcome back neighbor. I didn't expect to see you back so soon." I smile and hand her a small gift. We walk straight through her house out to the back yard and then to the green house.

Inside there are all kinds of wonderful herbs, vegetable and flowering plant growing. *See Sage Wisdom: Herbal Teas and Infusions. I am utterly amazed. Now I must add herbalist to the list of amazing things Luna is capable of doing. We chat about the different plants and how she initially started to study plants and healing. She explains that her mother taught her when she was much younger. *Much younger? What does that even mean? How old is she?*

"Did you get the pictures of your grandmother I sat on your porch some time ago. It is uncanny how much you look alike." She erupts into laughter. "You think it is my grandmother? No, sweetie that picture is of me. It was just a long time ago." I laugh with her. "You? That's impossible. You don't look a day over 80." We laugh together. She offers me some herbs to take with me. I pick various ones to fill a basket. I continue the joke. "So did you ever meet Harriet Tubman?" "Actually, yes I did. She was a brave and stern woman. But she had a kindness about her that was unmatched. People only remember the roughness of her but everything she did was out of her love for people." Of course, I know she is joking. I giggle. I follow her into the house until we approach that hallway. I stop while in mid step. "What's wrong?" she asks. I sigh and continue walking. "Nothing, I remember something."

"I want to show you something." We walk into a room that is very bright with crystals, bells, and glass everywhere. "This is my room of clarity. I come here whenever I need to clear my mind. You are welcome to use it whenever you like. It will help with your nightmares and so-called "hallucinations." *My friend must have told her about my dreams.* She continues. "We often have fears when we don't understand our gifts. We block our spirit helpers and see their "guidance" as something which is haunting us. If you listen carefully, while looking deeply, you will find the answers to all you seek. She guides me to a chair that sat in the middle of the room and motions for me to sit. Then she leaves.

At first there is a slight ringing in my ears. It gets progressively louder. I try to focus on the crystal but then I realize the hallucinations are back. I can hear voices. I close my eyes and calm my breathing. I can feel a warm sensation moving across my body. Did I fall asleep again? I think I am in a dream. I can still see Luna in her back yard from the window. She is dancing around naked in the sun. I can smell her with each passing breeze. She smells of lotus and maple flowers. She is laughing and for some reason it sounds like there are several children laughing with her. She turns to the window and waves at me to come out. As I walk towards the door I feel cool water running down my legs. When I open the door and step outside the sun warms my body. Luna lies on a bed of fluffy lavender pillows. She is still laughing and waves me closer.

When I get to her she pulls me on top of her and begins rubbing my now naked body. My juices flow as I nestle my nose between her legs and begin to lap the sap that flows out of her. Her moist center is very sweet and fruity. It is a strong taste that I have never before encountered. I push my tongue deeper insider her and she begins to involuntarily lift herself off the pillows into my waiting mouth. My tongue dances deliciously around, inside, nibbling gently around her mound that grows in size. We spin in the air while still embracing each other until we slowly descend back to the ground.

When the earth touches my back Luna ferociously kisses my lips. She places herself above me and laps up and down my wetness. Before I realize it she pushes inside me. In shock, I look down to discover Luna has a tekken. My legs open widely and wrap around her to receive as much of her as I can. Her sap is still on my lips and she begins to lick herself off my lips slowly. The cool water is pouring down my legs and I realize it is coming from inside of me.

I grab her shoulders as she moves in and out of me causing my legs to tremble violently. My arousal swells and before I understand, I explode in a kaleidoscope of colors, smells and energy as waves of orgasms hit me. My body is shivering and I am shaking. Not one, not two, not three but four, wave after wave hits me as I cum repeatedly. I awaken when her hand touches my shoulder. I am moaning and gyrating in her chair in the middle of her sacred room. To make matters worse, I am so wet my juices bleed through my clothes onto the seat. So many emotions pass across my face; embarrassment is one. "I am SOOOOO sorry, Luna."

"Apologies are not needed here. Each of us experience, what is needed in this space. One day I will share some of my experiences with you. But for now he is here to pick you up. He is excited to see you. I told him you are here." I look wide-eyed, satiated and apprehensive. I hope he did not hear me have the strongest orgasm I've ever experienced. "Don't worry he is just getting here." She winks as she watches my face smooth out before she walks out. I am still breathing heavily and can still strongly feel my wetness and arousal.

I take a few moments to gather myself, because I need them. I walk down the long hallway with my body pulsating with each step. I can see my friend watching me intently as I walk slowly towards him. He doesn't seem to mind how long it takes. Every few minutes I have to stop and lean my head against the wall to catch my bearings. His stillness is welcoming. He doesn't walk towards me to make this long walk any easier or shorter. He just patiently waits.

Finally I reach him. I embrace him tightly still quivering inside. He pulls me close and gently kisses my neck. I burst into another orgasm. I bury my face in his warmth and bite down hard on his shoulder. I grab his collar and try to hold in my moan. I lose the battle and moan loudly. Wordlessly, he throws me over his shoulder in a fireman carry style and carries me down the street to my house. He quickly enters the door and takes me up to my bed. *I must have left the door unlocked.* "I did not say goodbye to Luna." I whisper in his ear as my body continues pulsing in waves of energy.

"I'm sure she will forgive you." He smiles as he speaks. "Can I touch you?" He asks. I nod and he begins taking off my clothes. I am fixated on all the energy pulsing in my core. We have been intimate before but only in words. I know we will blend physically tonight. I claw at his clothing; I am unable to get them off fast enough. He is taking his own sweet time removing my clothing items. He kisses my lips deeply. Our lips move to music that only our hearts can hear. Kissing each part of my body he peels away each layer of my clothing. I orgasm three more times before my clothes are completely off.

All I see or hear is Luna. Her moans, her sap, her hands and her dick… but it is his dick in my mouth; his sweet dick that I suck, his dick that explodes in my throat as I swallow his essence. He jerks in my mouth and then wipes my lips as he finishes. He lies next to me and pulls me close. "I waited for you. I waited and I waited. I have waited **four entire** generations.... for you... and I am glad that I did." I beam as I think to myself that he must have meant "...for an entire generation". I drift off to sleep; only to wake in Luna's sacred room. I am still in the same clothes. Wasn't I wearing these clothes before when I left with my friend? There is a light knock at the door before Luna walks in.

"Well now. It has been almost an hour." "AN HOUR? *Only an hour?* But it seem like an entire day is past. Everything seems so real. At one point I think I am dreaming but after he and I are together I am no longer sure. "A dream?" I sigh deeply. I feel a little relief. I did not plan on blending with my friend this soon. I did not plan on blending with him under these types of conditions. Luna pours me a cup of tea and says "Each of us experience what we need to in this space." I interrupt and finish her statement, "one day I will share with you some of my experiences." We say the words together. Luna raises her glass of tea and nods affirmatively.

I must admit, all of this is a bit much. So, I return to my life as usual. Nothing out of the ordinary happens. My nightmares and hallucinations stop. I rarely look for Luna anymore. I know exactly when she will be outside. My aunt and I had planned on having lunch but she cancels at the last minute. Instead, I decide to do some landscaping with my free time. While tending to my lavender herbs Luna walks over. It is broad daylight. I close one eye trying to keep the sun from stinging both of my eyes. She steps into the beaming light and blocks it shielding my eyes. She hands me a letter and walks away. *This is a little odd.* I simply put the letter in my pocket and continue working. As the sun begins to set I head into the house and decide to take a hot bath. I open the letter as the water fills the bathtub.

The message inside is written on parchment paper:

You are welcome to a gathering of the divine crossing.
Tomorrow night.
Follow the sound of the bells and wear white.

I am very excited. I get to attend one of Luna's fancy parties and FINALLY see what they do in that house. I climb into the tub and the warmth engulfs me. My thoughts wander in a different direction. I think about my friend. I replay my dream about him as I gently rub my folds beneath the waters. I rock back and forth as the water swishes around me. The sensations build stronger and stronger; Even after I stop moving my hand the feeling continues. I get out the bath and wrap the towel around myself. The pulsing intensifies. I manage to make it to the bed and part my legs to insert my fingers. I move my fingers at a faster pace. I know that if I do not finish myself off the pulsing will continue. I slowly circle my love bud and envision him; I envision him and Luna. I close my eyes and the images come. My vision is clearer this time. This time they touch each other. I watch. Luna is on top and he laps up her juices while she dances on his face.

In my mind's eye, she glows as she nears climax. The more she glows... the faster I rub. Her glow turns into my flow. It is an indescribable whirlwind. We explode and cum together. I spend the rest of the evening cleaning my home. Over the past few months I have neglected both my home and work. My mind has been elsewhere. I stay awake almost all night. When I finally crawl into my bed it is nearly dawn. I feel a rush of anxiety. My heart pounds in my chest. My breathing is shallow and labored. I do not know what is causing it. Nor do I know how to stop it. I think of Luna's sacred room and how comfortable I feel when I am inside it. I think about the dream that I see in her room. Anxiety turns to arousal and I finally drift off to sleep with a pleasure-induced dream. I spring up when I hear my doorbell ring repeatedly. When I get to my front door there is no one there. I open my door to find a beautiful box; it is from Luna. Inside the box is a gorgeous flowing white dress with a crystal necklace, silver bangles and another piece of parchment paper.

It reads:

Dear Daima,
I didn't want you to be concerned about what to wear tonight. So
I gift you this small token of my gratitude as appreciation for
joining us. I look forward to seeing you.
With all my Love,
Ndelay

Ndelay? I read again and again. I finally have her true name…. Ndelay. I wonder what it all means. I can't wait to see what's in store next...

After Thoughts: Sage Reflections

Contest Winners

What's your Confession?

I would like to thank ALL the participants for the "Confessions..." contest. All the entries were wonderful and reached many people. Each participant shared a piece of themselves with the world and for that I am grateful! I am even more grateful that I did not have to decide because I LOVED all the pictures and "Confessions.." Once again Asante Sana (thank you very much) to the participants.

Uhuru Rahman
Magnetic sun
Anthony Stallings Jr
Kita Anthony
Fregilia Lane
Yashica McKinney
Maurice Minor

Words from the winners

Why did you enter?
First let me say, thank you. I entered for a few reasons: a favor to a friend and as an opportunity to express myself.

Why did you choose that photo and confession?
I chose the photo because of its simplicity and visual effect. I felt it tied into my confession.

What does it mean to you to win?
I'm honored to have won because you all took time out of your day to participate.

Anything else you want to share?
I look forward to sharing more confessions in a forthcoming book.

AND THE WINNER IS....... ~ Maurice Minor

Confession "I am a romantic sort. I believe in love at first sight. I believe that sometimes you just know."

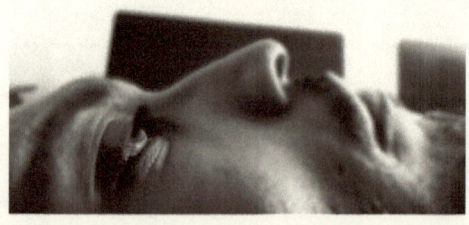

I love my body because ...

All so often we are obsessed with our bodies. Size, shape, height, weight... Society tells us that we are not beautiful without conforming to current beauty standards that are shallow and limiting. "Confessions..." is designed to rid us of our emotional, spiritual, mental, physical and sexual boundaries. With that in mine I had a "I love my body because..." contest

All the entries were beautifully honest and inspiring. I am grateful that I did not have to decide because I LOVED all the pictures and reasons why each participant loved their body. Once again, Asante Sana (thank you very much) to all the participants:

Anthony Stallings Jr
Kita Anthony
Ni-Ammun Onyemachi
Lakisha Boyd
Lakesia Kirk
Fregilia Lane
Curtis Royston
Robert Dillard
Sahir Bahar
Carlotta Blair

AND THE WINNER IS................ Curtis Royston III

"I love my body because . . .it is both my vessel and my tabernacle. It is how GOD represents itself wherever I am. I came of age in a time and place when light-was-right and thin-didn't-win and it caused me some trepidation about appearing underdressed in public. I tried everything within reason to "compensate" for what I thought were "shortcomings". However, as I matured I became more selective ...about what I allowed in and who I allowed near me. As my "vessel" or my body is a holy place that allows my spirit to participate in that natural world. As my "temple" my body allows me to fellowship with GOD wherever I am. I now realize how important it is to be aware of what I eat, drink, and mentally consume. It is my confession that it has been a long ride, but I'm happy with my journey thus far..." Thank You Very Much....

Support Black Businesses

Milele Enterprises LLC
4579 Laclede Suite 355   St. Louis MO   63108
www.confessionsbymilele.com
E-Mail: **jmlott@yahoo.com**
Milele Enterprises provides accounting, budgeting and tax services; notary services; intimacy counseling; writing, body butters and oil blends and financial management workshops.

Good Journey Development Foundation, Inc.
P.O. Box 23016, St. Louis, MO   63156
www.goodjourney.org
E-Mail: **Dionne.ferguson@goodjourney.org**
Good Journey Development Foundation is a youth leadership and community building organization. Good Journey creates programs and opportunities for young people (ages 8 -25) to develop, grow and lead in their communities. *Progressive serves as a business incubator for independent businesses.

Progressive Emporium & Education Center
1108 N Sarah Street   St. Louis MO   63113
E-Mail: **progressiveemporium@yahoo.com**
https://www.facebook.com/ProgressiveEmporiumandEducationCenter/
Progressive Emporium is a co-operative; the cultural arts center has a commercial component that sells books, afrikan imports, incense, personal grooming items, health items, cleaning items, tee shirts, essential oils, artifacts, handcrafted items, African art, spiritual oils and tools, specialty organic foods, herbal teas and drinks.

MwazaCarol*
1108 N. Sarah Street   St. Louis, MO   63113
www.mwazacarol.webs.com
www.mwazacarol.wixsite.com/mwazacarol
E-Mail: **mwazacarol@gmail.com**
MwazaCarol is a visual artist who manages a multi-media corporation that showcases   art work of Carol Thompson-Robinson. MwazaCarol provides workshops and classes. Mwaza means "creative, thoughtful, imaginative person" in Kiswahili.

Marie's Touch
4579 Laclede Suite 347 St Louis MO 63108
E-Mail: iris.m.dixon79@gmail.com
Marie's Touch provides professional comprehensive cleaning services to commercial businesses and residents across the St. Louis metropolitan area. Marie's Touch will leave your home or office in a pristine state because our motto is "Where Cleanliness is a Way of Life."

Sudan Illustrators, Inc.
1108 N. Sarah Street St. Louis, MO 63113
E-Mail: sudan.illustrators@yahoo.com
Sudan Illustrators is a cultural education organization that provide artistic and literacy based activities aimed to inspire and educate the entire black family. Sudan Illustrators, Inc. co-manages Progressive Emporium & Education Center, provides theatre/african drumming and dance activities and author book signings, lectures and other cultural activities.

Uhuru Lifestyles
1219 Waldron Avenue St. Louis, MO 63130
E-Mail: vbanks353@gmail.com
Uhuru Lifestyles provides african-centered graphic/logo design, writing, editing, designs business cards, business reports, curriculum development, research, communications, marketing services, grant writing and non-profit management and small business support services. Uhuru also creates custom-designed obituaries/display boards and memorial videos.

Freedom Creations*
1108 N. Sarah Street St. Louis, MO 63113
E-Mail: tpop80@hotmail.com
Freedom Creations builds custom designed structural, ornamental and carved art work, i.e., chests, book shelves, furniture, storage dividers, small carved display items, large Adinkra symbols (for outdoor decorations) big props (weddings and other ceremonies); Freedom Creations also provides home repair services.

Powertrip Productions*
1108 N. Sarah Street St. Louis, MO 63113
E-Mail: djwillpower314@gmail.com
Powertrip Productions is a musical entertainment and DJ Service corporation managed by DJ Willpower that provides record spinning and DJ services, musical/cultural workshops and selling of mixed music CDs.

TEACH Society*
1108 N. Sarah Street St. Louis, MO 63113
www.teachsociety.org
E-Mail: teachorg33@gmail.com
TEACH Society is a cooperative effort between certified professionals from
the fields of education, counseling, communications and preventive health
whose aim is to use cultural education to uplift and empower the Afrikan
American community; ceremonial/cultural celebrations are also provided.
TEACH co-manages Progressive Emporium & Education Center.

Zuri Life
4579 Laclede Suite 355   St. Louis MO   63108
https://www.facebook.com/pg/Zuri-Life-
1374941849202351/photos/?ref=page_internal
E-Mail: soontobeking@hotmail.com
Zuri Life provides an array of specialized services including Red Cross
certified swim lessons, custom designed t-shirts, baseball shirts/hats,
DVD duplication; Zuri Life also provides seasonal lawn care and snow
removal services.

Adero Wellness Services*
1108 N. Sarah Street St. Louis, MO 63113
E-Mail: aderowellness@gmail.com
Adero Wellness Services provides healing arts in Myofascial Release,
Neural Release (NRT) Therapy, Reiki, Therapeutic Massage,
Pathophysiology and Advanced Massage Therapy; specializing in cancer
clinic and pain management. Adero is certified to provide doula prenatal,
pregnancy, neonatal/post-partum and women wellness services.

Ngoma in Motion*
1108 N. Sarah Street St. Louis, MO   63113
E-Mail: DhatiKennedy18@att.net
https://www.facebook.com/Ngoma-In-Motion-231745604926/
Ngoma In Motion, aka NIM is a performing arts organization specializing
in Afrikan drumming and dance performances and workshops which
spans a gamut of the musical experiences; jazz, blues, traditional Afrikan,
R & B, Pan Earth, reggae, Afro Latin, highlife and Ngoma's own sounds —
which has fused a new genre coined the Mississippi Valley Music.

---

*Progressive serves as a business incubator for independent businesses.

Dhati M. Kennedy*

1108 N. Sarah Street   St. Louis, MO   63113
E-Mail: DhatiKennedy18@att.net
www.facebook.com/Ngoma.NIM?fref=ts
Artist/Master Drummer whose aim is to teach Afrikan culture, traditions and artistic expression through Afrikan drumming/music/dance as the lead of Ngoma In Motion.

Po Tolo Professional Services*

1108 N. Sarah Street   St. Louis, MO 63113
E-Mail: oheneaniwa50@gmail.com
PoTolo Professional Services provides manuscript editing and publication services for books and multimedia platforms.

By Drum Light*

1108 N. Sarah Street   St. Louis, MO   63113
E-Mail: mkbuch7@gmail.com
By Drum Light is a master artist who provides a variety of hand crafted products including carvings, paintings, batiks, t-shirts, cups, prints, hats, bags, CDs and other printed materials – some based upon his own art; By Drum Light also creates music/video productions.

Frannie's Brews*

1108 N. Sarah Street St. Louis, MO 63113
www.facebook.com/FranniesBrews/?fref=ts
Frannie's Brews is an herbal tea business that was established in 2015. The teas have medicinal benefits that can support and maintain optimal health.

Mase Roots*

1108 N. Sarah Street St. Louis, MO 63113
https://www.facebook.com/mase.roots?fref=ts
www.maseroots.com
Mase Roots educates the community about the importance of drinking alkaline ionized water and integrating alkaline ionized water as a healthier alternative for families. Mase Roots provides ionization systems for commercial, private, and residential communities as well as develop alkaline cultural lifestyles that prolong a healthier lifestyle.

Dr. Kamili Hayes*

1108 N. Sarah Street St. Louis, MO   63113
E-Mail: whayes@mytu.tuskegee.edu
E-Mail: drwkhayes@gmail.com
Historian/Educator who provides research services, lectures on historical topics and teaching about African Americans.

Sonja Robinson-Evans
www.sonjarobinsonart.com
E-Mail: SonjaRobinsonArt@gmail.com
Artist Sonja Robinson-Evans is known for customizing art to coordinate with decor (paintings, tapestry and home furnishings) that is sold throughout the country.

SaiRiseYoga (Saidia Therapylady)
Chicago, Illinois
https://www.facebook.com/saidia.therapylady?fref=ts
E-Mail: therapylady100@gmail.com
SaiRiseYoga provides Kemetic Yoga as a healing and regenerative fitness system characterized by a series of postures that creates alignment of the spinal column and corrects defects in the skeletal muscular system in order to relieve stress, increase blood circulation, nutrient and oxygen supply to vital body systems, and to allow internal life force energy and cerebral spinal fluid to flow more efficiently.

Stephen C. Bruce Creative
www.scbcreative.com
E-Mail: stephen@scbcreative.com
Stephen C. Bruce Creative works with non-profits and businesses to provide web and creative solution. The mission of Creative is to help clients communicate their missions visually through innovative and quality design; specializing in website development, logo design, cover design and photography.

Ojo the Storyteller
1219 Waldron Avenue   St. Louis, MO 63130
E-Mail: ojo.the.storyteller@gmail.com
Ojo the Storyteller is a professional Griot that has been educating/ entertaining families and communities for over 40 years. Ojo uses storytelling as a teaching tool to promote an understanding of African culture, increase literacy, foster deeper appreciation and respect for self.

Desserts Out The Jar
3830 Washington Blvd. St. Louis, MO 63108
www.dessertsoutthejar.com
E-Mail: DessertsOutTheJar@yahoo.com
Desserts Out the Jar emphasizes individually-crafted, home style gourmet desserts, conveniently packaged in authentic, traditional style Mason jars to lock in freshness and flavor.

Glossary

Swahili Terms

Arusi	Wedding
Habari Gani?	What's the news?
Njema Asante	Fine, thank you
Njema Asante na wewe je?	Fine, thank you and you?
Ndugu na Ndada	Brother and Sister
Mtoto/Watoto	Child/Children
Darasani	Class
Tafadali	Please
Una fahamu	Do you understand?
Ndio, La	Yes; No
Simama	Stand
Keti	Sit
Sikiliza	Listen
Sawa sawa	That's right
Alala	That's good
Fundisha	Teach
Kazi	Work
Mzuri	Good
Hodi Hodi	Knock Knock (May I enter)
Karibu	Welcome (You may enter)
Kula	Eat
Chakula	Food
Umuzi	House
Acha	Stop
Si jui	I don't know
Pamoja	Together
Nisamehe	Excuse me
Pole basi	I'm sorry
Sifa Ote Une Watu Weusi	All praises due to black people
Kwanini?	Why?
Tutaonana	See you later
Moja Mbili, Tatu	One, Two, Three
Kwanzaa	First fruits~
Kinara	Candle holder

Marassa Dialect
(Swahili, French mixture)

Nakupenda beaucoup :
I love you very much

Asante d'être venus et danser na mimi:
Thank you for coming and dancing with me

Kufanya maisha ya ajabu mon bel amour
You make my life wonderful
my beautiful love

Sikitu dada De rein:
You are welcome sister, it was nothing

Works Referenced

The Egyptian Book of the Dead: The Book of Going Forth by Day. Translated by Raymond O. Faulkner. Edited by Eva von Dassow. San Francisco, Chronicle Books LLC, 2008.

The Way of the Elders by Adama & Naomi Doumbia Ph.D., Llewellyn Publications; Saint Paul, Minnesota. 2004.

Topics on West African Traditional Religion, Vol. One by Kwabena Amponsah. Adwinsa Publications (Ghana) Limited, Legon-Accra. 1977.

Introduction to African Religion, by John S. Mbiti, formerly Proffeffor of Religious Studies, Makerere University, Kumpala, Uganda. Heinemann Educational Books. Portsmouth, New Hampshire. 1975.

The Lugbara of Uganda, by John Middleton, Case Studies in Cultural Anthropology, Holt, Rinehart and Winston, Inc. Evanston, Illinois. 1964.

Nile Valley Contributions to Civilization, Exploding The Myth, Vol. 1, by Anthony T. Browder, Introduction by Dr. John Henrik Clarke, Institute of Karmic Guidance, Washington, D.C. 1992.

Tropical and Southern Africa by Allen R. Boyd and John Nickerson, Scholastic Book Services, 1973.

Sacred Sexuality: Ancient Egyptian Tantric Yoga: A Neterian Guide To Love, Sexuality, Marriage, Relationships and the Secrets of Sexual Energy Cultivation, Sublimation, and Spiritual Enlightenment Fourth Edition, by Muata Ashby, Sema Institute of Yoga/C.M. Books, Miami, Florida. 1996.

Egyptian Yoga, The Philosophy of Enlightenment, Volume 1, 10th Anniversary Edition, by Sebai Dr. Muata Ashby, Cruzian Mystic Books, Miami, Florida, 1995.

The Spirit of Intimacy: Ancient African Teachings in The Ways of Relationships by Sobonfu E. Some, Originally published in 1997 by Berkeley Hills Books. Published by Quill William Morrow, New York. 1999.

The Healing Wisdom of Africa: Finding Life Purpose Through Nature, Ritual and Community by Malidoma Patrice Some, Author of Water and The Spirit, Putnam Special Markets, New York, NY, 1999.

Heal Thyself: For Health and Longevity by Queen Afua, A & B Book Publishers, Brooklyn, New York. 1992

Confessions of a Faithful Woman by Milele, Self -Published, 2012.

Sticks, Stones, Roots & Bones, Hoodoo, Mojo & Conjuring with Herbs Fifth Printing, by Stephanie Rose Bird, Llewellyn Publications; Woodbury, M.N. 2010

A Healthy Foods & Spiritual Nutrition Handbook: A comprehensive guide to good food and a healthy life style by Keith T. Wright, Health Masters, Philadelphia, P.A. 1999. Previous Edition Copyright 1989.

"*A*s those around you grow and improve,

you grow and improve."

-Milele,
Author/Educator

Author Bio & Contact
Milele

"Confessions of A Sage Woman" is the second book in Milele's "Confessions..." series. The author humbly says she is both a student and practitioner of the ancient sciences. Milele cultivates her innate sense of "sciences" during her initiation by studying numerology, herbalism, color therapy, afrikan divination, aromatherapy, alchemy, herbalism, crystal healing and much more.

Studies of these subjects are the cornerstone of a deeply embedded philosophy that Milele embraces and her attempt to share information through poignant stories, prose, poems and narratives about the ancient sciences.

"I am an organizer, educator, business woman, writer, healer, teacher, lover and liberator. I am also the mother of two Afrikan warriors who've taught me so much about myself and life. I began this journey to free minds and to challenge commonly accepted stereotypes about love, sex, relationships and humanity in general. Writing is only one of the many ways that I accomplish expression of both the arts and sciences. I also like to dance, garden, laugh and lay in the sun as much as possible. We must constantly find joy in life as we advance" Milele says.

The ancient sciences are not the only area that Milele has pursued and mastered. She graduated with honors both from Harris Stowe State University with a B.S. in Accounting and Webster University with a M.A in Management and Leadership. Milele works as an Accountant II for the Comptroller's Office of St. Louis. She uses her knowledge and experience of accounting defined as the "systematic process of identifying, recording, verifying, summarizing, interpreting and communicating financial information" to assist small businesses and non-profits under Milele Enterprises, a consultant firm.

Milele, which is the author's middle name, in Kiswahili means "For Eternity." The author attributes her early fascination with the sciences to early lessons taught by her mother in physics, aeronautics, engineering and the solar system. Her mother "Azima" formerly worked at NASA.

Milele also co-founded "Awakening the Ancient," AwTAN, which helps to provide a heightened consciousness and foster holistic understandings and practices involving intimacy, "sex," arousal, passion, sensuality, spiritual connections, exchange of energy and the "cosmic desire" to be fulfilled or satiated. The concept of "cosmic desire" taps into the energy of attraction that exists across the universe.

The goal is tantamount to what Milele hopes to achieve with her writings: to create a society of individuals with a love, honor, respect and appreciation for self and others where all can freely exist...... unfettered.

Milele's views and perspectives on sensuality, love, society, life, reciprocity, relationships and learning to relate sexually on a deeper more spiritual level can be followed on her blog: *Who I Am Affects You...* www.milelechanging.blogspot.com. Her vibrant and honest perspectives can be found on www.twitter.com/SimplyMilele. Milele self-published "Confessions of a Faithful Woman" in 2012 and will be publishing a delightful anecdotal book "Conversations with My Sons" in 2017.

Contact Info

Milele Enterprises LLC
4579 Laclede Suite 355
St Louis MO   63108

jmlott@yahoo.com

www.facebook.com/confessionsofa

www.confessionsbymilele.com
www.milelechanging.blogsport.com

simplyMilele on Twitter, Instagram

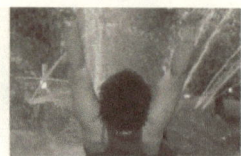

Confessions... of a faithful woman delves into arousal, taking written form as a collection of fictitious stories and poems written from versatile and unique perspectives.

As the first in the "Confessions..." series, it is the "foot in the door". It helps to blur the lines of conventional intimacy while creating a safe haven for many schools of thoughts.

The "Confessions..." series introduces and/or reacquaints the reader with some traditional Afrikan practices and perspectives surrounding elevating the mind, body and soul. Some of which are deeply inserted into our genetic material, and some of which we will bravely encounter for the first time.

The entire series will explore ancient practices, smash stereotypes and ultimately may change the way the reader thinks about relationships, attraction, arousal, sexuality, spirituality and views the world.

Edited by Veronica L. Banks, M.A.
© 2010 Milele. All rights reserved.

No part of this book may be reproduced, stored in a retrieval system, or transmitted by any means without written permission of the author.

Upcoming Book

"Conversations with My Sons"

Released in 2017